A Knot On My Dreams

Shyquana Bennett

A Knot On My Dreams
Copyright © 2020 Shyquana Bennett
All rights reserved.

Cover Design by
Red Raven Book Design

ISBN: 978-0-578-74301-1

❤Dedicated to Gran and Wayne❤

I've shed many tears losing the both of you to Covid, but every time you've popped into my dreams, it was nothing but laughter. I woke up smiling each time. It's what I needed to know that you both are in a better place. I hope I'm making you proud...

CHAPTER 1

KRISTEN

We were snuggled up on the couch getting ready to watch the season finale of Power. This was our show. No matter how hectic or complicated our week went, we made sure Sunday nights were dedicated to us. We would put our phones on silent and everything. I would always make sure dinner was done early and the kitchen was cleaned before it came on. I like to be relaxed with my glass of wine. He wasn't much of a drinker and neither was I, but I did enjoy a glass of wine every once in a while. I made sure to always have his favorite snacks available on Sunday nights. He's a Cheetos, popcorn, and Pringle's kind of guy. As long as I had one of those present, he was satisfied.

"Babe, do you think Tariq is going to tell his father who killed Raina?" Stephan asked me.

"Honestly, this boy does some of the dumbest things, but I'm going to give him the benefit of the doubt and pray that he tells Ghost who did it. If he doesn't, it better be because he got some of Ghost's blood in him and wants to handle it himself," I said.

"Nope, I doubt this fool is going to say anything. I bet you he's going to lie to his family because he's scared."

"Scared? Do you not know his mother and father? Tasha nor Ghost are punks. They are certified gangstas. There's no need for him to be scared," I said as I took a sip of my Moscato.

4

"Kristen, think about it. There's always that one child that comes out like you and one that comes out the complete opposite."

"True. Raina did boss up and approach the guy. You may be right, but I'm remaining hopeful that Tariq is going to handle this himself like he's Olivia Pope or something."

"Let's bet on it. Think of something you'd want to win and I'd do the same. At the end of the show, we'll see who won," Stephan says a little too eagerly.

I know this man oh too well. He is always trying to make a bet when we disagree on something.

"Deal!" I said while rolling my eyes at him. "If I win, I want to go away for a romantic weekend. What do you want if you win?"

"Well, when I win I'd like you to come with me to my family reunion," Stephan said smiling from ear to ear.

"Oh, Lord. I need Tariq to get it together this season because I'm not sure if I have enough sick days to take off after eating another piece of your aunt's unseasoned fried chicken."

Stephan nearly spits every drop of soda he had in his mouth out. We both shared a hearty laugh as he playfully slapped me on the leg.

"My family laughs at it all the time, but no one has the heart to tell her. She's been watching too many of those *Tasty* food videos on Facebook where they season all their meats with just salt and pepper."

"Well, I'm about to deactivate her Facebook until she activates her black card and season my chicken!"

I love Stephan dearly, but he knows his mother's side of the family cannot cook. I will go to the family reunion regardless, but if I win, I am making sure I am going there on a full stomach. You will not catch me sticking my fork in anything. His father is a great chef. Owns his own restaurant and everything. I just wish he had the heart to tell his wife and her sisters to let him do the cooking. Stephan said his father offered to do the cooking a few years back, but it ended in a big argument and his father decided to leave the topic alone.

"What are you thinking about?" Stephan asked, startling me as I was thinking of how to fake a stomachache or bad cramps the day of the family reunion. Just as I was about to think of a lie the theme music to Power came on.

"Saved by the show," I mumbled.

"Mmhmm."

As we were watching the show, I realized that I was losing this bet. I was still hopeful when Tariq told the investigators that he did not know who killed his sister. Growing up in the hood we knew better than to trust the cops with issues we can handle ourselves, but when he told Tasha and Ghost that he did not know, I knew I had to prepare myself for this tasteless family reunion. Stephan leaned over, kissed me on the cheek, and said, "We should wear matching colors." Like a little kid, I wiped off his kiss and rolled my eyes. We continued watching the show. Yelling and screaming at the screen as if the characters could hear us.

I nearly knocked my wine glass over when Tariq was on a hunt to find Ray Ray. I knew the good Lord was not going to let me suffer and lose this bet. I screamed out, "See, babe, I told you he was going to handle it himself!" I leaned over and kissed him on the cheek, mimicking what he did to me, and of course, his petty ass wiped it off.

"I don't understand how I was so close and then boom you end up winning the bet!" Stephan said.

"Oh, you almost had it. Gotta be quicker than that."

"I dislike that commercial now because you're always using that line."

Stephan and I have a great relationship. We weren't perfect, but in the eyes of others, we were the ideal couple. We have been together for four years and counting. Everyone always asks us when are we getting married, but truthfully we are both content with our relationship. It's not that we don't believe in marriage or never had the talk about it, we just knew it wasn't for us. Not yet at least. Even though we juggle back and forth between each other's apartments, it still feels good to have our own space. We have learned from previous relationships that being in one another's face all day and every day will become tiring and too much of a routine. I respected the days that he wanted to stay home by himself and vice versa. We honored the code that communication is key. Don't get me wrong, sometimes we'd argue over the smallest and unimportant things, but we didn't allow it to get to the point where we couldn't talk it out without too much time passing.

Stephan and I met at the pharmacy. It was an embarrassing moment, but it ended up being worth it. I had just left the gastroenterologist office after confirming that I had a bad case of hemorrhoids. Stupid me decided to take laxatives to help flush out my system and prepare me for a ten-day green smoothie challenge I was about to do. I didn't read the fine print that stated that this specific laxative isn't recommended for everyday use and of course I used it for four days in a row and was about to make it a fifth day when I realized my butthole was on fire. I was in so much pain. I could not sit or stand for too long. I was all over the place. When the gastroenterologist told me that the laxatives could cause hemorrhoids, I immediately felt stupid for not reading the entire instructions on the bottle. He sent me to the compound pharmacist across the street where they make special creams. He gave me the prescription to get a cream made that will help shrink and numb my hemorrhoids so I would not be in as much pain.

I nervously walked to the pharmacy, praying that it would be empty just in case the pharmacist had to explain to me how to use the cream. God answered my prayers because there was no one there but the workers. I gave the pharmacist my ID and my insurance card. He looked up the prescription and said he would need about fifteen-twenty minutes to get it ready since they make it there. I had some emails to catch up on anyway so I did not mind the wait. I work for the Board of Education as a Special Education Teacher. My class is small, only about ten students on average. I love my students, but those ten felt like twenty at times. I know you should not have favorites, but Anthony is mine. He is the class clown and protector. He would not let anyone from any other class make fun of his classmates. I had a class of sixth, seventh, and eighth-graders. Though they were middle school students, some of their reading and math scores were on an elementary school level.

Some of them were very bright, but behavior-wise they could not handle being in a normal-sized class. I was smiling to myself as I was thinking how happy they make me when I realized the pharmacist had been calling my name.

"Ms. Johnson?"

"Yes, I'm sorry." I put my phone in my pocket and headed for the counter.

"Your ointment is getting packaged. Your copayment is forty-six dollars," he said.

The one thing about working for the DOE is that their insurance sucks. I would sometimes be stuck with ridiculously high copayments. I had no choice but to pay it though. As I was placing my debit card back in my wallet in walked this fine man. It was just my luck that he stood behind me just as the pharmacist started explaining how to properly use the ointment.

I guess he saw the embarrassed look on my face so he tried to whisper the instructions. When he got to the part where I had to use Q-tips for my anal area, I almost fainted from embarrassment. There was no way this man was not eavesdropping. Before the pharmacist went towards the back to get my prescription he said, "I'll be right with you, Mr. Moore." I'm assuming he was referring to the man behind me because we were the only two there. I mumbled to myself, "This is so embarrassing."

"There's nothing to be embarrassed about. You'd be surprised how many people go through it," Mr. Fine man said.

"So you were eavesdropping?" I asked.

"No. He just doesn't know how to whisper properly, plus you're not the first person I've seen come in here for this kind of treatment," he chuckled.

"Oh so now I'm the laugh of the day?" I asked annoyed.

His chuckles quickly ended when he saw how serious I was. "No ma'am, I apologize if you took it that way."

I simply rolled my eyes, turned back around, and waited for the pharmacist to come from the back. Once he came, he gave me my package and I stormed out.

I called my sister and told her all about my embarrassing moment at the pharmacy.

"Kris, there's no reason to be embarrassed. Now don't get me wrong, you mainly hear about this with elderly people, but it happens to the best of us."

"It's easier for you to say, Monique because you're not going through it," I said annoyed.

"Listen, sis, I may not be going through it, but I've been there. Remember when I had the twins? They ripped me a new one. You don't think I had to go through the same thing. Besides, it's just a booty hole!" She said in her worst impersonation of Dina from the movie, *Girls Trip*. I should have never taken her to see that movie. Now all she does is quote it. Tiffany Haddish would be proud though.

I laughed and rolled my eyes at the same time. I can always count on my sister to make me feel better with her corny self.

"Thanks, sis. I needed that laugh. Hold on one sec. Someone is calling me on the other line." I looked at the caller ID and didn't recognize the number, so I let it go to voicemail. "I don't know who it is, could be a bill collector. If it's important they'll leave a voicemail," I said.

"Yup. Anyway, girl let me get back to work. Call me later. Love you lots," she said.

"Love you back."

Just as I was about to hop on the train I saw that I had a voicemail. My train was arriving so it was going to have to wait until I got off. I plugged in my headphones and listened to Tasha Cobb's album, Heart. Passion. Pursuit (Deluxe). I just love me some Tasha Cobbs. I raise the volume on my headphones every time *Gracefully Broken, Forever at Your Feet, I'm Getting Ready,* or *Your Spirit* comes on. Those were my favorite songs off that album.

I got off the train and now had two voicemails to listen to from the same number. My heart was racing. I was praying that I did not miss an urgent call. I immediately paused my music and began listening to voicemail number one.

Voicemail number one:

Hi uh, Ms. or Mrs. Johnson. My name is Stephan Moore. The person you just met at the pharmacy. I'm sorry for calling you but I wanted to apologize if I made you feel as if your situation was a joke. I was actually there for the same thing and the way you felt today was how I felt the first time I had the ointment explained to me with three people behind me who were definitely eavesdropping. Well, I just wanted to let you know that my neighbor suffers from the same thing.

Since he can't get around as much, I'm always the one who picks up his prescriptions. I'm not sure how...

Voicemail number two:

Sorry. I guess my voicemail was too long, but as I was saying, I'm not sure how long you've been suffering with yours, but I do know that besides the ointment, taking a hot bath works wonders for him. The doctors always tell you to buy a sitz bath. Yes, it helps at that moment, but think about it, how are you healing when you are sitting in the same position that is causing you pain? Anywho, if you are ok with us continuing this conversation instead of me being a creep and leaving a third one, then feel free to call me at 646-347-1718. Be blessed, lovely lady.

I was relieved that it wasn't an emergency kind of voicemail, but curious as to how this man got my number. Should I call back, block him, send a text, or act as if this call never happened? I contemplated on my walk home what to do and every time I thought my mind was made up, I second-guessed myself. I ended up calling one of my close friends, Eva. I would have called Latrice, but she's the wild one out of us, and in some weird strange way, she would have convinced me to call back, ask for his address, and finish the conversation face to face. I love me some Latrice, but that girl knows how to get what she wants and when she wants it. I on the other hand do not have the skills she does to lure these men in.

"You've reached Eva, tell me what you want or whateva," Eva sang as she answered the phone. This chick is always singing or trying to make something rhyme. I couldn't help but laugh at her stupidity.

"Eva, I'm gonna need you to get it together with all these lame sayings."

"You're supposed to be my girl, Kris. You know you don't want none of this!"

"Want none of what chick?" I asked.

"I don't know," she said laughing. "I just needed something to rhyme. Anywho, girl, what you up to?"

I filled her in on the doctor's visit, the embarrassing moment at the pharmacy with Mr. Stephan, and of course the voicemails.

"Damn, girl. He called twice to leave two voicemails?" She paused for a minute. "Hmmm, either he's sorry if you felt embarrassed or he's attracted to you and thought that your situation was a way to spark a conversation between you guys," she said.

"So what should I do?"

"I say call him back. What do you have to lose?"

"Nothing, I guess."

"So then call him back and call me after to let me know how it went."

"Wait, call him right now?" I asked.

"Uh, yea. What are you waiting for? You're grown, it's not like when we were younger and made them wait two-three business days before we responded to their call or text."

"You're right. Let me call him. I will call you back. Stay by your phone."

"Sure will. Go get your man!" she said a little too excited.

"Girl, bye!" I said before hanging up.

I cannot believe I'm about to call this man. My heart was raising with anxiety. I gained up enough courage and dialed his number.

"This is Stephan," he said answering on the third ring just as I was about to hang up.

"Hi, Stephan, this is Kristen. We met at the pharmacy a little while ago," I said nervously.

"I wasn't sure if you were going to call me back, but I am happy that you did," he said. I could feel him smiling on the other end.

"I just wanted to thank you for your message and the extra help you gave. It was really nice of you especially since you laughed at me," I said playfully.

"I do apologize for that. I felt like an ass after you left and had to make it right."

"How did you get my number in the first place?" I really hope he is not a stalker.

"Well when the pharmacist went in the back to get my prescriptions, I looked in the logbook and found your number."

"That makes sense," I said relieved that he wasn't that bad of a stalker.

"Yea. Sorry if that was a little weird."

The conversation continued from there. I felt like a little kid all over again. Asking twenty-one questions; what's your hobbies, favorite color, what you do for a living, own place, children, own car, etc. His answers surprised me. It made me even more attracted to him. We spoke on the phone for like three hours until I had to get myself ready for work the next morning. The next morning I woke up to a beautiful good morning text. That weekend we went out on our first date and have been together ever since.

My family loved him and his family loved me. We challenged each other in every way possible. Always holding one another accountable for reaching our highest goals.

"Kris? Babe? Hello!" Stephan yelled trying to get me out of my daze.

"Sorry, hun," I said embarrassed.

"What were you thinking about?"

"I was thinking about when we first met and the beautiful memories we shared and still are sharing. Stephan I know I don't say it much, but I truly do love and appreciate you. You've brought me out of many dark situations and I know God created you for me," I said teary-eyed.

"Babe, come here," he said as he pulled me into his embrace. "I'm more grateful for you then you think. I love that you appreciate everything I have done for you, but I don't think you understand how much you have done for me. I can never stop loving and doing for you. You are my Queen and though we aren't married, I vow to be by your side until death does us part," he said looking me in my eyes with nothing but love and passion.

We shared a long and passionate kiss. I don't think this man will ever fully understand how his kisses make me feel. He pulled me onto his lap and continued to kiss me. He knew where my spot was and he went right to it. As he was kissing and sucking on my neck, I had to pull away because I couldn't take it anymore. He looked at me and grinned. He grabbed my face and kissed me again. His hands roamed my body. As he unfastened the button on my pants, I helped him speed up the process as I removed my shirt. He laid me down on the couch as he removed my pants. He looked at me with lust in his eyes and I knew he was just as hungry for me as I was for him. He threw my pants on the ground followed by my panties. I was never a stick figure and I use to be very self-conscious about my body because of that, but Stephan showed me how to love myself and be proud of how God made me. I am beyond grateful for that because sex is much more enjoyable when you know you are sexy and beautiful in the eyes of your man. I pulled him towards me and kissed him as if I would never kiss him again. I felt the growth of his penis and knew just what to do. I unbuckled his pants as he pulled them down and kicked them off. Stephan knew exactly how to satisfy my every need, but tonight was all about him. I playfully pushed him onto his back as I took lead bringing

CHAPTER 2

KRISTEN

It was Saturday morning. Stephan was at work and I was bored out of my mind. I never liked being at home alone. I would always run errands just to pass time, but with having Thursday and Friday off because of Rosh Hashanah, I did all my errands already. That was the beauty of working for the D.O.E.; you get to have all these holidays off. So thank you to the Jews for creating Rosh Hashanah as a holiday. I decided to call Latrice. Everyone has that one friend that is always down for everything. Latrice was that friend. She knew how to have a good time no matter the time of day. She is exactly what I need to pass time.

"Hey girl hey!" she sang as she picked up the phone.

"Hey, girl. What you up to?" I asked.

"Trying to find something to eat. A bitch like me got a hangover and woke up hungry!" she said.

"When don't you have a hungover?"

"When I have to go to church the next morning."

"Now you know that's a damn lie. You've walked into the house of the Lord with dark shades on plenty of times."

"You ain't never lie, but the good Lord knows my heart and He ain't done with me yet, so go and judge someone else."

"You know I live in a judgment-free bubble, but it ain't me if I don't tell the truth," I said.

"True. I will give you that much. Enough about me, I know you called because you're bored and want to see my fine ass. I'll be ready in thirty minutes. Come scoop me up and we can go to IHOP so I can get my unlimited pancakes. I'll tell them you're my child so you can eat for free." Knowing her, she would do exactly that.

"I did call to drag you out the house so I'm going to let it slide. Just make sure you're ready because if I wait for more than three minutes I'm eating alone," I said half-jokingly. Latrice is never on time. Her thirty minutes can very well turn into two hours of waiting.

"You can't rush beauty. I'll hurry though because I'm starving," she said.

"Ok. I'll call you when I'm on my way."

I already showered and washed my hair this morning. All I had to do was get dressed and fix this hair of mine. I loved my shoulder length natural hair, but the maintenance could be overwhelming at times. My twist out or wash-n-go always changes. I can never make it look like the day before. Sometimes it's a good thing and other times its time consuming trying to make it look decent. Today was one of those days when it didn't want to cooperate with me. I ended up just doing a cute little high bun, slicked down my edges with Eco Style gel, and was good to go. I pulled up to Latrice's house forty minutes later. She must really be hungry because to my surprise she was already outside waiting for me.

"Took you long enough," she said while hopping in my car.

"Sorry, girl. I had to make sure these edges were laid!" I said.

"Well if IHOP runs out of pancakes, you and those edges will be in the kitchen making me breakfast." I knew she was not joking. Latrice does not play when it comes to her food.

We listened and sang along to the music playing on the radio as I drove us to IHOP. As usual, IHOP was crowded, but thankfully since it was just the two of us it didn't take long to be seated. We order the same thing every time so there was no delay in us making up our minds on what we wanted to eat. I always ordered the *breakfast sampler* that comes with turkey bacon, turkey sausage, scrambled eggs with cheddar cheese, pancakes, and hash browns. I always made sure the old-fashioned syrup was full because I did not come to eat dry pancakes. Latrice usually gets the *Split-Decision*, which comes with French toast, turkey bacon, turkey sausage, eggs over easy, and pancakes. We got our food a few moments later and we were tearing our food up as if it were the last supper. We were stuffed and satisfied. We paid and headed back to the car.

"Where we off to now, sis?" Latrice asked me.

"Well, we can take a drive out to Kings Plaza Mall. I want to get a few dresses for work. I need to redo my wardrobe. I have to keep up my appearance with my fly ass students."

"You and your badass kids. I don't know how you do it. I would have been slapped one of them for having such a smart ass mouth."

"And that's why God didn't place you in my field. He makes no mistakes," I said. "I love my babies. They are characters, but they have grown on me."

"I guess, girl. I'm fine with doing hair and listening to everyone who comes into the shop with their drama."

"Shoot, I enjoy coming into the shop and hearing the juicy gossip too. Even your white clientele be having some interesting stories."

"Ain't that the truth. They always into some freaky shit. I'm here for the entertainment though, so I keep on listening."

I spotted a man approaching my car, so I signaled Latrice so she can be alert. There are crazy people all around this world and I will not get caught slipping. I reached in my bag as if I was looking for my keys but I was searching for my blade. I felt for it, switched it open, and was prepared for whatever was about to happen. He was nicely dressed, but disguises are real.

"How may we help you?" Latrice asked sternly.

"I would like to get into my car. That's all ma'am," he said.

"Ok, so why are you by our car?" Latrice asked.

"I'm sorry, but this car is mine. There must be some sort of confusion."

"Are we being pranked or something? Sir, please move from my car before you get hurt," I said as I pulled out my car keys and pressed the unlock button. My car door wouldn't unlock though. I pressed the lock button and heard the lock sound. Latrice and I looked at each other and busted out laughing.

"I feel like a fool. I'm sorry, sir. Carry on," I said as we realized that indeed it was not my car. My car was parked three cars over. It was so ironic that he had the same BMW as me.

"It's ok. It's not every day that I get to be confronted by two beautiful women who mistook my car for theirs," he said.

"I apologize. We shall be picking our faces off the floor and moving right along," Latrice said.

"Well can I at least have your number so we can laugh about this moment over dinner soon?" he asked Latrice.

"I like how you tried to smooth that in. It's 718-555-7555," Latrice said.

I gave her a look of death and she knew why.

"Can I have a name to go with this number please?" he asked.

"Yes sorry, it's Kristen. K-R-I-S-T-E-N," Latrice said.

If looks could kill, she would definitely be dead.

"Ok great. Well, ladies, it was definitely a pleasure meeting you both, but I must hop in *my* car now," he said as we all laughed. "But, Ms. Kristen, I'd be sure to give you a call. My name is James by the way," he said as he shook both of our hands.

As we walked to my car, I couldn't help but give Latrice death stares.

"What did I do now?" she asked as if she were innocent.

"Since when did your birth certificate say your name was Kristen and not Latrice?" I asked.

"I wasn't sure if I wanted to entertain him, but he seems decent and a gentleman. So if he calls you, you can tell him the truth."

"I'm giving him your number, address, and social security number. Now if he ends up at your house, chops you up into pieces and throws your ass in the Hudson, don't come swimming to me because you want to play these games," I said.

"I'm too cute to be put in someone's dirty ass water."

We laughed at the whole situation as we got into my car. We blasted music while driving to the mall. We were so lost in the music that I wasn't sure if I was driving above the speed limit or not, but I knew I did something wrong when I saw flashing lights.

"Shit. The cops are behind me. Was I driving too fast?" I asked.

"I'm not sure, girl, but it looks like they want you to pull over. Thank God I didn't bring my weed with me."

I pulled the car over and put it in park. I nervously waited for the cops to approach my car.

"Damn, should I record this? You know how these cops are; one wrong word and they got their knees to our necks."

"No, girl. Just stay calm and let me do the talking," I said.

I rolled down both of our windows and lowered the music as well. It wasn't blasting anymore, but I didn't want to give them any reason to say anything crazy to me.

"License and registration please," the officer by my door said.

"May I ask what I'm being pulled over for?" I asked before handing over my information.

"Because you're black and driving a BMW. We need to make sure that your baby father didn't steal it or use his drug money to purchase it," he said.

"Wow! You racist son of a bitch," I mumbled.
"Just because you're a cop doesn't mean you can talk to people that way!" Latrice yelled from the passenger seat.

"I'm going to have to ask you two to step out of the car," he said angrily.

I knew it was risky going back and forth with a cop, but I am sick and tired of how they treat us, black people. I stepped out of the car as Latrice took her time. I didn't blame her for not being submissive. I was angry too. Little did he know, Monique is a cop. Wait until I tell my sister about this. As soon as I got out of the car and looked him dead in his eyes, he turned me around and slammed me against the car. Latrice leaped out so fast ready to defend me. Then I heard her burst into laughter. I looked up and there was Monique. I could have killed her for raising my blood pressure like that.

"Why the hell would you prank me like that, Mo!" I asked trying to calm my nerves.

"You guys were so angry with Mike that no one even realized I was standing right there," Monique said still laughing.

"Mike was about to get a Mike Tyson ass-whooping," Latrice said meaning every word.

"I must admit, if this wasn't a prank I would be scared of you feisty ladies," Officer Mike said.

"Well I'm glad you completed your prank for the day, but don't do that to me again, Monique!" I said.

"I won't. I apologize for raising your pressure, but I'm not apologizing for pulling you over. You did turn without signaling. I could give you a ticket for that, but I'd settle with a nice home-cooked meal instead," Monique said.

"Deal. Let me know what day and it's done. Mike, you're more than welcome to come too," I said.

"No the hell he's not. I'll be there in replace of him," Latrice said. I knew she was serious.

"Be nice, Latrice. I will have enough for all of you."

"Fine. But he's not allowed to get seconds," Latrice said.

We all laughed at her. Mike didn't seem the bit annoyed by her which surprised me. Latrice can be harsh with the tongue at times and not every man can handle that. Let me find out this white boy has what it takes to tame Latrice's wild behind.

We said our goodbyes and parted ways. You can tell Latrice was in deep thought so I let her have her moment.

"Listen, I know things like this bring flashbacks, but not all cops are the same. I don't think Mo knows about what happened or else she wouldn't have done this crazy prank," I said breaking the silence.

"I never told her the full story. She only knows the watered-down version. It's not easy to talk about. It was almost three years ago, but it feels as if it were yesterday," she said.

"We all heal differently. It can be ten years from now and still feel like it was yesterday," I said comforting her as she cried.

"You're right. Sometimes I tell myself that it's time to get over it and stop dwelling on it because people have been through much worse than me, but it's so much easier said than done," Latrice said as she sobbed.

"You don't owe anyone an explanation. Your rights as a human were violated and you cannot blame yourself for something you had no control over. The only advice I would give to you is to stop fighting yourself for trying to quickly get over this. When you feel yourself about to cry, do so. When you want to scream, scream at the top of your lungs. When you feel like being angry, be angry. Allow yourself to go through these emotions. Hiding them will only hinder your healing process."

Latrice may be one of the wildest people I have ever met, but she hurts just like the rest of us.

"You know what makes this easier to deal with?" she asked.

"What?"

"Having people like you, remind me that it's ok. Knowing that my support system is so strong helps me be a bit stronger. Yes, I have my moments when I feel like I'm going to crumble, but you are always there to pick up my fallen pieces," she said as she dried her tears.

"Well, my dear sister, please understand I will always be here for you. It doesn't matter how many cookies you've crumbled, together we will find a way to find every little crumb. You've held me down in some of my darkest hours, so it's only right to return the favor when I can," I said while rubbing her back.

We were now parked outside of her apartment and was sitting in my car talking. Latrice has always been a loyal friend to me so it hurts to see her hurt. I can't always take her pain away, but I'll do whatever I can to help. We finished our conversation and headed into her apartment.

As we got closer to her door, we realized it was cracked open. We both looked at each other thinking the same thing, *it's do or die*. We both knew what that meant. Whoever was inside was about to get the beating of their life even if that meant that one of us would get hurt in the process.

I quickly sent a text to my sister and told her it was a 911 at Latrice's apartment. I tucked my phone away and grabbed my switchblade. Latrice slowly opened her front door, slid behind it, and grabbed her metal bat that was hidden in a bucket full of long umbrellas.

As we got closer into the apartment, we heard noises coming from the bathroom. One thing about being great friends for years is that you can look at each other and tell what the other is thinking. She gave me the look that she was going to bust through the door and start swinging. I switched my blade open ready for whatever was behind that door. Latrice kicked open her door and what we seen before our eyes was the last thing we expected. I think Latrice was more shocked then I was. Once she saw what was going on in her bathroom she dropped her bat. I still had my blade in my hand, but I knew it wasn't going to be used anymore.

"What the hell is going on? Laurence, I ought to whoop your ass!" We both stood there with disgust and shock written all over our faces. We just witnessed Laurence bending Peter over the bathroom sink and clearly enjoying their moment of sexual behavior.

They both jumped up. Embarrassed that they have been caught. Laurence was Latrice's twin brother and Peter was her landlord.

"Peter, I asked you to check the pipes out in my apartment, not get pipe from my brother!" Latrice yelled.

"Latrice, let me explain..." Peter cried out.

"Save it, Peter. Just get the hell out of my apartment. Let this be the first and last time I catch either of you around each other or I'd be sure to let your wives know that their husbands are gay!" Latrice screamed.

"I'm so sorry. I didn't mean for this to happen," Peter said.

Just as he was about to walk out, in came Monique and her partner, Officer Mike Scott.

"What's going on here?" Monique asked with her gun drawn.

I explained to her the embarrassing situation with Laurence and the landlord. She listened on in disgust.

"I have no problem with people and their sexual preferences, but what disgusts me is that you lay in bed every night with your wives, yet you're out here craving sexual attention from another man. Both of you are married and should be ashamed of yourselves. Laurence, I'll leave it up to Latrice to figure out how she wants to deal with you. As for you Peter, I deal with idiots like you all the time. You just violated the TL-18 amendment for tenants. One of two things can legally happen. She can easily take you to court and the judge can very well make sure you will never be a landlord again or she can fight to get at least three-six months' rent-free. Latrice it is completely up to you. I can help you with the paperwork to make sure you win whichever one you want. On top of that, you have me as a witness; you can't get any better than that. The judge will quickly approve whatever request you make," Monique said.

"Can we just handle this outside of the courts? I don't think we need to involve any judge or jury into this," Peter pleaded.

"Well, Peter, how do you expect we handle this without the courts?" Monique asked.

"Ms. Walker, what is it that you want or that I can give to you that will have you forgive or have mercy on me for my actions?" Peter asked Latrice.

"You've been a shitty landlord for a long time now. Cutting off our hot water whenever you felt like it. My bathroom has not been fixed and it has been three weeks since I have put in my request form. The paint is chipping in multiple places in my apartment. Rent is just too damn high for me to pay someone else to do the job that we as tenants pay you to do. So, Mr. Landlord, I'm not sure this can be handled outside of the courts," Latrice stated firmly.

"Ms. Walker, I assure you that I can make sure those needs are met," Peter said still pleading.

"I'm not just fighting for me; I'm fighting for all of the other tenants in this building that you've wronged. You owe us that much," Latrice said as she stood with her arms folded.

"It's a done deal. I have a few handy friends that owe me a favor. We can get those jobs done for you and the other tenants within the next two-three weeks," Peter said.

"And if it isn't done within that time frame then what? I get to tell your wife how sorry of a husband you are and that you would rather screw my brother than be faithful to her? Oh, I think she'd love to divorce you and take half of whatever you have," Latrice said.

"Ms. Walker, please believe me that it will be done," Peter said.

"I think you should just take it to the courts. You should complain about the rent being too high. Show them pictures of work that has yet to be completed and how he's screwing people inside of your apartment. That part alone is a big one. Not only did he enter into your apartment without you knowing, but he also caused your anxiety to rise because you were so worried that someone had broken into your house. I am sure your doctor will not mind faxing over a copy of your documented anxiety attacks and how easily they are triggered. I'm sure the judge wouldn't mind you having a few months free of rent," I said finally getting tired of hearing Peter plead, but not believing half of what he said he'll do.

"That sounds like a good idea, sis," Monique said.

"Sounds like a good idea to me too. I can definitely appreciate a few months with no rent and the courts will still have him fix up my apartment. Yea, that sounds like the better option," Latrice said. The cheerful look on her face made him nervous.

"Please hear me out. I will have your apartment fixed first. I will install the new refrigerator, stove, cabinets, bathroom sink, shower, and toilet. I will have your apartment freshly waxed and looking brand new. My brother is the manager at a very nice hotel. I can arrange for you to stay there for as long as it takes me to set up your apartment. In the meantime, do not worry about rent. I will cover it. Just please do not take me to court. I'm begging you," Peter said with tears in his eyes.

Monique chimed in and said, "We will take that under one condition, this needs to be a typed agreement and notarized. My cousin is a lawyer and she will reach out to you when the agreement has been typed and ready to be signed."

"That is fair enough. Thank you, ladies, so much for this. I promise I will make the best out of this situation," Peter said.

"You can start by leaving my house. We will be in touch," Latrice said.

"Of course. I'm sorry again," Peter said as he gathered his belongings and exited Latrice's apartment.

We all looked at each other and then all eyes were on Laurence.

"I don't even know what to say to you, let alone want to look at you. Grab your shit and leave my house now!" Latrice yelled.

"I'm sorry, Trice. I didn't mean to disrespect you or your place like that," Laurence said as Latrice walked into her bedroom and slammed the door.

"Just give her some space and when she's ready to talk, I'm sure she'll be more open to hearing your apology. In the meantime go home and think of some nice things for you to do to get back on good terms," I said to him.

"Thanks, Kris. I'll leave, but again I'm sorry and I'm sorry that you guys had to be a part of it as well," Laurence said.

None of us responded. We just nodded and closed the door after he left.

"Ok ladies, I'm going to go back into the squad car. Officer King, take your time but not too much time," Officer Scott said.

"Yes, Mike, I'll be out in less than five minutes. Let me just make sure she's good," Monique responded to her partner.

Monique and I walked into Latrice's bedroom where she was pacing back and forth.

"Trice, sit down for a second," Monique said.

"Listen, I know you're upset and you have every right to be, but I am grateful that this was a controllable situation and we know who the unwanted guest in your house was. We worked together to make sure that you will be given the best treatment ever. You know I am a firm believer that God works in mysterious ways and he allows things like this to happen for a reason. Just think about it, your landlord would have been still dragging his feet when it came to fixing up your apartment. Now you're damn near getting a whole apartment makeover. This ugly situation is turning into a pretty good one if you ask me," Monique said.

"You're right. I don't know how to feel. I always knew my brother was a little curious, but of course growing up in a household like ours, being different was not allowed, especially when your father took pride in being the head Elder and your mother as the head deaconess. I do have a question though; if I took this to court do you really think I would have been awarded whatever I asked for because my rights as a tenant were violated?" Latrice asked Monique.

"I have no clue about any of this. I was just talking out my teeth. I am a cop. These dummies believe damn near every threat I throw. It's my specialty," Monique said laughing.

"Wait, so what about the TL-18 Law you mentioned that he broke? What was that about? That should be something that she can use if it went to court, right?" I asked.

"No, Kris. I made that up. I had to think quickly on my feet so I just put together the first thing that came to mind. The T stands for Tenant, the L stands for Landlord, and 18 stands for 2018. Damn, I'm good," Monique said while patting herself on the back.

"You had me fooled," I said.

"Shit, I must be a dummy too then, because while you were talking to him, I'm saying to myself damn Monique knows her shit. Wait so what do we do now? Since damn near everything you told him was a lie, how am I going to get a lawyer to type up the quote-unquote agreement? A lawyer is never going to agree on something that's not legally correct," Latrice said.

"When there's a will, there's a way. Call up Eva and explain to her the situation. She knows how to work her magic and make things like this come to life," Monique said.

"I forgot that Eva works in paralegal. I am definitely calling her. Thanks again, Monique. I owe you big time," Latrice said as she hugged Monique.

"Ok ladies, I'll leave you guys to handle that. I got to get back to work," Monique said as she hugged us goodbye.

As soon as Monique left, Latrice called Eva. Eva is a close friend of ours and I knew she would do whatever it was to make sure she could make this arrangement come true without it backfiring on any of us. It is hard to find great loyal friends, but when it comes to my small circle, I am always grateful for the loyalty they show. Eva was more than happy to help Latrice get what she deserved. All she needed Latrice to do was print out any text conversations and emails she has that showed proof of her request on what she needed to be done in her apartment. She also asked her to take pictures of her apartment and get clear shots of the problem areas. The pictures had to prove the date and time she took them so it would show that it was a current situation. We finished up our call with Eva and gathered what she requested. I stayed by Latrice for a few just to make sure she was good before I headed home.

CHAPTER 3

STEPHAN

I was in my office trying to type out the agenda for tomorrow's meeting when Samantha, my assistant, tapped on my door. I motioned for her to come in.

"Mr. Moore, you have a call on line three," she said.

"Smith's Bank. This is Stephan, how may I help you?" I asked as I answered the call.

"Hi, Mr. Stephan, my account seems a little lower than usual, I was wondering if there's anything I can do to get you to increase my balance?" the caller asked.

"Well maybe a home-cooked meal, with a nice warm bath with a beautiful woman in our jetted tub, and a much-needed massage for the both of us. How does that sound?" I asked.

"I think I can arrange that. I was thinking about chicken parmigiana, with spaghetti noodles, my famous sauce to go with it, and some good ole cheddar cheese biscuits. Now how does that sound?" she asked.

"Sounds like I need to pack up and head on home."

"That's the best thing I've heard all day," she responded.

"Now you said cheddar cheese biscuits, are you making them from scratch?" I asked.

"Of course not," she laughed. "They are the boxed Red Lobster ones that they sell at the supermarket."

"I should've known. My baby doesn't know how to make no damn homemade biscuits," I said laughing.

"My boxed biscuits are going to taste better than your aunt's unseasoned fried chicken and your sisters wanna be potato salad that looks more like potato soup," she said. She was laughing hysterically at her own joke.

I chuckled a little because it was very true, but I could not let her know I completely agreed with her.

"I'm glad that these phone calls are recorded so that I can let them listen to this recording at the family reunion," I said. Now it was my turn to laugh.

"Come on, babe. Don't be like that. You know I was just joking," she said.

"Nope too late."

"Ok, what can I do to have you forget about that?" she asked.

"Hmm, let me think long and hard," I said while I placed my hand on my chin and massaged my full beard as if I was in deep thought. I needed to use this moment to my best ability. "I can't think of anything right now, but don't worry, it'll come to me soon."

I heard her sigh over the phone. I knew she thought I was serious and it only made it even funnier. "On another note, how's your day going beautiful?" I asked.

"Well, it's been a day. So much has happened in just a short matter of time," she said and I knew by the way her voice changed that it was not the greatest day for her. I listened as she filled me in on everything that happened at the parking lot with the wrong car situation, getting pulled over as a prank, and what just happened with Latrice in her apartment.

"Damn, babe. It seems like I should be the one home cooking you a meal, running you a bath, and rubbing you down," I said meaning every word.

"Honestly, Steph, it wasn't a bad day, it was just too much happening in such a short time." I heard her sigh again.

"Even still, you need a mental break from everything. Let me finish up this agenda for tomorrow's meeting and I'm going to come home and help you cook," I said. Kristen knew I was a better cook then she was, but she can definitely throw down in the kitchen. She laughs at my family all the time because of their not so great cooking and how I can cook better than them. In my mother's defense, she was not the best cook, but she also never had to cook because my dad is a chef and loved cooking for the house or bringing home food he cooked at the restaurant.

I finished my conversation with Kris and promised her I would be there as soon as I could. We decided to do dinner at her place tonight. We both had keys to each other's apartment, but the majority of our time together was spent at hers. I didn't mind though. Her place is more home feeling than mine is. I know we kept our places for moments when we needed time to miss each other, but honestly, I cannot remember the last time that was. We were both wasting money having two apartments. That will soon change though, just wait.

I was determined to finish the agenda for tomorrow before I left for the day. Going over it a few times just to make sure I did not leave anything too important out. I think I got enough things on the list to discuss. If I left out anything, I would just have to add it in tomorrow. At this point, I was officially checked out of work and ready to be home with my woman.

Before I headed home, I made a quick stop to Lush. Kristen loves their bath bombs. I picked up three different kinds for her to choose from and her favorite facial scrub from there. I left my job at a good time so traffic wasn't too bad. A few blocks down was an edible arrangements store.

"Hi, I placed an order for pick up," I said to the lady at the front.

"Hello, what's your name sir?" She asked.

"Stephan Moore," I responded.

"Your order is ready. Let me go and grab it from the back," she said as she turned to leave.

When she came out, I thanked her and made one final stop before I headed home.

I got to Kris' apartment in no time and God was definitely on my side because I found parking right in front.

I took out the things I bought and entered.

"Babe, you're home!" she yelled as she ran towards me. I placed the bags on the counter and embraced her. One thing I love about this woman is how she loves me. You can always tell when someone genuinely cares and loves you. We hugged and kissed for a bit as I enjoyed taking in her scent.

"Of course I'm home. After hearing your voice earlier, work did not matter anymore. I knew I needed to come home to you," I said as I kissed her on her forehead.

"What did I ever do to deserve such a good man? Am I being pranked? Are you just in my imagination?" she asked.

"Nope. I'm not your imagination and God paid me a pretty penny to be with you. I already spent half of what he gave me so I can't leave you just yet, but don't worry I'll be asking him for a little more because some of it was spent on you."

She laughed and then slapped me on the arm. "Get settled in. I already started working on dinner. Come join me when you're ready," she said as she sashayed back into the kitchen.

Man, I love that woman.

I went to the bedroom to place my bags down, then walked into the bathroom and washed my hands. I was raised to always wash my hands when I come into the house before touching anything. Thankfully, Kristen was too. I did not understand how people could just walk off the streets, into their homes, open the refrigerator, and grab something. I wasn't a germaphobe, but I was very conscious of the many things my hands came across while outside. After undressing and throwing on some basketball shorts and a tee, I went into the kitchen where Kris was.

She had cleaned the chicken already so all I had to do was season it. I took over and told her all I needed her to do was prepare her boxed, I mean cheddar biscuits when the time came. She sat on one of our kitchen chairs and watched me go to work.

"It never ceases to amaze me of how good you are with your hands," she said.

"That's the only reason why you keep me around, so you can get a good home-cooked meal out of me," I said teasing.

"Well that may be true, but there are also other reasons too."

"Enlighten me, darling."

"Sure thing. Well for starters, I am not perfect and I know you are aware of my many flaws, yet you still love me as I am. You do so much for me and never intend to get anything in return. We have been in dangerous situations before where you have shielded and risked yourself for me. You are my best friend. The person I call when I need a voice of reason. I love that you are always willing to stop any and everything just to make sure I am ok and taken care of. We have been together for almost five years and you still do little things to surprise me or send me cute things just to make my day. Baby, I can go on all day but I'm hungry so I'll stop there," she said as she picked up a cracker and motioned for me to continue seasoning the chicken.

I was so stuck that I did not know what to say. Yes, I know she loves me and I love her as well, but to hear the many reasons why she does was refreshing. When you do things from the heart you do not look for a reward nor do you look for confirmation that they knew you had to move mountains just to make it happen.

"Thank you. Not just for what you said, but how you said it. I felt it and know you meant every word. Ditto, my love. Ditto," I said as I put the chicken down, walked over to her, and kissed her with everything within me.

I finished seasoning the chicken, put them in a Ziploc bag, and placed it in the refrigerator to marinate for a few while I cleaned up. Usually, I like my meat to marinate overnight, but these few minutes will have to do. I cleaned up the dishes and wiped down the counter with bleach and Lysol to take away any bacteria left from the chicken. Kristen prepared her homemade lemonade while I was heating my pot.

My pot was just about heated and ready with just enough oil so I took the chicken out and prepared it for frying.

I only had a few pieces left to fry, so I preheated the oven and prepared my sauce in another pot for the chicken and pasta. I put the noodles to boil. Once the chicken was done frying, I took the aluminum pan out of the oven and laid the chicken in it. I grabbed my saucepot and poured it over the chicken. I turned the chicken over and did the same. I topped it with freshly sliced mozzarella cheese and placed it in the oven to set in. The hardest part was over. Kristen had just finished preparing her biscuits and placed them in the oven.

"What shall we watch while we eat dinner?" I asked her as I grabbed the remote and turned the television on.

"The new season of Chicago Fire starts tonight. Let's watch the last episode of the previous season to refresh our memories and I'll record the new episode so we can watch it after," she said.

"Sure thing, sweets," I said as I searched on demand for the previous season.

By the time our eating area was set and the show was ready to be played, the food was done. I fixed our plates while Kristen poured us two glasses of her lemonade. I placed the food on the small eating tables we had in the living room. I reached for her hand as we prepared to say grace. "Dear Lord, we thank you for allowing us to see another day. We thank you for giving us food, shelter, great jobs, and most importantly each other. As we partake in this food, we ask that you continue to bless our hands so that we can continue to make meals with and for each other. We humbly thank you for everything you have done and will do. Please continue to keep us away from harm and danger, for this is our prayer, in Jesus' name we pray."

We both said, "Amen."

"Time to dig in," she said as she grabbed her fork and began to eat. "This is so good. You have to tell me your secret ingredients to this sauce."

"I put my foot in it. Especially this big toe with the hangnail. It scrapes up so much and adds such a great flavor to any and everything," I said.

She slapped me on my arm. "I dislike you a lot. Don't ruin my appetite. I know what that big toe looks like."

"I love you too," I said.

I pressed play on the television and we began watching Chicago Fire. I was deep into the show that I did not even realize that she was stealing a piece of chicken from off of my plate. By the time I realized, it was too late. She had already put it in her mouth while trying not to spit it out from laughing at her thieving ass. I could not help but laugh with her. Payback was coming though. I slickly pretended to reach for my lemonade as I grabbed hers and downed it.

"Now we're even," I said blowing her a kiss with my spaghetti breath.

"Babe!" she whined. "You drunk all of my lemonade. I only took a piece of your chicken. How can we be even?" she asked still whining.

"Well, the Bible says that if you mess with God's children, it would come back to you tenfold. So the Lord told me to get my tenfold worth of lemonade and what do you know, tenfold was all of it," I said shrugging my shoulders and blowing her another saucy breath kiss.

"I'm not so sure those were the exact words, but I do know you're going to pour me my drink back. I need something to wash down this dry ass chicken you made."

"By the looks of your plate, I can tell my chicken isn't dry, but since it is, I'll just eat the rest of yours."

"No! I was kidding," she said as she held onto her plate and moved inches away from me.

"I bet you were." I walked back into the kitchen to pour us both another glass of lemonade.

When I returned into the living room, she was rewinding the show since we missed a few parts fighting over food and drinks. Thank God for the rewind button. I love moments like this, but we get so lost into each other that we end up missing parts of our show or movie.

"Here you go, babe," I said passing her the glass of lemonade and another piece of chicken cutlet. Well, half of a piece because I broke it in half so I can have a piece too. She doesn't need to know that though.

"This is why I can't lose weight. You're always feeding me."

I knew Kristen was not the smallest of the bunch, but until she becomes ok with her size, the amount of times I tell her she is beautiful to me will not matter until she sees the beauty for herself. Now do not get me wrong, she knows she is beautiful, but she has her moments when she is not as confident as I would like her to be.

"I'm going to continue to feed you until you get so big that I have to roll you through the door and when you can no longer fit through the door, I'll come outside and feed you some more."

We looked at each other and started laughing.

"I love how you try to make me feel good about my weight and it's what makes me love you even more. Accepting me flaws and all. You are God-sent, but I need to get off of this weight," she said becoming serious.

"I get it, babe. This isn't something you have to do alone."

"So you're willing to make some life changes with me?" she said getting excited.

"I didn't mean me. Latrice has been drinking a lot lately and her belly is starting to show it. She always talking about how she is going to snatch up somebody's son, she can work on snatching up her body with you instead of snatching up a man for once. If that does not work out, you have Monique. I've seen how many donuts she can eat."

"Don't be talking about them like that!" Kristen said as she slapped me across my arm.

"I'm kidding, Kris," I said still laughing. "Listen, since this is something you are serious about, let us do it together. It is not about just losing weight. It is also about being healthy. We both come from a family with major health issues like diabetes and high blood pressure. So let us start by making healthier food choices. Instead of white, we will have wheat. Instead of juice or soda, we'll have water," I said trying to convince myself that I can make this change too. Soda is one of my best friends.

"I think we should meal prep as well. I have been watching people on Instagram do it and I think it is a great idea. Especially the days that we do not pack lunch. You know how crazy we get when we're trying to decide what we want to eat," she said.

"Very true. I'm always calling you trying to get an idea from what you ate or plan on eating," I said.

"Great, so meal planning it is."

"Yup. We can go to the gym twice a week and once on the weekend. I say twice because you know how crazy our schedules can get, mine especially. Twice a week is a good goal to start with. Plus, sex at least three times a night. Sex is great cardio," I said.

She looked at me like I was crazy. "Who the hell told you that sex is cardio? I hope you meant three times a week."

"Think about it. When we have sex, you be sweating, panting, and trying to catch your breath. Your body be sore for days. That is just like going to the gym. See, baby, we've already been working out."

She slapped me on my arm again. "I don't be panting and out of breath. That is all you! Sore for the next few days? Oh, you're flattering yourself Mr. I caught a cramp in my leg."

"It was only one time that I caught a cramp." She was not about to play me. I always put it down on that ass.

"Let's not talk about all the times you claim to be tired just so that I could climb up and do all the work," she said

"Well, I do be tired. You don't be complaining when I give you these long strokes."

"How can I complain when in the midst of these long strokes you be choking me? Of course, I don't complain, I can barely speak, let alone breathe."

"I guess that makes two of us," I said giving her the eye.

"What you mean by that?" she asked.

"Oh, you know. All those times I have to go to work with my shirt fully buttoned. Trying to hide the marks on my neck. Funny thing is, it's not from you kissing it, but how tight your legs be wrapped around it," I said while massaging my neck acting as if I could still feel the soreness.

"That's not my fault. No one told you to find where my spot is."

"You're right. As your man, that's my job to do so. And I must say that I do a damn good job at it," I said as I patted myself on the back.

"How did we get on this topic anyway?"

"We were talking about burning calories," I said winking at her.

"Right! Now back to the real issue, me losing weight."

"Trust me, baby. I didn't forget about the real issue, but right now we have a bigger issue to take care of," I said as I guided her hands inside my boxers.

She gave it a nice squeeze. That only made it jump and crave for her even more. I pulled her on top of me and kissed her deeply. I love to hear the little moans she makes. I lifted her face to look deep into her eyes and whispered, "I love you and all of your curves." I placed my hand on her chin and pulled her lips back to mine. I felt him growing even more and knew it was only a matter of time before I had to release him from my boxers. She purposely positioned her love box right on top of him as she continued to kiss me deeply. This woman knows exactly how I like it. Damn, how did I get so lucky? I cupped her butt with both hands and pushed her down further onto me. She needed to feel how ready I was. I held her by her back as I flipped her onto it. She felt how ready I was and I needed to feel if she had matched my readiness. I continued to kiss her as I positioned myself on top of her. She pulled her shirt off and I unfastened her bra and released my titties. I sucked on her right one. "These are mine and all mine, right?" I asked her in between licks and sucks.

"Yes, baby. No one else's," she replied as she fought to catch her breath.

"Good girl."

I wasted no time pulling off her leggings. I had to stop for a minute as I realized she had on one of my favorite cheeky panties. I love the way she looks in black underwear. I made her stand up and she knew exactly what I wanted her to do. The sexual connection we have is like no other. Without exchanging words, we both knew what to do to keep the other satisfied. She slowly spun around and stopped when her ass lined up with my face. I placed my hands on her round butt and slowly caressed her cheeks. She let out that soft moan again. I continued to massage her cheeks as I slipped a finger inside her love box. It felt like she was ready but I had to be sure. I stuck another finger in and slowly moved them in and out. I felt her walls clench around my fingers. I played with her a little more before I removed them. When I looked at my fingers, the wetness covering them proved that she was more than ready. She turned around as I stood to my feet. I kissed her again before I bent her over the couch. She positioned herself just the way I liked it. Nothing turns me on more than seeing her back arched the way she does it. I placed my hand on the small of her back as I positioned myself to enter her. Her warmness and wetness always make me weak. I slid in and out of her just the way she likes it. Long and slow with deep strokes. I continued as I dug as deep as I could. I picked up the pace and continued going in deeper. She reached behind her and placed her hands on my stomach.

"Move your hands, you're going to take every inch of me," I said as I picked up the pace even more. Her moans and cries only turned me on. I grabbed her shoulders as I pumped even harder and faster. I felt myself about to explode and slowed my pace. There was no way I was about to cum when she didn't yet. I squeezed her breast as I went back to giving her long strokes. I moved my hand down to her clit and started making circular motions as I continued to stroke her. I felt her love box tighten against my penis and knew it was only a matter of time before she climaxed.

"Baby, please don't stop. Please, just like that!" she said as I felt her tighten up even more.

Her wish was my command so I did just that. It was too damn good though and I knew if she didn't cum any minute that I would. There's something about that feeling I get when I feel her tighten up against me. Feeling her wetness increase. Not only does it confirm that I am doing my thing, but that she is close to climax. I grabbed her by her hair and pounded away. She was close to climaxing and I was going to make sure I came right with her.

"Come on, baby. Come on daddy's dick, just like I like it," I said.

"Daddy, I'm cuming!" she screamed as I felt her body begin to shake, and at that point, I lost it and came right with her. I felt her body go limp as she collapsed on the couch.

I kissed the back of her neck as I got up from the couch and went into the bathroom. I turned on the jetted bathtub and grabbed her bath bomb. I dropped it in the tub when the water was at the right temperature and height. I called for her to come into the bathroom and when she saw the bubbles, pure excitement filled her face.

"You never cease to amaze me," she said as she grabbed my beard and pulled me in for a kiss.

"That's my job, babe. Now step in and have your moment. I'll join you in a minute," I said as I left the bathroom. I went into our bedroom and grabbed the bag from the last store I went to and placed it on her dresser for her to see when she gets out of the bath. I went into the kitchen and grabbed the edible arrangement box of strawberries, bananas, apple wedges, and pineapples all dipped in chocolate. I entered into the bathroom, sat on the edge of the bathtub, and fed her some fruit.

"Come join me so I can feed you too," she said while winking at me.

I wasted no time undressing and hopped right in. She took the box of fruit and did just as she said she would. She mimicked the scene of the movie *Lady and the Tramp,* where the dogs ate the same spaghetti and ended up kissing each other. It was cute and corny in its own way. She got up from facing me and sat in front of me as she laid her head on my chest. I kissed her on the cheek and gave her body small massages.

We spoke about what I did at work today and she went into further detail about all the events that happened with her day.

After our nice long bath, we headed back to the room where we prepared for bed. I sat on the edge of the bed and just admired her beauty. She spotted the bag and almost leaped out of her skin.

"Aww, babe! You really went out of your way today. You know how much I love Victoria's Secret!" She pulled out the lingerie I bought her and her new panties. Kris had an addiction for Victoria Secret panties and I just added to her addiction. I love that she takes care of herself and always aims to please me, but the real issue is where are these panties going to go? She barely has any room left in her underwear draw. I shook my head as I watched her try to stuff them in the draw. She made it work though. She then grabbed her favorite lotion from The Body Shop, *Coconut Body Milk*, and began to lotion her silky smooth skin. I love the way it smells on her.

"What are you thinking about, babe?" she asked.

"Just thinking of how lucky I am to have such a beautiful woman like you," I said.

She walked up to me and kissed me passionately. I pulled back soon after because I felt myself getting excited again.

She winked at me and continued getting ready for bed. I moved from the edge and laid on my side of the bed as I turned the television on and watched the Sports Center. I didn't bother to ask her what she wanted to watch, I knew as soon as her head hit the pillow she was going to be done for the night.

She was finally done with her nightly routine when she grabbed the remote and put it on mute. I knew exactly what that meant. I got out of bed and we kneeled by the bedside. She grabbed my hand and we bowed our heads as we prepared to say our prayers.

"Dear Heavenly Father, we come to you as humbly as we can. We thank you for the many blessings you have showered upon us. We are forever grateful for you showing us the way and never leaving or forsaking us. We ask that you forgive us for all of our sins that we have and will commit. May we never go astray. We pray that you will continue to bless our relationship and make us stronger in unity. May we always be open and honest with one another and may we not let anyone or anything come in and tear us apart. Bless our home, families, friends, coworkers, and those we provide service. Please keep us away from all harm and danger and please watch over all of us as we travel to and from our destinations, for this is our prayer in Jesus' name we pray, Amen."

"Amen."

She kissed me goodnight and tucked in on her side of the bed. I cut the lights off and did the same. I turned the television back up a bit and continued watching the Sports Center. It was almost finished so I put on Martin. I usually watch him at night until I fall out as well. The only bad thing about watching this at night while Kris is sleeping is having to hold back my laughter. This was the episode when Pam's cousin Tammy escapes from the mental hospital and pretends to be her. I watched as much as I could but felt my eyes getting heavy. While it still played in the background, I prepared myself to knock right out. I turned over and wrapped my arm around Kris as I pulled her into me and inhaled her scent. The clock read 11:15 p.m. Not bad. I'll get a few hours of sleep in.

It felt like I was just about to get into a good deep sleep when I felt Kris tossing and turning in my arms. I thought she just wanted room so I moved my arm as I drifted back to sleep. It could not have been any more than two minutes when I heard her scream and her arm came slapping me across my chest. It is rare when she has episodes like this and I know how bad her anxiety will be for the rest of the week because of it. I also knew this meant we might not be getting much sleep after all tonight.

I grabbed her arm and tapped her repeatedly. "Kris, baby, you have to wake up," I kept repeating. I shook her a little harder. "You are dreaming, baby, wake up." I kept shaking her as she kept screaming, crying, and fighting in her sleep. After a good shake and calling out her name, she finally woke up. She seemed relieved to see me as she buried her face into my chest and cried. It was a normal routine when she has bad dreams. This was another reason why we never stayed apart from each other. If I was not here when she had one of these dreams, best believe I would be in my car within the next five minutes. She would not be able to go back to sleep if I was not there. I rubbed her back as I reminded her that it was just a dream. It usually takes her a few minutes to calm down before she could tell me what happened. In the meantime, I continued to rub my hands up and down her back, soothing her. She lifted her head a few minutes later. I grabbed the box of tissues I kept on the nightstand. They are on my side of the bed for moments like this. She laid back down on my chest for a few more minutes and then got up and went into the bathroom. She climbed back into bed and laid on her side facing me.

"I hate when I have bad dreams," she said.

"I know, babe. I wish I knew why you get them. I think you should consider talking to your doctor about it," I said.

"At my next appointment with her, I will."

"Let me know when it is and I'll go with you," I said

"Ok, I will," she said.

"Are you ready to talk about it?"

"Not right now. What I want is a glass of wine to help my nerves."

"One glass coming right up," I said as I got up to head to the kitchen to pour her a glass.

I handed her the glass of wine and she took a few sips as she adjusted herself on the bed. We sat in silence for a bit before she began to speak.

"I had a dream that Latrice and I were in some club having the time of our lives. We were dancing and singing along as if we were the only two in there. Out of nowhere, a fight breaks out and everyone is running away from the fight because innocent people were getting hit and hurt in the process. You know when danger like that comes, I'm out. The last thing I need is to get arrested over being at the wrong place at the wrong time, especially since I work for the Department of Education. Anywho, Latrice and I gave each other that look that said let's get up out of here. As we were heading towards the exit, we see the bouncers arguing with a group of girls. One girl jumps up and slaps one of the bouncers after he shoved her out of his face. The other bouncer grabbed the girl by her neck and was shaking her. Her friends started pouncing on them. Then the next thing I know, Latrice and I got pushed out of the way by a group of guys. I'm assuming they were with the girls because they came for the girl's offense and started fighting the bouncers. More security came out of nowhere and it ended up being a nasty brawl. They were blocking the exit so we could not get out. Latrice and I were trying to get around them and squeeze our way through when the cops came in with guns drawn. They were yelling, telling everyone to freeze and get down on the ground. Latrice was yelling that we were not part of the fight and that we were trying to leave. This mean-looking black cop comes up to her and screamed in her face, 'no one asked you about your involvement. Get on the ground and do as we say!' So I jump in the conversation and say 'Officer, with all due respect, we weren't involved. We were trying to leave and go home when we got blocked in.' He grabs me by my arm and says, 'Did I ask you for your input? I think not!' I was trying to shake him off me but he grabbed me harder and pushed me onto the ground. My face was being mushed to the floor. Latrice was trying to pull him off me when he backhands her and sends her flying across the floor. I leaped up and slapped him so hard when I woke up I still felt my hand stinging," she said shaking and squeezing her right hand.

"Damn, babe. That's some crazy-ass dream. I would hate for you to get involved in real life with a cop. As a black person, male or female, they do not give two shits about us and think we are all the same; a criminal, drug deal, smuggler, you name it. They'll call us anything in the books, but educated," I said getting upset just at the thought of how people of color are perceived. I had to mentally tell myself to calm down as Kris was telling me about the cop putting his hands on her and Latrice. I felt my fist bawl up and my chest tighten. I had to remind myself that it was just a dream.

"But wait there's more," she says.

"Continue," I said preparing myself for whatever comes next. At this point, I needed a drink too.

"So after I hit him he grabs me by my neck and then I hear someone yell, 'if you don't get your hands off of her I will have your badge!'"

"I'm sorry detective; they weren't cooperating with my orders. I had to restrain them," the black cop said.

"I looked up and there was my sister. Nothing made me feel safer than seeing her. I felt like I could breathe again. She assured me that she was going to handle him. Latrice and I chatted with Monique briefly and then headed to the car. I called you instantly and you told Latrice and me to get home ASAP and that you were going to stay on the phone until we arrived. You told Latrice she had to stay by us and you were not taking no for an answer. When we pulled up to the house, you were outside waiting. I ran into your arms and just cried. You held me and then said not to worry that you will take care of it. I asked you what you mean by that as I saw the seriousness in your face and right when you were about to tell me, I woke up."

"Well I'm pretty sure awake or asleep I would never allow someone to disrespect you like that and get away with it."

"I know, Steph. I wish you could've felt how relieved I was when Monique showed up right on time."

"I believe you, love. It is calming knowing that your sister is a cop. Well, a detective now as of last week. Even though I still worry about you when you're out and about, I know that she'll shut the whole city down for you in two point five seconds," I said.

"That's very true, but because I know the title she holds it also makes me worry about her. She has put away some dangerous people and I fear retaliation. Not only retaliation from them, but also from people who hate cops. The sad part about it is that I can't even be a hundred percent mad about people feeling a type of way about them because there are some dirty cops out there and they get away with murder, literally."

I shook my head in agreement with her as she continued with her rant. Lord knows I want nothing more than to get at least four hours of sleep, but how can I when she is feeling this way? I have a big meeting tomorrow and I know me not getting any sleep is going to show. I should have put a sleeping pill in her wine glass.

"Babe, are you listening to me?" she asked as I snapped out of my thoughts.

"Of course I am."

"So what did I say?"

"Kris, I was paying attention. Let's watch some t.v. until you drift back to sleep," I said trying to change the subject and not get caught.

Thank God, she did just that. I turned up the volume and pulled her into me and we watched Martin until I heard her light snores and knew she was out for the count. I turned down the volume and tried to get into a comfortable sleeping position without waking her.

CHAPTER 4
KRISTEN

I woke up with my head pounding. I hate the nights when I have nightmares. It always seems to mess up my whole day. Sadly enough, every time I have bad dreams they always seem to come true in some way. The hard part is not knowing when it's going to happen and who it will involve. My dreams usually come true, but never with the same people that are in my dream. It scares me because I don't know who to warn or how to stop it from happening. The only thing I can do is pray about it and ask God to help me focus throughout the day.

I cannot begin to express how grateful I am to have Stephan in my corner. I do not know how I would manage sometimes if it were not for him. Sometimes I think about what my life would be like if I stayed with one of my exes. I highly doubt any of them would be as supportive as Steph, especially during my nighttime episodes. It most likely would have scared them off. I cannot blame them though.

Today ought to be an interesting day. For starters, it is testing week. The week of testing should be the easiest week ever, but for some reason, it tends to be the most drama-filled week all school year. Last year during testing week, four fights broke out. I had a conversation with my colleagues about what we thought made testing week always a crazy one. I stated that it's because they are locked in a classroom for hours. During testing week, the students are seated for a long time, not able to speak to one another, and having to take a test that I am sure none of them is excited for. When they can stretch their legs and interact with one another, they are filled with so much energy that they use any way to release it.

"Yes, babe. I'm sorry," I said after realizing he had been calling me a few times.

"How are you feeling?" he asked.

"I'm ok. I have a slight headache, but that's nothing new."

"Just take it easy today and try to take your mind off of it."

"I will try my best. It's testing week, so I'm going to take advantage of my quiet time and get some writing done."

"That sounds like a great idea. You haven't shared any poems with me in a while. I miss reading your work."

Hearing that he misses reading my work makes me melt. Not everyone appreciates a good writer.

"I'll make sure I have one for you to read by the time I get home," I said.

"I'll be waiting on it," he said as he leaned in and kissed me on the forehead. "I should be home at a decent time today. After I wrap up today's meeting there are only small things to do."

"Sounds good to me. I'll text or call you later to discuss dinner," I said as I put my blazer on, grabbed my bags and car key.

I grabbed my lunch bag and past his to him. We kissed each other goodbye and hopped in our cars.

I started up my car and Tamar's album, *Bluebird of Happiness* started playing. I just loved me some Tamar, but it was routine for me to play my gospel music in the morning and my R&B as I drove home from work. I let my phone connect to the cars Bluetooth and started my gospel playlist. I hit shuffle and the first song that came on was, *It's Not Over*, by Israel & New Breed. It's something about these kinds of gospel songs that puts me in a grateful and humble place. I turned the volume down as I said a quick prayer asking God to give my loved ones and me traveling mercy. I thanked him for waking me up this morning. It's so easy to ask God for things, but I'm learning to just say thank you for what he's already done for me and the great things I know he will do. I turned my music back up and drove off.

Traffic was on my side today. It only took me twenty-two minutes to get to work when on a bad day it can take thirty-five minutes. I found a good parking spot on the block of the school and put my D.O.E. plaque in the window so these traffic cops won't give me a ticket. I swear they be out here looking to give anyone a ticket, just got meet their quota. I don't mind the hustle, but leave my car alone, please! I grabbed my bags and headed to the entrance of the school.

"Good morning, Ms. Johnson. How are you?"

"Morning, Agent Adams. I'm well and you?" I asked as I walked through the front door.

"I'm hanging in there," he replied.

"That's all we can do. Just take everything one day at a time," I said smiling at him.

"You're absolutely right," he replied smiling back at me.

Agent Adams has been working at John Franklin Middle School since I was attending many years ago. I don't know any school safety agent that works as hard as him. He puts the young agents to shame. My school isn't one of the worst middle schools, but they sure aren't angels. They say it takes a village to raise a child and boy am I happy for the support system we have here for our students.

I went into the main office, said my good mornings, and grabbed my attendance folder and everything else that was in my mailbox.

"Ms. Johnson, who you all dressed up for today? You got a hot date or something?"

I turned around to see little Miss Amber coming up the stairs behind me. "No date, it's called looking nice for yourself and not anyone else."

"If you say so, but I can tell you got a man," Amber said smirking.

"And how can you tell I have a man missy?" I asked.

"Because you got that same glow my momma has when she and her man friend are on good terms," she said giving me the side-eye.

I could not help but to chuckle at her theory. These kids swear they know it all and they may be right sometimes, but you cannot let them know that.

I got off on the fourth floor and told Amber to enjoy the rest of her day and to behave herself. When I got upstairs, I realized I still had a few minutes to unwind before I went to the gym to greet and pick up my students. I walked to my classroom, hung my stuff up, and put my lunch in the refrigerator. I opened the window and sprayed some Febreze, the gain scent. It is something about a good smelling room that relaxes me. I put some words of encouragement on the board and tidied up the room a bit before I went to get my students.

"Good morning, Ms. Johnson. How are you today?" asked Kendra Boyd, the assistant principal.

"I'm great, Mrs. Boyd. How are you?" I asked.

"It's day one of testing, so I'm good but anxious for it to be over already," she said as she placed her hand on her forehead as if she was already over this day. Little did she know, I too was ready for testing to be over.

"How is Malcolm doing in your class?"

"Malcolm is doing better. He is not quite there yet, but well on his way. He's determined to graduate this year so he's been staying out of trouble and trying to be on time," I responded honestly.

"That's great. That boy has been through it! I am happy we have not lost him to the streets. I am hoping and praying that he stays on the right track. It is so easy to revert to old ways. I am grateful that he is comfortable enough to talk to you and Mr. Jones. Having a teacher and a guidance counselor they can trust does a lot for our students," she said as we headed for the door.

"Yes, he has come a long way and I will continue to do all that I can to make sure it stays that way," I said as I followed behind her so I could grab my students from the gym.

"Your work and dedication will forever be appreciated," she said as she turned to face me and smiled.

I smiled back at her as my way of saying thank you.

"Good morning, Ms. Johnson!" Kamaya screamed from across the gym.

"Good morning, Kamaya!" I yelled back.

Coming to work in a bad mood or feeling down does not last long because of my students. They tell me all the time how much I mean to them, but I do not think they truly understand how much they mean to me.

Once all my students saw me enter the gym, they started heading towards me. I greeted them and we headed to our classroom. Once outside the classroom, I greeted them with our individual handshakes.

To release some stress and get their minds right for today's test, I dimmed the lights, put on some calming music. I had them sit at their desk, close their eyes, and meditate. We usually have *Meditation Mondays*, so the students know the routine when it comes to meditation. When I first tried it with them, I did not think they would be into, but it was satisfying to see that they appreciated it. Only God knows what my students go through on the weekends and what their lives are like when they are not in school. When Monday's come around and we start with our meditations, they know it's to erase any negativity that has happened the week before and over the weekend. It is our preparation for a calmer week. Sometimes I need it more than they do and after that crazy dream I had, I need this. I set the timer for five minutes. I sat at my desk and joined them in meditation.

As I closed my eyes, I put myself in a happy place. I imagined I was laying on the beach. I had this huge umbrella blocking the sun. The temperature was perfect. It wasn't too windy and not scorching hot. Steph was on his cot next to me. Not many words were shared between us. We both were just appreciating our view, each other's presence, and the beautiful weather.

The timer went off and we all opened our eyes. We did a quick whip around about how we were feeling when we woke up this morning and how we are feeling now. Just as Seth was sharing his feelings, in walked Malcolm. I smiled at him and the class told him good morning in unison. I was relieved to know he made it in time to take the test. I filled him in on what we were doing and he was fine with going next.

"This morning I woke up feeling tired and groggy," Malcolm said.

"What time did you go to bed?" I asked.

"After midnight."

"After midnight? What made you go to bed so late?" I asked.

"Not really in the mood to talk about it," he said as he put his book bag behind his seat.

"I won't force it out of you, but as always, when you're ready to talk about it I'm here," I said feeling bad knowing it must not have been a good thing.

"Ok class, as we wait for admin to walk around with the test, you can take out the iPads and unwind." Taking a test is nerve-wracking enough, so I can only imagine how some of my students feel with taking the state test. I allowed them to use the iPads just to wake up their minds, relax and put them in a better mood, especially Malcolm.

I walked around to see what each of them was doing. Adam was on Facebook looking at his girlfriend's page. I just shook my head and laughed as I walked by. Jason had his headphones in, listening to music on Sound Cloud. Octavia was reading a book. I admired her. She loved to read and did not waste an opportunity to do so. Steven was looking up Gucci sneakers. I do not know where he was going to get the money from to buy a pair, but hey, I will let the boy dream. Samiyah was on YouTube looking at natural hair tutorials. I have had endless conversations with Samiyah about beauty school. To be so young and talented, I only pray she makes it far and not get caught up in the negative things this world offers. Her hair is always done. It was not until the end of last year that I found out that she was doing her own hair and her sisters. If it were not a conflict of interest, she would be doing mine too. She has beautiful dark brown naturally curly hair and she clearly embraces her roots. I ended up staying by her desk longer than I expected. Watching the tutorial with her from one of her favorite YouTubers, *TheChicNatural*, doing a twisted updo. I may have to try that style on my hair. I touched my shoulder-length hair and remembered that washday was soon coming. That is the worse part of being a natural girl for me. After the tutorial, I walked to Justin's desk. He was playing some zombies game. It did not take me long to move right on to the next student, Malcolm. Malcolm was listening to music. His cousin and oldest brother are underground rappers. I can tell by the mixtape cover that he was listening to one of their songs. He looked up at me and I mouthed to him *are you ok?* He nodded his head and said, "Yes." I rubbed his back and walked to Anthony's desk. He was watching an episode of

Wild-N-Out. As they were doing their own thing, I decided to pick up my book and read a few pages before admin stopped by with the tests. Kendall Ryan is a great author and she had me hooked with her book, *Filthy Beautiful Lies*. Just as I was diving deeper into the book, there was a knock at the door.

"Come in," I shouted from across the room.

In walked Mr. Jones, the guidance counselor. I joke with Stephan all the time that if he ever did me wrong, I would leave him for Mr. Jones. Stephan knew I was not into light-skinned men and Mr. Jones was just that, but it was something about him that made me do a double-take every now and again. He had all the women drooling over him at work and he did not pay them any mind. There is no ring on his finger and he did not let many people into his personal life so no one knew what his relationship status or preference was. He was often the topic of discussion, but I did not engage like the rest of the women. Mr. Jones was a fine-looking man, but I loved the man I had at home.

"Hey, Ms. Johnson. Here are the tests and pencils. Call my extension or A. P. Boyd's if you have any questions or if someone needs to be escorted to the bathroom," he said as he handed me the materials.

"Great. Thank you, Mr. Jones."

"Not a problem, Ms. Johnson. Good luck guys. Make sure you read everything carefully and thoroughly. You got this!" he said as he exited the room.

We had about five minutes before testing began. The students turned their tables into testing positions and prepared for me to hand out the tests.

"There's no doubt in my mind that you all will do well, but it's up to how well you focus, think things through, and how bad you want to do good that will determine how well you do. Good luck and remember to stay positive and take deep breaths even when you get a question you may not know or understand," I said to them as I handed out the packets.

Testing began and so did the quietness. I sat at my desk and wrote out my to-do list for work and home. Just as I was about to put my cellphone on silent, I got a text from Steph, *Don't forget to write a poem. Love you and good luck to the kiddies*. We were not supposed to have our cellphones out during testing, so I quickly responded, *Thanks for the reminder. Love you more and see you later*. I took out my journal and realized it has been months since I have written in it. I need to get back into writing. It was my safe haven. I did not know what I wanted to write about so I just started writing. I was just going to let my creative juices flow and see where it took me.

After writing for some time, I ended up with two poems. Writing the second one made me glance up a few times to make sure none of my students was reading what I was writing.

When I finished writing, I reread some of my old writings. Before I knew it, it was time for the students to take a break and go to lunch. Some of my kids were done with their tests, while others had to eat lunch and finish it in another room. Mr. Jones came into my room and collected the completed tests. He took the unfinished tests and handed it to the teacher that would hold all the students who needed extra time.

I dropped my students off to the cafeteria and went outside. I packed my lunch from the night before so I did not need anything in particular from outside, just air. I pulled out my phone and called Stephan.

After three rings, he finally picked up. "Hey, love. How was testing?"

"It went fine. I was honestly caught up in writing that I didn't realize how fast time flew by."

"That's great. I'm glad you took time out to write."

"Yeah, me too. It was needed. How's work going for you?"

"It's going. The meeting went as planned. Kevin was not in today, thankfully. You know when he's in attendance he likes to drag the meeting."

"That's a good thing," I said as we both laughed at how extra Kevin could be. He was one of those coworkers who needed people to know that he knew his job and knew it well. He was indeed one of the best staffs that Stephan has because he really did know his work, but no matter how many times Stephan told him that his work would show for itself, he didn't get it.

"Any thoughts on what we're having for dinner tonight?"

I was thinking about that as well and had no clue. "Not sure. Something quick and easy. Any thoughts on your end?"

"I know we spoke about eating better and working out, but I've been craving for a good homemade burger," he said.

"Damn, that does sound good. Tater tots with melted cheese or some curly fries?" I asked as I envisioned biting into a well-seasoned juicy burger.

"I know you love tater tots, so we can have it with that."

I jumped for joy in my head. I loved it when I got my way with him. Some would call it being spoiled, but I call it being satisfied.

"Don't pretend that you don't be busting down those tater tots with me!"

He laughed and said, "You got it, love. Tater tots for the win. You do know that I'm making the burgers, right?"

Little did he know, I was going to volunteer him to do it anyway. I can throw down in the kitchen, but so can he. We knew the dishes we did better than the other and there was no shame in my game.

"Music to my ears. Not a problem with me."

I finished my conversation with Stephan, went back inside, and ate my lunch. The rest of the day went by with a breeze, only with a few middle school kids running around in the hallway acting up.

Since Steph was cooking dinner, I didn't have to head straight home. I decided to go to the nail salon to get my nails and feet done. I was supposed to get it done over the weekend but never got around to doing it.

After getting pampered, I went to pick up a bottle of wine and headed home to spend the rest of the day with my love.

CHAPTER 5

STEPHAN

After my meeting, I was mentally checked out. It did not take me long to realize that I was not going to get much work done. I told Samantha that I was leaving for the day and that I will see her tomorrow.

I pulled into the parking lot of Food Bazaar and grabbed a cart. I headed straight to the meat section. I looked for the perfect packaging of ground beef. When I found it, I went to pick up the bread. Nothing tastes better than Martin's potato roll bread. I am so going against everything I said to Kris yesterday about eating better. As I was making my way to the dairy section to pick up the cheeses we needed, my cart bumped into someone else's.

"My apologies," I said to the woman whose back was turned towards me.

She turned around and said, "It's ok don't...Stephan? What a surprise! How are you?"

Great, this was just my luck. "Hey, Chasity. I'm great, how have you been?"

"I'm doing well. I can't complain," she said looking me up and down.

We stood in silence for a second just reading each other. "Well, my apologies again. Have a great one," I said as I pushed my cart and went around hers.

"Stephan, it really is great seeing you. The last time we saw each other wasn't pretty and I'd like to make up for that," she said as she tilted her head to the side and waited for me to respond.

"There's no need. That is in the back of my mind. Again, have a great one." I turned back around and kept it pushing, literally.

Who would have known that I would run into Chasity? It has been years since we have seen each and I was not about to let her re-enter into my life. I damn sure was not going to tell Kris that she is back in town. I know we have this no lying to each other rule, but telling her this will potentially harm what we have built.

I decided to push Chasity to the back of my mind and continue my food shopping. I picked up everything I needed for tonight's dinner and got some stuff to make for our lunch tomorrow. I got some green grapes, apples, and oranges as well. Those were the only fruits I knew Kris and I did not mind eating daily.

Just as I hopped on the line for the register, I looked to my left and Chasity was in line next to me. It did not take her long to notice me standing there.

"I am truly sorry and I would love to make it up to you. I know you are surprised to see me and I did not expect to run into you either, but take some time and think about it. Give me a call when you're ready to accept my apology."

I gave her a blank stare and simply said, "Ok." I had no intention of calling her. Her name and number have been long gone erased and deleted. Kristen made sure of that.

I placed my items on the register as the cashier rung everything up. I paid for my groceries and made my way to my car. I put everything in my trunk and started up the car. As I sat there waiting for my car to warm up a bit, I checked my phone and seen four missed calls from Samantha.

I pushed the call button on my car and returned her call. She answered on the second ring. "Samantha, everything cool?"

"Hey, boss, yes, umm, I just got word that Chasity is back in town," she said sounding worried.

"Yes, I'm aware. I just ran into her at the supermarket, unfortunately."

"Did she say anything to you?"

"That she was sorry and wanted to make up for her wrongdoings."

"Boss, you know she's trouble."

"I'm fully aware. Trust me, I didn't entertain it, but I appreciate you letting me know."

"Of course. Have a goodnight, Mr. Moore."

"You too, Sam. I'll see you tomorrow," I ended the call and pulled out the parking lot. Just as I reached a red light, a silver Honda pulled up beside me and there was Chasity, yet again.

She winked at me as she drove off. This is one hell of a psycho chick and I had to make sure I was smarter this time around.

Everyone has that one crazy ex. Chasity was mine. We had been broken up for almost a year when Kris and I got together. When Chasity found out about it, she started calling me at all times of the night and popping up at my job. I told Kristen that I would handle it, but it only got worse. She ended up popping up on Kris at the mall while she was with Latrice. She said one bad thing to Kris and ended up getting her ass beat. After that, I never heard anything else from her, until now.

God must have felt sorry for me running into her because I found parking right in front of our apartment building. I grabbed the groceries out of the trunk, locked the car, and made my way to the apartment. The apartment always smelled like one of the candles that Kris lights. I know how much she loves to walk into a good smelling home. After setting the bags down and washing my hands, I found where she had her candle and lit it. This one was the watermelon lemonade scent from Bath and Body Works. I must admit, she does have good taste when it comes to scents. I did not care about those things, but hey happy wife, happy life. She was not that just yet, but it did not hurt to get some practice in.

I stripped out of my work clothes, threw on a t-shirt and some basketball shorts, and headed to the kitchen. I seasoned my meat, made them into patties, and let it marinate in the fridge for a bit while I worked on our lunch for tomorrow.

"It smells amazing in here," she said as she walked in and kissed me.

Kissing her back I said, "I haven't started dinner yet, but lunch for tomorrow is done."

"What's for lunch tomorrow?" she asked as she lifted the cover to the pan after washing her hands.

"Well nosey, I sautéed some shrimps and finally used our salad chopper and chopped up a good ole salad mix."

She opened the salad bowl. "Cucumbers, tomatoes, lettuce, spinach, croutons, and shredded carrots. That looks really good! Nice and simple, just like I like it."

"I bought shredded mozzarella cheese too to add to the salad. I just did not throw it in there yet. I wish you ate onions and peppers that really would have made the salad good. "

"And I am thankful that you know that I don't like onions or peppers because you would've been eating this salad by your damn self," she said laughing, but I knew she meant it.

"You just don't know what good food is," I argued back.

"Put onions and peppers in my food and it'll be the last time you have *good food*." She said mocking me.

We both laughed. "I'll start dinner as soon as I finish washing up the dishes."

"Sounds good to me. I'm going to get out of these clothes and take a shower."

"Ok. Make sure you wash my body good. I don't need to be tasting no saltiness tonight," I said winking at her.

"Boy, please! You ain't never tasted any saltiness over here," she said as she slapped her ass and walked away.
"It was that one time," I said jokingly.

She walked back to the kitchen, flipped me the bird, and said, "Now the candy shop is closed since you want to be a smart ass."

"Come on, baby, you know I was just joking," I said as I ran after her and wrapped my arms around her waist. I pulled her in close. "Trust me, I wouldn't be with you if I ever had to second guess how you smelt, let alone taste."

"I know, but don't joke like that or else the candy shop will be closed and reopened for its new owner," she said as she turned around to face me.

"New owner? That would be the last piece of candy he will ever have and the last piece of candy you would be distributing. Try me if you want to." I said half-jokingly.

She leaned up and kissed me. "Then don't let that happen again."

She walked into the room and I went back to the kitchen to finish washing up the dishes. I heard the shower turn on and her music start to play. She was playing her favorite old school playlist. I dried my hands and set the George Forming to heat. This was my opportunity to make it up to her.

I made my way to the bathroom, turned the knob, and let myself in. The music was blasting from the speakers so she did not hear me come in. I quickly undressed and stepped in the shower.

"Shit! You scared me, Stephan!"

"Shhh," I said as I placed my lips on hers. She kissed me back and allowed my tongue to roam her mouth.

I pulled her in closer to me and grabbed the back of her neck as I kissed her deeper. Soft moans escaped her mouth as I slid my hands down her back until I reached her cheeks. I gripped them with both hands and kept on squeezing them. I felt my penis poking at her box and knew I would not be able to hold out much longer. I needed to feel inside of her, but I know foreplay is what gets her juices flowing and I needed to have her at her wettest. I slid a finger inside of her and placed another on her clit as I massaged her. Her soft moans let me know that I'm doing something right. I felt her body relax as I played with her. I sat her on the edge of the tub as I kneeled on the ground of it. Placing her left leg on the rim of the tub, I parted her lips and tasted what I have been waiting for all day. My tongue roamed the insides of her love box and played with her clit. I loved how she grabbed my head every time my tongue sucked on her love box. I did not want her to cum just yet, so I kept teasing her, licking and sucking, and repeating just that. I felt her thighs tighten around me as I slipped a finger inside of her while still teasing her. I knew it would only be a matter of time before she came. I picked up the pace, stopped teasing her, and ate her the way she loved. In seconds, I felt her muscles tighten around my fingers as she gripped my hair. Her body trembled as she called out my name and told me she was cumming. I picked up the pace, sliding my fingers in and out of her as my tongue continued to suck and pull on her clit. I didn't stop until I knew she was done cumming. I felt her muscles pulsating around my fingers. I leaned up and kissed her deeply.

She looked at me with lust and hate in her eyes.

"I hate that you can make me cum so hard like that, but I love you for knowing just what to do," she said as she got up and kissed me passionately.

I wasn't done with her just yet. "That was just the first part. Turn around." I felt my penis throbbing and knew I would not last more than ten minutes inside of her.

"Not so fast, daddy," she said as she dropped to her knees.

"Shit." Ten minutes went down to seven. Kristen dropped to her knees and took all of me into her mouth. I felt my knees grow weak while she was sucking me and playing with my balls. Her warm mouth felt so fucking good. She started tongue kissing the tip of my head and I could not help but moan. Hearing her moan while giving me head only made it harder for me not to bust all in her mouth. She slid the rest of me back into her mouth and picked up her speed. *God, please do not let my knees give out on me now.* I could not help but to grip her hair and push my way deeper in. I felt my dick hit the back of her throat and the way she gagged, I knew I was only seconds away from releasing all of myself into her mouth. I needed to hear that gagging sound again. I kept feeling myself hit the back of her throat and could not help but let the moans escape. She was gagging but still taking it like a champ!

"Damn, baby, I'm about to cum," she looked up at me with satisfaction and determination to make me cum. She picked up her pace as I gripped her hair a little tighter and pounded myself in her mouth. Her gags and moans increased and it sent me over the edge as I came all in her mouth. I could not help but let out sounds of satisfaction.

She got up from off her knees and pulled me up. I slapped her on the ass a few times. *Damn, that was some great head.* I knew I had to fuck her good for that, but I needed a few moments to reset. I took my time kissing her on her neck and sucking on her breast. *Damn, how did I get so lucky?* With her right breast in my mouth, I let my tongue roam freely over her nipple.

Kristen pulled my head away from her right breast, "Daddy, don't leave her lonely," she said as she placed my mouth on her left breast. I gave it even more attention than I did the right one.

"Yes, just like that!" she cried out. *That won't be the only crying you'll be doing tonight.*

My penis was resting on her love box and the warmth from it turned me on even more. It's something about the way she moans that gets me every time. I was done with the foreplay. I needed to be inside her and I needed that to happen now. Picking up her right leg, I entered her nice and slow. I started with slow pumps until she got comfortable. Her warmth and tightness felt too good. I needed to think of something to stop me from coming inside of her right now. *Shit. A is for Apple, B is for Blueberries, C is for Carrots...Fuck it.*

I was being greedy tonight and was taking advantage of her every way I could. I lifted her with both legs now on my shoulders and dug into her. I felt her muscles grip my penis as her moans increased. *Shit.* I heard myself moaning too. I kept digging deeper and pounding into her. A few pounds in and I felt her tightening even more.

"Baby, I'm about to cum," she cried in my ear.

"Cum for me, baby," I said as I pounded deeper into her.

"Cum with me please," she moaned and pleaded.

Fuck. That was all I needed to hear. I came inside of her as I felt her juices sliding down my cock. I slowed down my pace but kept her in the same position until her body collapsed and I felt all her body weight on me. *Now that's how it's supposed to be d*

CHAPTER 6
KRISTEN

I felt my whole body go limp. I had to gather my energy as Stephan helped me back to the ground. The water temperature was perfect, but by the wrinkles on our hands, I knew we have been in this shower far too long. I grabbed my washcloth and handed Steph his. I lathered my washcloth with my Dove soap and began to soap up my body and Steph did the same.

"Turn around," he said in a low deep tone. His voice alone just sent a chill through my body.

I did as I was told. He took my washcloth from me and washed my back with the cloth. I let him wash my whole body and then returned the favor. I turned to let the water run down my body. With my back facing Steph, he started massaging my shoulders. He went from massaging my shoulders, to my back, and then my butt.

I reached behind me and grabbed his hands, "Don't be starting nothing," I said as I turned to face him.

"I wasn't starting. Just making sure I give your body the attention it needs."

I could not help but smile at him. "Trust me, you've given my body more than enough attention."

"It's my job to and I take pleasure in doing so," he said as he kissed me on my forehead.

We finished showering and was ready to leave the bathroom when Steph realized he forgot about grabbing his towel.

"That's what you get for sneaking into the bathroom," I said laughing at him as he stood in the tub contemplating what to do.

"Not funny," he chuckled. "Can you be such a doll and bring me my towel please?"

I grabbed my towel and dried myself off. "What do I get in return for doing such a nice deed?"

"You'll get your dinner cooked."

I gave him my thinking face. "I can make my own dinner. You did the hardest part already, which was seasoning the meat." I was loving every minute of this. "What would you have done if I weren't home and you forgot your towel?"

"I'd figure it out."

"Well, pretend I'm not home and *figure it out*," I said.

"Oh, so this is how you want to play? Ok. No worries, love." He grabbed his washcloth, wrung it out, and dried his feet off. He stepped into his slippers as I watched his naked body drip it's way to our bedroom.

Knowing Steph and his petty self, this was not going to be the last of this. He was going to get me back for not getting his towel. I love that he has such a great sense of humor. I have never been with a man who has great character traits as he does. He has a great sense of humor, an amazing heart, his mannerisms are through the roof and he has a bit of street to him. The street side of him does not come out often, but it's come out enough for me to know that my baby can hold his own.

While lathering my body with lotion, we chatted about our day at work. We both were finally dressed in our house clothes. Steph threw on a pair of basketball shorts and a T-shirt. I threw on my matching pajama set from Victoria Secret, shorts, and a tank top with the big *PINK* logo on the butt. I followed him to the kitchen where I sat at the island table and watched him cook.

The aroma in the apartment smelt amazing. My stomach was talking to me, begging me to hurry up and put some food inside. He pulled out the bacon from the fridge and prepped the pot for frying. *A bacon cheeseburger?* I felt my body doing the happy dance. He looked back at me and just shook his head and laughed at me because he knew exactly how excited I was for dinner.

I heard the text tone of my phone go off twice. I got up to retrieve it from the room. Of course, it was from Latrice. I let my iPhone recognize my face so it could unlock it and see what she wrote.

Message one: *Hey, girl. You home? Can I stop by?*
Message two: *Kris, please be home. I'm like ten minutes away.*

Great. Latrice knows I do not open my door for pop up visits. You have to call in advance, confirm that I am home, and see if I am ok with having company. For her to already be heading my way only means two things, something really bad must've happened or she has to pee and couldn't wait until she reached her house. I laughed to myself because she has definitely popped up here twice just to pee. I doubt that was the case this time though. I sent her back a quick reply.

Hey, Trice. Yes, I am home. See you when you get here.

I took my phone back with me to the kitchen and told Steph that she was on her way here.

"Let me guess, she got to pee and our house was closer than hers?"

We both laughed. "I don't know. The semi urgency in her text didn't sound like this was an *I have to pee* visit."

"Oh boy. I swear I don't know anyone who has as much drama as Latrice," I knew Stephan loved Latrice on the strength of me, but he could not understand how she could get herself caught up in crazy situations. To be honest, neither did I, but I loved her nonetheless.

Shrugging my shoulders, "True, but we'll see. Maybe it's not as deep as we are expecting."

"Nope. *We* won't see anything. That is your friend and your job to listen. I will be watching the game while y'all chat. I'll make her a burger though because you know the first thing she's going to do is comment on how good it smells in here and how she wishes she could have a home-cooked meal."

I could not help but join him in laughter. He knew Latrice just as well as I did when it came to her greedy self. I do not know anyone who can eat as much as she does and not gain one single pound. I can look at a burger and gain three pounds.

"You are absolutely right. Better make some tater tots for her too. I'm not sharing any of mine." Steph knew how serious I was about my tater tots.

Ten minutes later Trice was coming through the door.

"You guys living like y'all are Martin and Gina. You need to lock your doors," she said as she walked in.

"I unlocked it a few minutes ago when I knew you would be close," I said as I got up to hug her. She hugged me back but held me a little longer than she normally does. Latrice was not the type to show compassion, let alone a long hug. Something was definitely up.

"Hey, Trice," Steph said as he leaned over to kiss her on the cheek.

"Hey, brother," she said as she took her jacket off and put it behind the chair next to me. "It smells good in here. Boy, you have no idea how much I miss a home-cooked meal."

Steph and I looked at each other and busted out laughing.

"I'm making you a burger now," Steph said while still laughing and shaking his head.

"Thank you. I sure am hungry!"

"When are you not hungry?" Stephan and I asked in unison.

"That's a good question. When I find the answer to it, you'll be the first to know," she said winking at me.

I had to change the subject or we would be talking about Latrice and food all night. "So what brings you by?"

Her face got serious. "We can talk about it after we eat. You got any wine?"

"I believe so." I got up and went to the wine and liquor rack to see what I had. I pulled out a bottle of Chardonnay and a bottle of Chablis. We weren't heavy drinkers here, but I tried to always have a new bottle of something anytime we had guests over.

I showed her the bottles to see if she approved of either. She grabbed the bottle of Chablis.

"Yes, this will do. Shit, at this point anything will do. I just need something to help ease my mind."

"The burgers and tots should be done in a few minutes. You ladies can have the living room. I'll be in the bedroom so you can chat."

"Thanks, babe."

"I appreciate it, Steph," Latrice said as she helped me set the table.

The food was finally finished and we were ready to dive in. Steph prayed over the food and before we could even say *amen,* Trice was popping a tater tot into her mouth. It burnt her tongue. That is what she gets for being so damn greedy.

We talked about everything from under the sun; Trump and the government shut down, new memes and videos on Instagram, work, the weather, you name it-we spoke about it. Latrice chimed in like she usually did, but as her closest friend, I knew whatever it was that happened was still troubling her. When you truly know someone, you can look past the laughter and jokes and see their true hurt or anger. I said a silent prayer that God would give me the appropriate words to say to her when she finally reveals to me what brought her here.

Steph seasoned the heck out those burgers. Every bite was full of flavor. I had to stop the juices from running down my mouth a few times. Even the tater tots were baked to crispy perfection. He topped it with melted cheese and bacon bits. I wish I had room in my stomach to have another serving. This is why it's so hard for me to lose weight. Starting tomorrow, I'm going to do better.

I washed up the dishes from dinner and cleaned up what was left to be cleaned in the kitchen. I loved it when Steph cooked. He always cleaned up while he was cooking, so there wasn't much for me to clean. He and Trice chatted a bit while I cleaned. After I was done, Stephan excused himself and left us to chat.

"So what's going on?" I asked as I grabbed a seat on the couch next to Latrice.

"I told you that Chanel and I were going out for dinner and drinks, right?" She asked eyeing me.

"Yup." Chanel is Laurence's wife.

"Ok, so." She was hesitating and I could tell whatever was about to come out of her mouth was something I may have to take to my grave.

I shifted in my seat, trying to get comfortable without showing how uncomfortable this story sounds like it's about to get.

"So we went to Red Lobsters for their unlimited shrimps and of course their biscuits. We were eating and having a great time. We paid for dinner and ended up going to the bar a few blocks away from the restaurant. As we are sitting at the bar, these two well-dressed men walk in and of course, spots us. They approach us and try to make small talk. You know me though; I'm going to play nice so we can get some free drinks. These men were really into us and because they were easy on the eye, I was enjoying it. We got free drinks and even though we just ate, they bought us appetizers too. I wasn't hungry but I sure wasn't going to pass up free food."

I wanted to say *when do you ever pass up free food?* I decided to keep that to myself and allow her to finish with her story. So far, nothing seemed too alarming to cause her to be at my place.

"So as we are laughing and drinking, one of the guys notices Chanel's wedding ring. He asked her how long she has been married and if her husband would be ok knowing that she's at some bar taking free drinks from random men. I was about to get real defensive, but I waited to see what she was going to say. She takes a sip of her drink and tells him, 'my husband isn't worried about me. He is probably out doing the same thing; getting or giving free drinks.' We all had that same puzzled look that you have on your face right now. So the same guy, Keith, goes 'getting free drinks? Well, you must have a good-looking husband. I thought I was good looking, but no woman has ever bought me a drink before.'"

I had that crazy feeling in the pit of my stomach that this story was about to turn for the worse real quick. I poured myself a glass of wine to calm my anxiety.

"We were all waiting for her to respond. She picks up her glass and sips again before saying, 'Well if you were gay and into gay bars, I am sure you will be able to find someone to buy you a drink with no problem.' Kris, when I tell you that I almost spit out everything in my mouth!"

"You're lying! So she knows your brother is into men? And here we were just the other day, threatening him that we were going to tell his wife and she already knew!" I poured us another glass of wine. My mind was spinning just from hearing this. I could not imagine what I would do if I ever found out that Stephan was gay.

"Girl, I wish you were a fly on the wall and could've seen my face!"

"Damn, T, so what happened next?" I needed to know what happened after that. I felt my anxiety increasing.

"Keith goes, 'Damn, love. Sounds like you need something stronger than what you're having.' So he asks the bartender for shots for us and I tell the bartender to make hers a double. I gave her that *I'm sorry* look and she tells me that she's known for a while. I asked her how she knew. She said one day she was looking at their bank statements trying to dispute some fraudulent activity and came across charges from a place called *Peaches*. She thought that was one of the fraudulent activities and added that to the list of things that needed to be disputed. The bank ended up doing their investigation and realized that she did have fraudulent activity on her account but Peaches was not one of them. They told her after further investigating that it was a charge made from her account and they pulled charges made previously from the same place. The customer service representative told her to speak with her husband about those charges."

My heart ached for Chanel. It is one thing to be in a relationship with someone, but to be married and have this happen; I do not know how she has not lost her cool yet.

"Damn, Trice. I really feel bad for her. I mean, I know we knew and it was only a matter of time before she found out, but to find out this way, that's embarrassing and hurtful."

"Girl, I was so at lost for words. It puts me in an uncomfortable position as well though because he's my brother. I don't care that he's gay, but it does bother me that he's out indulging with other men while he has a wife at home. If you want to be with a man, fine, but let your wife go and be free. You have her thinking that you guys are going to spend together forever when you have a whole different agenda. But there's more."

My eyebrows instantly raised. "Oh Lord, go on I'm listening."

"So she continues to tell us how she went to Peaches one day and showed a picture of Laurence to the bartender and asked if he had seen him there. The bartender told her that he is a regular and a great tipper. While she is going into details, the other guy we were with, Trent, tells her that he's heard enough. He proceeds to tell her that he is a lawyer and has good connections if she wanted to get a divorce. When he said lawyer, all the sadness and anger I felt disappeared real quick. He just became even more attractive."

I could not help but laugh at Latrice. She did not always make the best choices with men, so the fact that she spotted someone with a great job was a good look for her.

"She took his business card and said when she's ready to file, she will. You could tell that she did not want to divorce my brother, but knew it was only a matter of time before she had to. After a few more drinks, we were all tipsy. Chanel said she did not want to go home, so I told her she could stay at the hotel with me. She agreed and we ended up exchanging numbers with the guys before hopping in an Uber. Not even ten minutes after settling into my temporary room at the hotel, I got a text from Trent asking if we were inside safely. I told him that we were and asked if he and Keith were good. He said they were still at the bar. Our texting went from checking in with each other to him and Keith outside my room door."

I could tell by the look on her face that this conversation was about to get even more interesting. I opened up the other bottle of wine and poured us both another glass. I'm sure I was going to need it. I nodded for her to continue.

"I can't remember full details but I do know that when I woke up this morning, Trent was lying next to me, while Chanel and Keith were laid out on the sofa bed. I woke up with the worse hangover."

"Wait, what you mean you don't remember full details?" I asked looking at her puzzled. "Did you guys have sex? Did Chanel have sex? These are important details I need you to remember." I don't know why I cared to know the details, but I was intrigued.

"All I remember is bits and pieces. We did have sex and according to Chanel, it was more of an orgy party. I asked her did she and I do anything together and she told me we only shared a few kisses, just to tease the guys."

I almost spit out my wine. Just a few kisses? Since when did either of them get down like that? Maybe I heard her wrong.

"You said you guys shared a few kisses?"

"Yes, you heard correctly. I really have to stop drinking. You know my motto has always been *strictly dickly, never let a chick lick me.*"

"You definitely need to stop drinking. If not, then just limit how many drinks you have. A few kisses could've very well led to unforgettable things." I cringed at the thought of her and Chanel kissing. They were practically sisters.

"Trust me, Kris, it was my wake up call. I felt sick to my stomach when she told me that."

"I bet you were."

"But on a much lighter note, despite the terrible hangover I had this morning, I managed to make it to the shop to do my client's hair. I must say, hangover and all, my skills are one of kind." She fetched for her phone to show me pictures of her client's hair. That is one thing I could say about Latrice, that girl knew how to do hair. I've allowed her to straighten my hair a few times. Stephan loves my naturally curly hair, but I know he also loves it when it's straight. His eyes always light up when he sees me with it straightened. I don't do it often, but when I'm ready to switch it up for him, I let her straighten it. Thankfully, she knows how to take care of natural hair as well, so I do not have to worry about heat damage.

"Damn, girl. Your fingers are blessed!"

"Thank you, sis. If I don't remember to thank God for nothing else, I sure remember to thank Him for this talent."

"Amen to that!"

"There's more, so while I'm doing my client's hair, I hear my text tone going off and of course my hands aren't free so it has to wait until I'm finished. I finally get finished with installing and styling her weave and when she leaves I grab my phone to see who has been texting me." She pauses while she picks up her glass of wine to take a few sips.

"Well, who was it?" I was growing impatient.

"It was Trent. His first text was asking me how I was feeling this morning and then his second text he wrote that he wanted to take me out on a sober date and get to know me better."

"Well, what did you say?"

"You know me, I usually block numbers to those I've had a one night stand with, but for some reason, it was something about him that felt different. I responded and told him that I would love that."

"*You* responded?" I was shocked. Latrice was notorious for acting as if she never met her one-night stands. Even if she saw them in the street and they stopped her, she would act as if they got the wrong person. He must have really made an impression on her.

"I sure did. Shocked the hell out of myself. I do not know what it was about him, but he kept my attention all night. Usually, I just want to get my fix from a man and then send him packing, but not Trent. I'm actually looking forward to going out with him."

"Wow, this is shocking. Who would have known that someone could hold your attention like that? Do you think it's because of his good job or was the sex just that great?"

"Honestly, neither. I don't remember how good or bad the sex was, nor do I know what level of a lawyer he is. It was just his attentiveness and how he made eye contact every time I spoke. Usually, a man's eyes are so focused on my cleavage that they miss what I'm saying. He paid attention to every detail of what I said and didn't miss a beat."

"I can't begin to tell you how happy I am. I have been waiting a long time for you to find a man to tame your ass and get you to see your view of men differently." I found myself getting too excited. I was already hearing wedding bells.

"Slow your roll, Kris. All I agreed to was going on a sober date with him. I can see the excitement written all over your face. You're probably planning my nonexistent wedding in your head."

We both busted out laughing because she read me correctly. "When is this sober date?"

"Tomorrow. I'm meeting him for brunch. He has an early morning case and wants me to meet him after. It worked out perfectly because tomorrow is my day off."

"Great! This means I need to pick up more wine just in case you end up knocking at my door again."

"Yes! Get some more Chablis. I like that better than Chardonnay."

"The nerve of you to have a preference. You sure didn't mind helping me finish my bottle of Chardonnay."

"Well it was offered for free and I like free, but if I had to choose, Chablis will win every time."

I could not help but to shake my head at her. I heard the door to my bedroom open and out came Stephan.

"Sorry ladies, don't mean to intrude, just needed some water and a snack." I watched him as he poured himself a glass of water and grabbed a can of sour cream and onion Pringle's. Damn, this man is fine. I couldn't help but be grateful to have someone like him. I hope this Trent guy treats Latrice like a queen, so she can finally know what it is to be with a man and not a boy.

"No need to apologize. I need to get going anyway. While you're up, pass Kris a paper towel please."

Confusion was written all over my face. "What do I need a paper towel for?"

"To wipe up all that drool running down your mouth as you stare at Stephan." She and Steph busted out laughing.

I got up from my seat and opened the door to my apartment.

"I guess that's my cue," she said as she grabbed her stuff and headed for the door. "Have a goodnight, Steph. Kris, I'll call you tomorrow."

"Please do. I need full details."

"I'll be sober so I'll remember everything. Love you," she said as she hugged me.

"Love you back," I said hugging her and locking the door behind her.

"That girl is something else," I said to Stephan as I took a Pringle out of his hand right before he was about to eat it.

"She sure is. Was everything ok with her though?" he asked concerned.

"Babe, you have no idea the night she had last night."

"Oh boy, I don't even want to imagine."

One thing I appreciated about Stephan was that despite Latrice's wild behavior, he always looked out for her wellbeing. He has even come to her rescue a few times.

"Well I know you don't like knowing about our girl chat and I won't fill you in on the details, but I am going to hope and pray that the guy she met would be the one to help tone her down."

"I admire you for the amount of love you have for her. It's great to know that she has someone who is genuinely looking out for her best interest."

"She's been by my side when I had no one. It is only right to want to see her find true happiness. She's had a rough life and even though I've been her shoulder to cry on, no one knows how much hurt, disappointment, and even anger she carries with her."

"Alcohol and men seem to be her escape from all of that."

"Exactly and because it's her escape, she tends to make the worse decisions when she's under the influence. I just want my friend to find true happiness. She does not believe in therapy but I wish she would consider it. It might just save her." Stephan walked over to me to wipe the tears that have escaped from my eyes. I just wish that Latrice could see the potential that I see in her.

"Well tonight when we say our prayers, let's lift her name up and focus our prayer on her."

"From our lips to God's ears," we both said in unison.

He gave me the warmest hug and kiss and told me that Latrice is going to be fine. Call me crazy, but hearing that, put me at ease. I cut off all the lights in the living room and followed him back to the bedroom.

We were snuggled up in bed watching Martin and laughing at an episode I am sure we have seen thousands of times. It was not long before I felt my eyelids grow heavy and knew it was only a matter of time before I would be drifting off to sleep.

CHAPTER 7
KRISTEN

I think I drunk way too much wine last night. The sound of my alarm gave me an instant headache. I just wanted to push the snooze button one last time but knew I couldn't. I heard the shower running and knew Steph beat me to the bathroom. I got up and entered the bathroom. I peeked inside the shower to tell him good morning. After brushing my teeth and washing my face, I went into the kitchen and packed Steph's lunch bag and mine. It was routine for us. If I got in the shower first, he would pack our lunch bags and vice versa.

Today was day two of testing. Even though I would have loved an extra five minutes of sleep, I needed to leave a little earlier to pick my kids up a treat. I think they would love some donuts from Dunkin Donuts. I hope that the sugar rush would keep them up and focused on the test.

I searched my closet for something to wear and decided on my dark blue flare dress from Fashion Nova. Thankfully, it did not need ironing. I honestly hate ironing and usually bought clothes that did not require any. Stephan on the other hand wore button-ups all the time. He did not mind ironing though, but lately, I have noticed that he has been dropping off his shirts to the cleaners to be cleaned and pressed. I wonder if it is because I accidentally dried one of his good shirts and made it shrink.

We weren't big at-home breakfast eaters. We would usually pick up something on our way to work or pack something to go. We did cook a lot at home for our lunches and dinner meals, but not so much for breakfast.

After packing our lunches and picking out my clothes, Stephan was finally out of the shower. Thank God I didn't pay for water, because my water bill would be high every month with how much water we waste.

"Good morning, sunshine." He came out of the bathroom with his towel wrapped around his waist and body still wet.

"Good morning, handsome," I said as I wrapped my arms around his neck as he pulled me in for a kiss. "I like the way that body wash smells on you." I felt like a creep as I sniffed his body. Oh well, he did smell extra good. I made a mental note to check which body wash that was so I could buy him a few more bottles.

My shirt was damp because of his wet chest, but neither of us seemed to care. He held me longer than usual and I felt my body crave for him and felt his erection poking me.

"Don't start nothing, Steph," I said giving him the side-eye.

"All I need is five minutes," his voice was low and sexy. That sent an instant wave of excitement through my body.

"It'll have to wait until I get home. Plus you already took your shower." I was thinking of every excuse to use.

He ignored every excuse I gave him. His hands gripped both of my cheeks as he kissed me hungrily. I felt my body caving in and knew I had to stop him.

"Steph, you're going to make me late."

He silenced me with another kiss. This time I did not bother to stop him. I just let him have his way.

"Five minutes, baby and that's it. That's all I need," he said as he pushed my head down and had me bent over the bedroom dresser.

Eight minutes later, we were panting and trying to collect ourselves.

"Five minutes my ass!" I said grabbing my towel and hitting him with it.

"I tried, baby. I did," he said laughing.

I do not know why I believed we could do this within five minutes. That has never worked for us and today was no different. Now I was going to be late if I didn't hurry up and get in the shower. I wanted to exfoliate my whole body with my new dove exfoliator, but that would have to wait until I got home. I jumped in the shower and quickly lathered my washcloth with my dove soap.

Steph entered the bathroom right after me to grab his washcloth and clean himself off. Moments like this made me wish I could be a man. Just put my penis in the sink and run the water over it. For me to clean up in the sink, I would have to test my flexibility by putting one leg up on the sink while the other leg supports my balance. That requires too much work, so I always end up back in the shower.

I had to cut my shower short, making sure I got the important parts. By the time I got out, Stephan had already put on lotion and had his boxers and undershirt on. We spoke briefly about the rundown of our day, then he kissed me goodbye as he headed to work. I had ten more minutes to finish getting ready. I think I can do it. My hair was going up in a bun today. That definitely saved me time.

To my surprise, I was dressed and ready to go within nine minutes. I grabbed my bags and headed to my car. As my car warmed up, I said a quick prayer for traveling mercy. Traffic was light, thank God. I got to Dunkin Donuts in no time.

"Welcome to Dunkin Donuts, what can I get for you today?"

I told the woman at the cash register to give me a dozen assorted donuts and hot chocolate. Moments like this are when I am grateful for Apple Pay. I did not have to go searching for my wallet in my pocketbook. Malcolm walked in as I was waiting for my order to be completed.

My heart warmed at the sight of him. For him to be so young, he has been through more in life than I have. He grew up in a house of five boys and two girls. He is the second to last. All of his brothers were gang bangers and they took pride in making sure the world knew who they were. His two sisters are just as ruthless as the boys are. His second oldest brother was gunned down two years ago. Malcolm was filled with rage. He joined his brothers in finding who was responsible for his brother's death.

He was absent a lot from school when that happened. No matter how many times we reached out to him and his parents regarding how important it was for him to continue his education, it all went on deaf ears. Mr. Jones and I tried to reason with the mother, trying to get her to see the path that he was going down. She always promised that she would talk to her husband and Malcolm, but he still never showed. The school even made home visits. He would show up the next day and not again for the remainder of the week. We had to involve ACS, but his family had such a bad reputation, that their caseworker was afraid to push any further.

It wasn't until last year when Malcolm witnessed his cousin get stabbed to death that he realized that this lifestyle wasn't for him. He wanted better for himself. The next morning he was the first one in my class, clearly waiting for me to get there before the others. As soon as he spotted me, he ran to me and buried his face into my chest as he cried. I did not know what was wrong but I allowed him to get it all out. That is when he told me about his cousin dying right in front of him and how helpless he felt because he could not help him. He told me that he wanted to graduate and move with his grandfather down south so he could start a new life.

Unfortunately, because he missed so many days of school he had to repeat what was supposed to have been his last year. He has been doing a lot of extra credit work, staying later to get tutoring, and really focusing on class. He was determined to graduate this year and I did everything I could to help him make that happen. So far, he was on the right track and all I needed was for him to stay on that track.

"Good morning, Ms. Johnson," he said as he hugged me.

"Good morning, Malcolm. How are you today?" I asked.

"I'm ok. Ready to take this test and be done with it."

"I understand. What you came here to get?"

"A bacon, egg, and cheese on a croissant with some hash browns."

I ordered his breakfast for him and paid for it.

"Ms. Johnson, you didn't have to pay for my breakfast. My oldest brother gave me money this morning." He tried to hand me a five-dollar bill, but I moved his hand away.

"Keep your money. Buying your breakfast is the least I could do to show you how proud I am of you."

"Thank you, Ms. Johnson. You mean a lot to me. I am going to miss you when I graduate. I am going to graduate right?" He looked at me with worry in his eyes.

"Yes, we are already halfway through the school year and your grades have been great. You are above average. Just make sure you stay focused." I gave him his food and grabbed the box of donuts and my hot chocolate.

Just as we were heading to the door, Anthony came running in. He looked terrified.

Malcolm and I were asking him what was wrong. He was trying to tell us, but couldn't catch his breath. Just as he was telling us what he saw, we saw it for ourselves. It was a gang of teenagers coming down the block. Some had baseball bats in their hands and other objects I could not identify.

My heart instantly went into my stomach. "Who are they looking for?" I asked nervously.

"They are looking for you," Anthony said looking at Malcolm.

I ran to the counter and asked if they could lock the door. I was panicking as I was searching for my phone. I finally found it and pulled it out to call Agent Adams. He picked up on the second ring. I explained to him what was happening and he said he was going to radio it in and that hopefully, they will have youth officers nearby. He told me to stay put and to try to keep Anthony and Malcolm as safe as I could without putting myself in harm's way.

One of the workers ran to the back to get the keys to the front door. She locked it just in time as one of the teenagers tried to grab it open. They were pulling and banging on the door, threatening to bust the windows open if we did not let Malcolm out.

"Ms. Johnson!" Anthony screamed towards me as he ran to the side door that we clearly did not think about. We all ran to the side door to hold it close just as one of the boys tried pushing his way through. Only his right arm made it through the door. Malcolm and Anthony were pushing the door on his arm as if they were trying to break it. The boy was screaming out in agony. One of his friends was threatening to kill us if we did not release the door and set his arm free.

Malcolm and Anthony were filled with rage and determination to not let them get inside. One of his friends started hitting the window with his bat repeatedly. Glass was shattering everywhere. My heart dropped as I searched for safety for us. Malcolm screamed for us to hide in the bathroom, but he wasn't letting go of the door. Anthony pulled my arm as we ran to the bathroom. I screamed for Malcolm to come with us. After seeing that they had broken through one of the windows he finally let go of the door and ran towards us. Just as he reached the door, one of the guys slammed the baseball bat into Malcolm's shoulder. He immediately dropped to the floor in agony. The guy swung his bat again, this time aiming for Malcolm's head. He hit Malcolm so hard,

I swore he had crushed his skull. He lifted his bat again, but Anthony tackled him to the floor before he could hit Malcolm. Malcolm got up, stumbled a bit, and picked up the baseball bat and began beating the guy with it.

One of the guy's friends came through the window and came charging at us. I reached for my hot chocolate that was on the counter and threw it at his face. I started beating him with my bag. It was the only thing I had in my reach. My MacBook was in there so I hit him with full force so he could feel every bit of it. His other friends moved the friend whose arm was stuck in the door out the way and they came running through the door heading towards us until they heard the sirens. They ran out of the Dunkin Donuts shop and scattered.

I was so relieved that the cops were pulling up that I did not even notice the guy I as beating run out. He did not get far before the cops caught him. Malcolm still had the bat in his hand but was now stomping out the boy who hit him. I was trying to pull him off the boy, but he would not stop. The cops came in with guns drawn, screaming at Malcolm to drop the bat. I jumped in front of Malcolm and was trying to explain to them that he's the victim. It was going on deaf ears. Malcolm realized what was going on and stopped stomping out the guy and dropped the bat.

The cops came rushing in and two of them pushed Malcolm to the ground. I was screaming towards the cops that he was only defending himself. Malcolm was screaming in agony as they tried to cuff him. You can tell just by the looks of his shoulder that something was wrong.

Without thinking, Anthony tried to pull one of the officers off Malcolm. The other cop drew his gun, pointed it at him, and told him he would shoot him if he did not get off his partner. I jumped in front of Anthony and before I could utter a word out, I heard a familiar voice, "Officers, these are the victims!" Agent Adams screamed as he ran towards us. "You're safe now, Ms. Johnson. There's a patrol car outside waiting for you guys."

"I'm not riding with these cops. They just threatened to shoot my kids!" I was furious and if they thought I was going to trust them to escort us, they thought wrong. "I will drive *my* car with Anthony and Malcolm."

"Ms. Johnson, it's safer if you drive with them." I guess it took him a minute to soak in what I said about them trying to shoot my students. "You are in no shape to be driving. If it's ok with you, I'll drive you and the boys in your car."

"That's fine with me."

I still had Anthony behind me. We went to help Malcolm up, but he was in too much pain.

"My shoulder, Ms. Johnson. It hurts so badly." He was holding his shoulder, but what concerned me most was this big knot on his head.

"He's going to need to get that checked out. I'm going to radio for them to send an ambulance." The officer who pulled his gun out on Anthony said.

"Oh, now you care about his wellbeing?" He made me mad all over again.

"Ms. Johnson." Agent Adams gave me the look that told me to cool it. I obeyed only because I did not need this officer to delay calling the ambulance for Malcolm. *Lord, please let him be ok.*

The officer radioed for them to send an ambulance. We forgot all about the boy who hit Malcolm who was lying on the floor in a fetal position. The officer looked down at him and pressed the button on his radio. "Make that two ambulances."

Agent Adams sent the other agent he came with back to the school to give the report. He needed them to contact Malcolm and Anthony's parents to inform them of what happened.

"Did they catch any of those guys?" Anthony asked.

"They caught a few of them," one of the officers responded.

"A few of them? What about the others?" I asked concerned.

"Don't worry, we will do everything we can to catch them, but we do need to get you guys out of here," one of the officers said.

We heard over the radio that the ambulance was en route. A sigh of relief escaped from me. They also mentioned that we all needed to go to the hospital to get checked out. I explained to them that I was fine and no physical damage was done to me. I did agree to go to the hospital, but only to ride with Malcolm until his parent's arrived. Anthony had minor cuts and bruises so they wanted him to get cleaned up and checked out.

We heard the sirens blaring from down the block and I knew it was only a matter of time before they came to take

Malcolm. It felt like forever, but when they finally arrived, they asked us a few questions about Malcolm and what happened. I told them the briefest story and mentioned how the young teen slammed his bat into Malcolm's shoulder and head.

Thankfully, they allowed Anthony and me to ride in the back of the ambulance with Malcolm. I gave Agent Adams my car keys and he promised he would put it in the school's parking lot. It felt like the longest ride to the Hospital. There was not much traffic, but my anxiety made it feel like it was taking us forever to get there. I called my principal while we were on the way to the hospital. I told her the hospital we were heading to and to have their parents meet me there.

Once we got there, the nurses came and looked at Anthony and me. They cleaned up his bruises and we sat outside of the room where they had Malcolm as we waited for both of their parents to arrive.

"Do you think Malcolm is going to be ok," Anthony asked. You could see how concern he was.

"I'm sure he is going to be fine. That boy has been through a lot. He's a trooper."

"I hope you're right. He looked like he was in so much pain."

"He did, but he's in one of the best hospitals, they'll make sure he's ok," I said as I squeezed Anthony's hand. "How are you though? That was a lot for you to take in this morning."

"I'm ok. I'm a bit shaken up now, but while everything was happening, I was determined to make sure they didn't get to

Malcolm. I just wanted to help as much as I could," he said teary-eyed.

"You did more than just help. You risked your life for a classmate. That is the bravest thing you could have ever done."

"I did it because I know if it were me, Malcolm would have done the same thing, if not more. I just hope he's going to be ok."

Seeing Anthony this emotional only made me more emotional. I pulled him in for a side hug. "He would've done it for all of us and he will pull through. I have already said a prayer to God and I know he will hear me. We just have to be strong and have faith." I wiped the fallen tears from his eyes.

Just as I was calming Anthony down, in walked Malcolm's family, his *whole* family. My heart dropped and for some strange reason, fear filled me. I did not know what they were going to do when they saw him. I know how ruthless his family is and they made sure everyone knew it. The fact that someone crossed one of their own only meant that this would not end well.

I tapped Anthony so he could sit up. I got up from my seat and approached the family. My heart was beating more than normal and I tried to think of what I should say.

"Mr. Brown, how are you?" *Damn Kris, why would you ask how is he? You know he isn't great. He's clearly beyond pissed off. Great job Kris.*

"Ms. Johnson, where is my son?" Mr. Brown asked me with anger-filled eyes.

"He's right this way," I said as I guided them to the room Malcolm was in.

He walked into the room, not holding the door for anyone.

"Thank you, Ms. Johnson," Malcolm's mother said as she hugged me. She followed behind her husband and so did the rest of the family.

I returned to my seat and sat with Anthony. We just stared at each other briefly and exchanged no words. Honestly, I did not know what was left to say. The look on his father's face made me nervous. I knew revenge was on his mind, but how far he was about to go to get it was what I was afraid of.

Only moments went by before Malcolm's oldest brother came bursting through the door. He walked up to me and all I could see was red. He told me to tell him everything that happened and not leave out any details. I told him everything I could remember.

He looked at Anthony and thanked him with a pound of the hand for stopping the boy from hitting Malcolm again with the bat. He walked away from us after I was done telling him what happened and pulled out his phone and made some phone calls. I can only imagine the kinds of calls he was making. Anthony and I were trying to eavesdrop as best we could, but could only make out a few words here and there. It was definitely noted that whomever he was on the phone with had to find out who was responsible for what happened.

Anthony's mom came rushing in and you could tell she had been crying. She ran to where we were and hugged her son as if she was afraid she was never going to see him again. It sent chills through my body. We sat her down and filled her in as best we could. She cried the whole time we were telling her what happened. Boy was her reaction so much different from Malcolm's family. Fear filled her eyes and rage filled theirs.

"Anthony, when did you become this brave soul?" she asked in her thick Spanish accent as she cupped his face.

"I don't know, mom. I got so caught up in the moment and knew I had to help somehow."

"It's that adrenaline rush that takes over you in times like that," I said as I thought back to when I jumped in front of Anthony when the officer had his loaded gun pointing to him.

We heard the door to Malcolm's room open and saw the nurses bringing his bed out. We got up from our seats to see what was happening.

"Where are they taking him?" Anthony asked.

"He has to get a CT scan done. He had a seizure while we were talking to him. The doctor wants to rule out that he does not have internal bleeding in his head. If he's hemorrhaging then they'll have to do surgery," his mom said as she started crying.

Mr. Brown pulled her into his chest. "Don't worry, whoever is responsible for this will learn to never mess with my family again."

"That's the problem now. You guys walk around like we are bulletproof! Yes, our family name holds weight in the streets, but it is not like how it was back in the day when your father and uncles ran the streets and everyone feared them. This generation is always in competition to be at the top. I don't want to have to watch my back every time I leave my house and neither should my children!"

"What do you expect me to do? I did not choose this lifestyle. It was chosen for me. I taught our children what was taught to me. Do you think I like for my family to be tested like this? Our bloodline is in too deep for me to pull out of it now. I have to find who did this to my son and make sure they know that the same fear that was installed decades ago, remains!"

"And how do you expect that to happen?" she asked with tears still falling from her face.

"Kevin is making a few phone calls now and I will handle the rest once we are out of here. I will not discuss the details in front of people we do not know." He looked around the waiting area as if one of us were wearing a wire and ready to turn him in.

"If anything happens to my baby, you better make sure whoever is involved pays for it. I don't care who you have to go through to get to them, it better be done." Her tears were no longer falling and this time she had that same look that the rest of the family had.

"Now that's the wife I married! Trust me, it'll be handled." He kissed her on her forehead as he signaled for his oldest son to meet him at the house.

"I'm going to take my son home. He's heard, seen, and been through enough today," Anthony's mom said as they got up and headed to the nurse's station to see about his discharge papers. They waited over there for a few minutes before he waved goodbye to me. That should have been my cue to leave, but I felt frozen. Now that Anthony was gone, I felt alone.

Malcolm's family was so busy plotting and making phone calls that no one acknowledged that I was still there. *Shit. I didn't call Stephan!*

It took me a while to find my phone. I looked at my phone and seen I had seventeen missed calls from him and four text messages. I opened my text messages from him and read the four he left me.

Hey, babe. You never texted me and told me you reached to work safely.

It's lunchtime, no phone call today?

Ok, I have not heard from you at all and it is now 12:37 p.m. Just let me know you are good.

I called the school, they told me bits and pieces of what happened. I'm on my way. Please do not leave until I get there.

Tears filled my eyes as a wave of relief hit me. Nothing at that moment felt better than to know that he was coming to get me. I got so caught up in trying to make sure that Malcolm and Anthony were ok that I didn't bother to think to call someone on my behalf.

Just as I was about to call him and let him know I would stay and wait for him, Monique walked in with Mike. She spotted me almost immediately and made her way towards me.

"Great. Here come the cops," Mr. Brown said, as my sister got closer to where we were. "Listen, I'm going to tell you just like I told the others, we have nothing to say nor do we want to press charges."

"Relax. I'm not here for you," Monique said shooting him a look that told him to cool it.

I got up from my seat and met her the rest of the way. Before she even embraced me, she checked me out to make sure I was not physically hurt.

"Are you ok?"

"I am now. How did you know I was here?"

"You do know I work for NYPD right? We heard the chatter over the radio this morning, but it's not my district and they had all the youth officers on it already. It was not until Stephan called me and said that the school told him that you were involved in this madness that I started putting pieces together. Didn't take long to know that you were here."

"He should be here any minute. I'm sorry I didn't call you guys. It was just so much happening at once that my safety and informing you and Steph was the last thing on my mind."

"Listen, I get it. Am I upset that you didn't think to call me, yes, but again I know how it feels to be caught up in that moment. I'm just glad you're safe." She finally embraced me and I did not want to let her go.

"Can I interrupt this real quick?" My head popped up so quickly at the sound of his voice.

"Baby!" I ran into his arms and buried my face into his chest.

"Kris, you had me so worried. Are you ok? Why didn't you call me? What happened? Are the kids ok? Did anyone get hurt?" He just kept asking questions and I had to silence him and told him that I will tell him everything he wants to know once we got out of here.

Forty minutes later, they brought Malcolm back to his room and told us they would review his CT scan and keep us posted. Monique got a call on her radio and had to leave. She promised she would come by the house later to check on me and to hear how Malcolm was doing. Stephan stayed with me while I waited to hear what the results showed.

I called my assistant principal in the meantime and gave her an update on everything. She told me that she already put in for a sub for me for the rest of the week and for me to make sure I was mentally ready before I came back. I assured her that I was ok and did not need any days off, but then I saw the look that Steph gave me and decided to just take the days. I mentioned to her that Malcolm and Anthony missed their state test and she told me she already worked it out for them to retake it in a few weeks. I felt the weight lift from my shoulders. That would have devastated them if they missed it and did not have the opportunity to make it up. We spoke for a little while longer and ended the call with me promising to keep her updated.

I rested my head on Stephan's shoulder and closed my eyes. I felt his lips touch my forehead as he kissed it. His presence alone put me at ease and made me feel safe. I felt myself drifting off and allowed my body to do just that.

I could not have been asleep for more than five minutes before I felt Stephan tapping me. I lifted my head. My eyes felt so heavy that it took a while for them to fully open and adjust.

I looked at him and his eyes went from mine to Malcolm's room. We saw the doctor entering and I got up to hear what the doctor had to say. I did not care if I was family or not.

I stood by the door as the doctor explained to us that he did have internal bleeding inside of his brain, but it was not severe and just needed to be observed. The doctor told us that they are going to keep him overnight and monitor his progress. He said he didn't want to get our hopes up, but if everything goes as planned then the internal bleeding can stop on its own. The family thanked him as he left to go see another patient.

The nurse hooked him up to an IV filled with medicine that would help bring the swelling down and reduce the amount of pain he was in.

"Malcolm, baby, mommy is going to stay right here," his mom said as she held his hand in hers.

We all went back into the waiting area and had small talk. I did not realize how much time had passed until the nurse on duty came over to us and said visiting hours were over. No one wanted to leave, but honestly, there was nothing else for us to do. Malcolm would be here for a few days being observed. No new information would be given to us until tomorrow anyway.

Stephan helped me to my feet as I grabbed my coat to put it on. I guess going home was not a bad idea. A wave of sleepiness hit me as I zipped up my coat.

I went over to speak to Mrs. Brown. "You have my number. Please call or text me if there are any changes with Malcolm, good or bad."

"I will, Ms. Johnson. Thank you for loving my son as if he were your own. He's really lucky to have another mother figure like you in his life."

I leaned down to hug her. "I will always be here for him. Again, please keep me posted and let me know if you need anything."

"I will. Thank you again."

"No need to thank you. We'll talk soon." She nodded at me and I grabbed my bag and headed to the exit with Stephan's arm interlocked with mine.

The drive home was a quiet one and I appreciated it so much. The only noise was the radio playing softly in the background and the sound of the blinker every time he made a turn. I had my window cracked enough to get a relaxing breeze through the car. As I rested my head on the window, I could not help but replay everything that happened. I wondered how my students did today. I was not there to mentally prepare them for the test with our classroom meditation or given them their iPads to unwind. I don't even know who they called to cover my class at such short notice. I wish I could just hear their voices. I felt myself smiling at just the thought of them. I hope whoever they got to cover my class treated them well. My students do not deal well with change and they feed off everyone else's energy. I can only pray that they put someone with my students who would mesh well with them.

"Babe, we are home." I was so caught up in my thoughts that I did not even notice that we were parked outside my apartment. I grabbed my bag and unfastened my seatbelt as Stephan came around and opened my door.

"Thank you, hun," I said as I took his hand as he helped me out the car. I couldn't wait to get inside to just take a bath and relax.

I didn't even bother to search my bag for my keys. Steph took out his set of keys and let us in. I kicked my shoes off as soon as my feet touched the inside of my apartment. I went straight into my bedroom and undressed. I stripped down to my panties and bra before I went into the bathroom to wash my hands and run my bathwater. I set it to the perfect temperature; hot enough to calm me. I went into the bin where I kept my bath supplies and found my twilight bath bomb. This one was my favorite for when I needed a great aroma and something to calm me mentally and physically. It has this pinkish-purplish color to it. When you drop it into the bathwater, the water turns blue and pink. The swirling of those colors is simply beautiful. The edgy aroma, a vanilla scent mixed with a bit of lavender is so pleasing to my senses.

I grabbed my iPad and my beats pill and prepared myself for a long bath. I needed to try to take my mind off everything that happened today. I turned on my Apple Music, connected my beats pill, and put my old school R&B playlist on shuffle. I dipped my toe into the tub and the water temperature was perfect. Slowly easing myself into the water, I felt my muscles thanking me for this heat.

I had my music playing and my iPad opened. I clicked my kindle app and it took me right to the current book I was reading, *Dirty Little Secrets*, by one of my favorite author's, Kendall Ryan. I only had a few pages left and was determined to finish it while I was soaking.

Between the aroma, the music, the atmosphere, the temperature of the water, and my book, I felt like I was lost in another world and loved every second of it. My hair was tied up in a loose high bun so I sunk as deep as I could into my bathtub without getting my nape too wet.

It did not take me long to finish my book and the way it ended had me in my feelings. I could not wait to purchase part two. I needed to know what happened between Emma and Gavin once she found out the truth about how his ex died. I grabbed my phone and sent a tweet to Kendall Ryan, *Just finished reading Dirty Little Secret and I must say @KendallRyan1 you are one of my favorite authors! But how could you end the book like that?!?! Now I have to end my bath early to go purchase the second book. I need to know what happened!*" I love Apple, but I hate that I cannot buy Kindle books off my iPad. Kindle and Apple need to come together and make an agreement to make that happen. Now I have to grab my laptop just to buy the second book. I will though because I need to know what happened.

I soaked in the bath for a few more minutes, promising to leave after a song had finished, but Pandora kept playing my tunes. I knew Stephan must have been out there shaking his head at me singing like I was the next Jennifer Hudson. Finally, a commercial came on and I took that as my cue to get up and shower. I grabbed my Dove exfoliating body polish and gave my body a nice scrub. The kiwi seeds and cool aloe fragrance smelled amazing and had my body feeling extra clean. After rinsing off, I grabbed my Dove bar soap and washcloth and gave my body the washing it needed. My bathroom smelt amazing with all these different fragrances.

"Babe, your dinner is going to get cold." I heard Stephan yell from outside the bathroom door.

My dinner? I know he did not cook anything. I wonder what he ordered. I grabbed my towel and dried myself off before exiting the bathroom. I walked into the kitchen to see what was for dinner and my eyes lit up as if it was my birthday. Jamaican food from *Island Tropics*! I swear I did a happy dance in my head.

"Welcome to the Island of Jamaica," Stephan said in his fake Jamaican accent.

"It smells amazing in here. My stomach is doing summersaults just thinking about diving in." I walked over to where the food was and could not help myself from grabbing a piece of fried dumpling, my favorite.

"That's for your breakfast, ma'am. You eat that now and you won't have any for tomorrow."

"For my breakfast?" I gave Stephan a look of confusion.

"Yes, you're going to be home tomorrow and I don't want you in here stressing about what you're going to eat and you may not even feel up to cooking."

Boy did I love this man. I forgot that I'd be home for the rest of the week. He was right; I may not be in the mood to cook tomorrow and I'm not even sure if we have anything to cook. We were supposed to have gone food shopping after work today.

"You're such an amazing man. Thank you for being you and treating me better than I deserve." I felt my eyes begin to sting as he walked over to me to catch my tear from falling.

"None of that tonight. You've had a day from hell and the least I could do is bring you some of your favorite dishes." He tilted my chin up to kiss me and at that moment, I knew I needed to put it all behind me, even if just for tonight.

"Ok, no more mushy stuff. What you ordered us?" I was beyond ready to chow down. The way my stomach was dancing around right now reminded me that I did not eat at all today.

"I ordered a few of our favorites. Usually, we have our separate dishes, but since I did not know what you were in the mood for today, I ordered a few things. We can have a mini thanksgiving. We have jerk chicken, oxtails, stew chicken, and curry goat. I also ordered rice and peas, white rice, sweet plantains, and cabbage. Oh, and I got your favorite, carrot juice."

"Babe! That must have been expensive. You really outdid yourself. Thank you so much!"

"It's no biggie, sweets. It's enough for us to have lunch for tomorrow as well."

"And you mentioned breakfast for tomorrow. What's on the menu?"

"Check and see." He did not have to tell me twice. I lifted the aluminum foil and seen ackee and saltfish. I should have known he got that when I spotted the fried dumpling. "How did you get them to make this at dinner time? They only serve ackee and saltfish for breakfast."

"You know the chef of Island Tropics and my dad go way back. I called him directly and he told me he was prepping the food for tomorrow before he left. I asked would it be too much for him to whip up some ackee and saltfish and fried dumpling for us and he said he would do it just for me. Of course, now that means that I owe him a favor."

"Imagine he asks you to be one of his guest chefs when he does his annual cooking competitions?" I got excited at the thought of it. That would be great exposure for Stephan. I have been trying to get him to consider opening up his own restaurant, but he always turns down the idea.

"You really think I'm that good of a cook to compete?"

"Why do you think I still keep you around?"

"I can think of a few reasons," he said winking at me.

"Don't be nasty when I'm trying to be serious." I gave him my side-eye, even though he was right. I did keep him around for those reasons, but that was not the point I was trying to make. "I think you're an amazing cook. It is in your blood. Not on your mom's side though." He reached over and slapped me on my butt as we both fell out laughing.

"You better leave my momma and her sisters alone."

"I'm leaving that conversation alone. We can go all night about their food." We shared a good hearty laugh just at the thought of it. Thank God he picked up after his father. "Let me go put on some clothes so we can eat. I'll be right out."

I'm so used to putting on lotion right after I finish drying off from my shower, so it felt weird putting on lotion now. I did it anyway because I can only imagine how dry my skin would feel if I didn't. I grabbed a pair of shorts and a tank top to put on. I did not bother putting on any panties or a bra. I was letting everything breathe tonight.

I walked back into the dining area and the table was laid out with all of the food. He even had a glass of wine poured out for me. "You didn't have to go out your way, but I am so appreciative of you."

"I put your carrot juice in the fridge. Figured you needed a glass of wine more than the carrot juice."

"I sure do need it more. It'll come in handy for my lunch tomorrow." I grabbed a seat at the table as he reached out his hand for us to say grace. He said grace and it reminded me that I need to say a special prayer tonight for Malcolm and to just thank God for not letting this situation be worse than it could have been.

"Time to dig in." He didn't have to tell me twice. I already knew what I wanted to grab first, the oxtails. I took a little bit of everything. Biting into everything before it even hit my plate. I felt like I was in food heaven. Nothing felt better than being hungry and having everything on your plate tasting amazing. No words were exchanged between us as we both dug in and enjoyed the many different flavors hitting our mouths.

Our silence was broken by my phone ringing. We both looked at each other shaking our heads. It never failed, every time we were about to eat or eating, someone was ringing one of our phones, mainly mine. I looked at the screen and it was Monique. I forgot she said she was going to come over after her shift.

I quickly wiped my hands and sent her text. *Hey, sis. Steph and I are having dinner and I'm sure I'm going to knock out right after. Are you able to stop by tomorrow instead?* I picked up my fork and continued eating while I waited for her to respond.

A second later she responded. *Sure, no problem. Just wanted to make sure you are ok.*

Yes, I'm fine. I'll be home all day tomorrow so stop by when you want. Great, now all I need is for Latrice to make no pop-up visits and the rest of my night will be fine.

"Everything on my plate was so good." Stephan laughed at me as my eyes rolled to the back of my head just reliving how great everything tasted.

"I can't even lie, it definitely hit the spot. Those oxtails were on point and putting the oxtail gravy on my rice, man that was good!" I couldn't help but laugh at Stephan, but I understood what he meant though. This food was made with love.

I couldn't force anymore into my mouth. I was stuffed! We sat at the dining table for a bit just having small talk and enjoying each other's company. Stephan was about to pull out a board game until it hit me that today is Wednesday. It's time for ratchet t.v. Black Ink Crew was about to come on. When I told him why we couldn't have game night, he rolled his eyes. He usually goes into the room while I watch my ratchet shows, but tonight he cleared the table and joined me on the sofa.

"Wait, so you're not going into the room like you usually do when I watch my ratchet shows?" I asked as he placed my legs on his lap. A good foot rub is exactly what I needed and I was getting just that from the perfect person.

"Nope, I decided to see what all this ratchetness is about. I need to see what you ditched our game night for."

"Well prepare to be entertained." I turned up the volume just as the show began.

For someone who always had something smart to say about some of the shows I liked to watch, he sure was glued to this one. I was showing him how to use the hashtags on twitter to join in on what people were saying about the show. He took over my phone and was tweeting about everything that was going on. I can't even lie, I've been a huge twitter user for years and always joined in on the hashtags, but this is the first time that my tweets got this many likes and retweets. The sad part about it was that I wasn't the one tweeting, it was Stephan! I couldn't help but shake my head and laugh at him. I guess he will be joining me next Wednesday night.

After watching Black Ink Crew, we headed for bed with Martin playing on our television. I muted the television as we kneeled for prayer.

"Dear Heavenly Father, we come to you humbled and grateful for all that you have done for us. Lord, today was not a great day, but it could have been so much worse. I thank you for not letting me witness what worse could have been. I lift up Malcolm at this time. I am asking that you send your angels down to watch over him. Yes, he is in the hands of nurses and doctors, but Lord, we know there is no doctor like you. Please heal him and please do not let this set him back to his old ways. I am lifting up Anthony as well. Thank you for giving him such a brave heart, but most importantly thank you for not letting him get injured as well. Thank you for keeping me safe throughout it all. Please watch over each of our families and loved ones. Thank you for Stephan. Lord, he is the best thing that has ever happened to me and I ask that you continue to bless our relationship. Let no man or woman come between us as we continue to build our foundation. We thank you and we praise you. Amen and amen."

"Amen. Felt like you were about to start preaching on me."

"I'm sorry. I just had so much to be thankful for. Only God knows what else could've happened today."

"Let's not dwell on what else could've happened and just be grateful that you're ok."

"You're right, babe." I leaned over to kiss him as I snuggled up under him. Tonight I needed his body heat. The comfort of him would surely put me to sleep.

I thought about all the fun times Stephan and I shared as I tried to put my mind in a happy place. We are due for a trip soon. I am going to plan a weekend getaway for us while I am home tomorrow.

I felt my body drifting into a deep sleep until something dwelled on me. It had my mind replaying everything from the last couple of nights.

"Steph, are you sleep?"

"Not anymore, wassup?" I felt his arm loosen around me as he shifted to lay on his side.

I turned around to face him. "It just hit me."

"What did?"

"What happened today. It was my dream all over again."

"I'm confused. Your last dream was about you and Latrice at a club when something broke out. How does that add up to..." The look on his face proved that he understood how I made the connection.

"Think about it, in my dream Latrice and I was in the club when the fight broke out. We got stuck inside because the bouncers thought we were involved and wouldn't let us leave. That's just like earlier. We were stranded inside the store because of those teens who were trying to fight Malcolm. It's as if Anthony and I were Latrice and I. Then the cops come in and attack Latrice and me. Earlier today, the cops came in and treated Malcolm as if he wasn't the victim. Plus, I had to jump in front of Anthony when the cop pointed his gun at him. Luckily Agent Adams came inside at the right time, just like Monique did in my dream." I kept going on comparing my dream to what happened today. I hate that I have dreams and they end up coming true in some weird way. I just never know with who, when, or exactly how it'll play out. It's as if my dreams give me a snippet of what's to come. Sometimes it's worse than my dreams and sometimes it's not as bad. I just wish there was a way I could know who is involved so I could warn them, but would that be cheating life?

CHAPTER 8

KRISTEN

It has been almost four weeks since that crazy day in Dunkin Donuts. It took me a while to get back into the swing of things at work. I won't lie, I've been extremely paranoid every time I got close to the school. I hated that this situation made me feel so unsafe. Anthony was handling it better than I was and I knew I had no choice but to not let it get the best of me.

Malcolm is coming back today. The class and I are having a little welcome back party for him. I've been visiting him at the hospital almost every day and the medical staff kept saying how lucky he was and how much of a miracle his story is, but I know my God and I know it was all Him. Prayer works!

Unfortunately, his family will not allow this situation to rest. I've overheard them on a few occasions talking about all the people they've made pay for this so far. When will this ever end? I don't think they cared that this will only become a never-ending battle. Someone is always trying to rise to the top and will stop at nothing to make it happen.

April was here and the weather was finally warming up. The cold was not for me and I was beyond happy to hang up my winter coat. I loved the spring and fall season. Since today was not so cold, I decided to take my students to our outdoor yard. I had everyone grab their independent reading book as I grabbed mine. We found a nice shaded area by the benches and enjoyed some fresh air.

I loved the fact that my students enjoyed reading. It not only benefited them but gave me time to read as well. I just started a new book, *Mask Off*, by Darlene Arrington. I loved supporting black authors. She had me glued from just the first page.

I was so engrossed in my book that I did not realize Malcolm was here until I heard the class shouting his name. I looked up and he was closing the door to his father's Jeep. It didn't take him long to spot us and when he did the biggest smile crept across his face. It made me so happy to know that he was in good spirits. I walked over to the gate of the yard to let him in. His father got out of the Jeep and walked over to me. He apologized for Malcolm's lateness. I was just happy that he was here. I did not care if he was late. He explained to me that even though he's back at school he still needs to take it easy and that his wife came to the school earlier to drop off a note to the school letting them know that he cannot participate in any vigorous activities, which meant that going to the gym was definitely out the question. The doctor was ok with Malcolm staying home for a few more days, but Malcolm was ready to come back. His dad said they debated for a while, but settled on letting him come back with some restrictions. I assured him that we would make sure he was good. It felt good when he told me that I was one of the very few people outside of his family that he trusted with his child. He also mentioned that one of his sons or himself would be dropping him to and from school until things cooled down. I knew exactly what that meant and I did not bother to push the issue. I simply nodded and said I understood. We spoke about his progress for a bit and then he departed.

I walked back over to our shaded area where the kids were all surrounding Malcolm asking him how he was and filling him in on everything he missed while away.

We stayed outside for about twenty more minutes before I decided it was time for us to head back upstairs. It was time for social studies, which meant I was going to be teaching this subject for two period's straight, *great*. This was not their favorite subject and it was not my favorite to teach. On the bright side, after social studies, they had art class and I had my prep.

It felt like hours passed by before the end of third period rang. I don't know who packed up their social studies textbook faster, them or me, but it was clear we've all had enough. The class lined up by the door as they waited for me to tell them to proceed.

"Octavia, you can lead the class to Mr. Stevens' room." The class walked silently to their art class and waited for him to come outside and greet them. Once Mr. Stevens came out of the classroom, he greeted them as they entered.

"See you all in a few. Please behave!"

"We will," they all sung in unison. I sure hope they were going to be on their best behavior. I love my students, but I know they aren't angels. They had their days where I felt like every strand of my hair was going to turn grey. I can't lie though, they bring pure joy to my life despite the moments they make me want to pull my hair out.

As I walked back into my classroom, I grabbed my cellphone from off my desk to text Stephan.

Hey, my love. How's work going?

Almost instantly he wrote me back. Hearing his text tone always made my heart smile, especially when it's out the blue.

Hi, babe. It's going. Sitting in this meeting, listening to these fools lie about all the great reasons why I should grant them a loan.

Lol, and you're being rude by texting while they are pleading their case.

They think I'm calculating everything up. Would you rather me stop texting you and pretend to act like I'm considering their case?

Nope keep the text coming. Just dropped my kids off to their art class and though I'm supposed to be prepping my lessons, I don't feel like it.

Oh, so you're using me to keep you company?

Pretty much.

Ouch! I don't appreciate being used.

It's all in love, baby. What time are you getting off today?

By the look of things, I should be getting off between six-thirty and seven.

Ok, so I'll make sure dinner is ready when you get in. Do you have a taste for anything in specific?

It took him a while to respond, so I decided to get some classroom work done in the meantime. Time was slipping away from me so I had to work faster than I expected to.

I was almost finished with prepping for my next period class when I heard my favorite text tone.

Sorry, babe. I'm back. I had to wrap up that meeting. What I have a taste for? You, duh!

Ha! Can you not be nasty for once? You do know I'm at work and so are you!

And?! Ok, I'll stop until I get home (wink). Honestly, it's been a long day and I think a night out will do me good. How about you go home after work, freshen up and take an Uber to my job? I can drive us to that Italian restaurant I told you I wanted us to try.

I couldn't help but smile at my phone. He and I haven't been out to eat in a while. I was so wrapped up in thinking about what I was going to wear that I didn't realize I never responded.

I heard his text tone again. *Are you ok with that???*

Yes, babe. I am more than ok with that. Can't wait!

We wrapped up our conversation and then I headed to Mr. Stevens' classroom to pick up my students.

Thankfully, he didn't have so much of a bad report to share with me. I wasn't surprised that Anthony, my class clown, was a chatterbox in his class. This boy always has stories for days but never wanted to speak up when he was called on to answer a question. *How ironic.*

Justin led the class back to our classroom.

"You may enter the classroom. Please grab your math notebooks and pull out your math homework."

"Math homework? We had homework for math yesterday?" I heard Anthony whispering to Jason.

"Yo, why you never pay attention to your homework sheet. It's listed there." Jason shook his head at Anthony and I couldn't help but shake my head either. It was clear who was getting an incomplete grade for their homework today. This was nothing new with Anthony. I adored him, but he picks and chooses what he wants to do sometimes and his grades reflect just that.

I went around collecting everyone's homework and began the lesson. Since they all learned on different levels, it wasn't always easy getting through the lesson. I had a combo of sixth, seventh, and eighth graders in my class, but for the most part, they were on the level of elementary students. Nonetheless, I always pushed them to go above and beyond. I did fear for them once they graduate from here. I can only hope and pray that they get the services that they need. Some high schools allowed them to opt-out of being in a special education class and into a regular classroom. Truthfully, many of my students wouldn't do well with opting out. They needed and strived with a smaller class and being able to get one on one help. In high school, they may not have that luxury.

This lesson was a bit of a struggle and just by glancing through their homework, I can tell that they weren't grasping the concepts. I stopped teaching and allowed them to go on their laptops to give their brains a break while I searched up an easier and fun way to teach them variables. It didn't take me long to find the perfect fun way to get them to understand what they needed to learn.

Ironically enough they were enjoying the learning activity. I think they were having too much fun with the lesson and it made me smile knowing that our day was not wasted. I gave them their homework back and told them that I expected to see the corrected answers. Of course, Anthony was excited because now he had an opportunity to make up his homework and was no longer receiving an incomplete grade.

The period ended shortly after and it was time to drop them off to the cafeteria for lunch. I had Anthony lead the line this time. I grabbed my jacket, wallet, and phone as they waited for me to tell them to proceed. I forgot my lunch at home so I had to go out and buy lunch today. I hated spending unnecessary money and my mind was already set on what I packed. Now I have to go and find something to eat. *Annoyed.*

After dropping my class off to the cafeteria, I walked to the supermarket down the block. They serve hot food in the back. It was just a matter of what my eyes locked on. I didn't want to get anything too heavy since Stephan and I were going out to eat later. I decided on a piece of salmon, spinach rice, and broccoli. My meal came up to $11.57! This is exactly why I pack my lunch. I don't believe in spending this much on lunch. I remember back in the day when I use to buy a sandwich from the corner store for three dollars and get a free can soda and a bag of chips. Now, the corner store charges five dollars to make the same dried sandwich and the chips are no longer apart of the packaged deal. Some stores don't even include the soda.

I paid for my lunch and headed back to my classroom. When I came back from washing my hands, I called Stephan on FaceTime but he didn't pick up. *Strange.* I put my music on shuffle as I pulled out my lunch to eat. *Damn, this honey-glazed salmon is good. I guess it is worth the money. I need to learn how to make spinach rice.* I sent a pic of my lunch to Stephan and told him we needed to make spinach rice one day.

Three minutes later he called me back on FaceTime. "Hey, babe."

"Hey, darling. Sorry I didn't answer when you called. I was making the reservations for tonight."

Reservations? Damn, that means I can't be late. I need to think about what I'm going to wear. "What time did you make the reservations for?"

"For seven o'clock sharp, so don't be late. I finished up some work faster than I anticipated, so I should be done with work by six the latest."

"I'll be on time. I just need to figure out what to wear, but I have time." I made a mental note as to what he had on and I think I knew what I was going to wear.

"Good. I'll be ready when you get here."

"Sounds good to me. Did you get the picture of my lunch? I'm so mad I left my lunch at home."

"Yea I did. That looked good."

"It was great. I was mad that I had to spend money on lunch because I left mine at home, but I must admit that it was worth the money."

Stephan and I chatted for a few more minutes before Malcolm walked into my room. I told Steph that I would call him back.

"Hey, Malcolm. What's going on?"

"Nothing. The class is at gym and I can't participate, but I also don't want to sit in the gym while everyone plays. Is it ok if I stay here with you? I promise I won't be a bother."

"Sure you can stay here. You're far from a bother. Let me just tell Mr. Greene that you'll be staying with me for this period." I walked over to the classroom phone and called the gym teacher to let him know that Malcolm will be staying with me.

Malcolm grabbed an iPad and headphones as he sat at his desk. I couldn't help but stare at him. The side of his head showed evidence of what happened that day. It was a few weeks ago, but it still felt like yesterday when I saw all the blood rushing from his head. Now that spot will be a permanent scar. I have God to thank for him not giving up. This could have been a major setback for him, but instead, it made him even more motivated to graduate and move far away from here. I hurried and wiped the tear that was threatening to escape.

"Ms. Johnson, you know what I was thinking..." The smile on his face faded when he saw the sadness written on mine. "What's wrong, Ms. Johnson?"

"Nothing, Malcolm. I'm ok."

"You're not. I can see the tears forming in your eyes. Are you about to cry?" And just like that, a tear escaped from my eye. I couldn't look him in the eye and lie to him.

"I'm ok. I'm just grateful that you're sitting here with me and not elsewhere." Another tear slipped away. *Get your emotions together. Stop crying!* "I'm so proud of you and how you've taken charge of your own life."

"Thank you, Ms. Johnson." He got up and walked to me as he wrapped his arms around me. *Great! There go more tears.* "It's because of people like you that I didn't give up. Please don't cry. I'm going to make you proud on graduation day, just watch."

I hugged him back and squeezed him a little tighter after his last statement. "You can't make me any more proud than I already am."

He sat down at the chair next to my desk. "My dad likes you. He's such a hard shell, but I can tell that he does."

I had to sit up in my chair for this one. "How can you tell that he likes me? And when you say like me, like me how?" I gave him the eye.

"Not like that, Ms. Johnson." We both laughed. "I mean he likes you as an individual. He knows how much you look out for me. He doesn't trust many people, but he knows you have my best interest at heart. He won't say it, but if we disagree on something about school and I mention your name, he'll drop it and let me be."

His father barely spoke to me every time I came by to check on him. When they did show up to parent-teacher conferences, it was usually his mother who spoke. This was news to me.

"What have you spoken about with your dad that you had to mention me to get your way?"

"He was against me going to Saturday class for tutoring. I was telling him what I would be getting extra help and he didn't budge. Then I said, Ms. Johnson thinks tutoring will help me get above-average grades. When I said that, he just said 'fine' and walked away."

"Well, I'm glad that your father knows that I'm always going to look out for you."

"Yes he does and I know it as well."

"Now that we got that out that way. What were you trying to tell me before you asked me what was wrong?"

"Oh, I was going to say, you know what we never got?" He started laughing and I sat there puzzled.

"What did we never get?" I wanted to laugh too.

"We never got to eat those donuts you bought for us from Dunkin Donuts that day." He started laughing again and knowing that he was making light of this situation made me feel more at peace.

"You're absolutely right. I wonder if I go back there would they give me a free order?" I was half-joking. I forgot all about the donuts I bought for my kids. It was the furthest thing from my mind and I haven't been back there since that day. I wonder if they got their glass window fixed. I'm going to have to see it for myself. *One day.*

The rest of the school day flew by with a breeze. I reminded my students of their homework assignments and walked them downstairs for dismissal. I spotted Malcolm's' dad's jeep as I waved to him. He nodded his head in my direction. I guess that was his way of saying hello. What a strange man.

I forgot today was Monday, which meant I had to stay at work for an extra hour for professional development time. Thankfully they didn't have a PD planned for us and were allowing the teachers to use our PD time for classroom setup. I went upstairs, cleaned up my classroom, and prepped it for first period tomorrow. I printed out the lesson plans I needed, sharpened a few pencils, and even swept my floors. I'm sure the custodian will appreciate not having to clean my room today.

I grabbed my bags and headed to the main office to clock out. It was now three-thirty and that meant I only had two and a half hours to get ready and be at Stephan's job. It felt like a lot of time, but knowing me, time will fly right by. I hope that the traffic would not be bad.

I walked into my apartment and inhaled the great scent of my plugin from Bath & Body Works, Waikiki Beach Coconut. It's a great feeling to walk into your house and be hit by a pleasant smell. I kicked my shoes off, dropped my bags on the counter, and headed to the bathroom. I looked in the mirror as I ran my fingers through my curls. These curls are not going to last after my shower. I didn't have time to twist it, so a sleek bun it is.

I scanned through my closet looking for the perfect outfit for tonight. I remembered what Steph was wearing and wanted to match his fly. I searched through my closet until I found one of my dresses from Fashion Nova. I laid my dress on the bed and went to find a sexy panty and bra set. *Bingo! He is going to drool when he sees me in this.*

I gathered everything for my shower and headed to the bathroom. I let the water run as I stripped out of my work clothes and placed them in the hamper. My hamper was getting full. I hated doing laundry and it was one of the reasons why I knew Stephan was my soulmate because he didn't mind it.

I decided to co-wash my hair. I had a lot of products in it and knew adding gel on top of it would leave that nasty white residue. While the conditioner soaked into my hair, I decided to shave my body parts that needed shaving. After I got every strand of hair off, I exfoliated my skin. Nothing felt better than hair free smooth skin. I washed out the conditioner, tied up my hair, and finished my shower.

I dried my hair with an old T-shirt and added my leave-in conditioner. Just as I thought, time was slipping by me. It was already 4:37 p.m. I had less than an hour to leave my house. I needed to blow dry my hair. I decided to lotion my body first and then dry my hair. I wish I had time to use my diffuser, but time was not on my side. I set my blow dryer on the medium setting, sprayed my heat protectant into my hair, and quickly dried it. I added my setting lotion so it would help make my waves pop. I used my Eco Style gel to lay down my hair and my edges. Thankfully it didn't take me long to perfect my bun. I grabbed my scarf and tied down my hair. I had twenty minutes left to get dressed and to do my makeup. *Where did the time go!*

I did my makeup before I put on my dress. I gave myself a natural glow. Stephan wasn't a fan of women with too much makeup. He appreciated natural beauty, but tonight was a makeup kind of night. I just made sure I kept it cute and simple. I slipped on my dress and heels. I walked over to my full body mirror and couldn't help but smile at how good I looked.

I grabbed my phone off the charger and ordered an Uber. It was coming in three minutes. That means I had two minutes to throw everything into my little purse and put on some perfume.

I heard my phone ping and knew that meant the Uber driver was here. I l looked at myself once more and headed to the door.

CHAPTER 9

STEPHAN

There was a light knock at the door. I told whomever it was that they could open:

"Mr. Moore, sorry to bother you. I need you to sign off on a few documents before I close up for the day," Samantha said as she stood by my office door.

"What am I signing off on?" I stopped what I was doing as I looked at the documents Samantha was handing to me.

"The top page is the numbers for today, underneath that is the amount that each teller had in their drawers at the end of their shift, plus what I added to their draws for tomorrow. Then there's time off request..."

I had to stop her right there. "A time off request from who?" As soon as I said that, I saw the name in the left-hand corner, Denise Jennings. "Denise wants another day off? I'm not even sure if she has any days left."

"I already checked. She has exactly seven hours left." She flipped the page over and showed the next page where it showed her remaining hours.

"I wish you would've told me this earlier. I'm not even sure if I could find someone to cover her shift at this short notice." I hated being the bad guy and denying people a personal day, but they knew my rules. The customer always comes first. I had to make sure when my customers walked through the door, that they didn't have to wait too long to be serviced. If I can't find someone to cover her shift, then I may have to deny her time-off request.

"Mr. Moore, I already got it covered. You didn't hire me as your assistant for no reason." She flipped over the next page and it showed the schedule for tomorrow.

"You're right, Samantha. I underestimate you sometimes and I apologize. Ok great, Thomas Avery will cover for her. Thank you for handling that. It's one less headache I needed." I signed off on all the documents and handed them back to her. I checked my watch and it was now 5:52 p.m. Kristen should be here any minute. I finished up what I was doing before Samantha walked in and organized my documents before shutting down my computer.

I didn't realize how long I was holding my pee until it was too late. I got that instant rush which made me jump out my seat and head towards the bathroom. Of course, this is the time that the button on my slacks wanted to get stuck. I felt myself doing the *pee-pee* dance. I finally got my button loose and that release never felt better. I fixed myself and washed my hands. I had to check myself in the mirror to make sure I still looked decent. I ran my hands through my locs. *Kris is going to have to tighten these up this weekend.* I shut off the bathroom light and headed back to my office.

When I reached inside my office, I could not believe my eyes. Not only was Kristen on time, but she looked beyond beautiful. I stood there speechless.

"Hey, daddy. You like?" she said as she spun around and walked towards me. I was still stuck as I felt her lips touch mine.

I had to pull her back and look at her again. "Damn, baby. You look beautiful."

"Thank you, babe." She was smiling from ear to ear. She looked stunning. "Are you ready to go?"

"I don't even want to go out anymore. I just want to take you home." I couldn't help but lick my lips. If I had not made the reservations and had her come all the way over here, we would have definitely gone home. I didn't even have an appetite for food anymore. I had a taste for her.

"Well, I didn't get dressed up to just go home. We have plenty of time for that." She winked at me and that made *him* jump.

"You're right, my love. I am keeping my promise and taking you out, but best believe when we get home, that ass is mine." I pulled her into me and kissed her deeply. "I love what you're wearing and on top of it you know red is my favorite color."

"I'm glad you approve of my look. When we were on FaceTime, I was struggling in my head on what to wear. I saw what you had on and it clicked that I had this red dress in my closet that I haven't worn yet."

"Well, my dear, you have made a great choice. That dress was made for you." I took her by the hand and made her twirl around for me. I sat down at my desk and asked her to model her way to me. She did as she was told. I wrapped my hands around her waist and pulled her into my lap. She grabbed my face and I felt the passion in the way she kissed me. She wanted it just as bad as I did.

I slid my hand up her thigh and was welcomed with warmness. I was inching my way up further when she grabbed my wrist. "Wait until we get back home. You're not about to mess up my outfit nor this hair." She kissed my cheek and got up from my lap.

"You're just going to leave me like this?" I asked as I looked down at how happy *he* was.

"Trust me, baby, I will take care of him tonight." She winked at me with her sexy brown eyes. "Now are you ready to go? We have reservations."

"Yes, we can go. The faster we get there, the faster I can get you back home." I grabbed my suit jacket and briefcase as we headed for the door. Samantha was shutting down the last computer when we walked out of the office. "Have a great night, Samantha. I'll see you in the morning."

"You too, Mr. Moore. Kristen, you look beautiful! I hope you guys have a great night out."

"Thank you, Samantha," Kristen said smiling back at her.

I held Kristen by the waist as I led her out the door. My car was parked two cars down. I unlocked the doors as I opened her side of the door. I closed it behind her and walked over to the driver's side. Before I could even pull my car out of the parking spot, she had already disconnected my phone from the Bluetooth and connected hers. She had Summer Walker's album, *Last Day of Summer*, playing as we drove to the restaurant.

It was good that we left the time that we did because traffic was picking up. I called the restaurant to let them know we were en route but maybe a few minutes late. They assured me that our table would be ready and waiting for us when we arrived. As we drove to the restaurant, we filled each other in on our day.

We pulled up to the restaurant's parking lot twenty-three minutes later and was seated at our table. The atmosphere was even more beautiful than it looked online.

I was so hungry that everything on the menu was calling my name. We decided on getting an order of calamari as our appetizer. Kris ordered her favorite, chicken parmigiana with spaghetti noodles and I ordered the house famous spaghetti and meatballs. I don't know what they put in their sauce, but I heard it was to die for. My mouthed watered just at the thought of it hitting my tongue.

Our calamari didn't take long to come, thankfully. Hands down they had the best calamari. Their breading wasn't too thick or too thin. It was perfect. I ordered a bottle of wine. They say wine goes perfect with this kind of food.

We were so lost in our conversation that we didn't realize that we both reached for the last calamari. I let Kristen have it, but instead of eating it, she grabbed her knife and cut it in half. We laughed as we both took our half into our mouth.

I couldn't help but stare at how beautiful my woman is. Brains and beauty. Forget drooling over the food, I was drooling over her.

I stopped her in the middle of her telling me about work. "You're really beautiful. I hope when you look in the mirror you see what I see."

She blushed. "That was so random, but thank you for always making me feel better about myself."

"You shouldn't need me to make you feel good about yourself. I want you to see what I see. Falling in love with yourself is the best kind of love there is."

"Since when did you become a preacher on self-love?" she asked jokingly, but I knew it was her way of turning the attention from herself.

"No preacher here, baby. Just stating the facts." I grabbed her hand and held it to my lips, kissing it softly. She blushed.

Our food arrived and the aroma was amazing. "Saved by the waiter," she said. We both thanked her for bringing our food. That calamari was just a teaser. I could not wait to dive into my plate. They loaded my plate with meatballs. My stomach thanked the chef.

I picked up my fork to dive in when Kristen stopped me. "We never said grace." *Crap. Sorry, Lord.* We held hands as she blessed our food. When we said amen, I picked up my fork, twirled my spaghetti around it, and took my first bite. *So damn good.* It should be a sin for food to taste this good. By the looks of Kris' face, her food must be good as well. We were silent for a while as we both enjoyed our dishes. Occasionally she would feed me from her plate and I did the same.

"That was great. Like everything on my plate and even your plate was good. I can't eat anymore though, I have to save room for a slice of their red velvet cake," Kristen said. She wasn't a big cake eater, but she did love a good red velvet cake and this was definitely the place to get it from.

"I may have to take mine to go. I forgot about dessert."

"More for me." She winked at me.

"No, I said I'm taking mine home, which means you can watch me eat mine later." How dare she think she was going to take my slice too? I love her, but I don't play when it comes to my food.

I sat and watched her dig her fork into her slice of cake as she made soft moaning sounds to every bite. I knew she was teasing me on purpose. She'll get what's coming to her sooner than she thinks.

I paid for the bill, asked for my slice to go, and grabbed our doggie bags as we headed for valet parking.

I tipped the guy when he pulled up in my car. I opened the door for Kristen to get in and hopped in on my side. Again, she wasted no time putting on her playlist. At least she wasn't blasting her music this time. We didn't talk much on our way home. We both seemed to be lost in our thoughts. I'm sure what was on my mind, wasn't on hers, or was it?

We pulled up in front of her apartment in no time. I motioned for her to get out so that I could find parking. I didn't know how long that would take and didn't want to have her walking for long in heels if I couldn't find a close parking spot.

"I'll drive around with you."

"No, babe. You have on heels. Go inside and I'll be there when I can."

"Sounds like you're trying to get rid of me," she said as she pouted her lips.

I held her by the chin as I pulled her in for a kiss. "I'm not trying to get rid of you. What I am trying to do is give you time to get that ass upstairs and be ready for me as soon as I walk through the door." I winked at her and she knew exactly what I meant.

She wasted no time getting out of the car as she sashayed her way to the apartment. I couldn't help but laugh to myself. I drove off once I saw she made it in safely.

I drove around for about a good fifteen minutes before I saw someone pulling out of a parking spot at the end of the block. I reversed the car and stopped when I reached behind the moving car. I was not about to risk losing this spot by going all the way around the block just to come around. The driver pulling out gave me a head nod and I returned the gesture. I pulled into the parking spot and shut the car off.

Kristen had fifteen minutes to make sure she was ready for me. I'm planning on sleeping well tonight. I had some great food with my beautiful lady. Now all I needed was a good nut and I would be out for the night.

As I walked into the apartment, I realized all the lights were out. I know damn well she did not fall asleep on me. She was supposed to be in the house getting ready for me to tap that ass. As I got closer to the bedroom, I heard soft music playing. I opened the door and took in the aroma of the lit candles. On our king size bed, there she was, the most beautiful image on earth. She was bent over the bed, wearing nothing but a red thong, assuming her position and ready for me to take charge.

It was going to be a great night...

CHAPTER 10
KRISTEN

Work flew by today. Before I knew it, I was in the main office clocking out. I sat in my car thinking about how great last night was. My mouth watered at the thought of the food we had. I ate the rest of it for lunch today. I don't know what Stephan had for lunch because he ate all of his last night. Speaking of last night, I know he was shocked when he came into the apartment, saw me on all fours, bent over, and ready for him to take charge. I'm not a fan of thongs, but this was a special occasion. I needed to show him how much I appreciated him. He wasted no time stripping out of his clothes and bringing me to ecstasy. He made sure I got mine and then he got his, twice. Each time he came, I came too. I was exhausted, but beyond satisfied. It's not every day that I can have multiple orgasms. Last night was one of them. When I came back from freshening up in the bathroom, there he was on his side of the bed, eating his slice of red velvet cake. I felt like a five-year-old, wishing I didn't eat all of mine. Knowing Stephan, he was going to make sure I knew how good his slice was. He made every moaning sound as he took a bite of his cake. I just looked at him and rolled my eyes as I turned my back towards him. I felt the bed vibrate a bit as he laughed at me. I opened my eyes as I felt something pressing against my lips. It was him feeding me a piece of his cake. I didn't hesitate on taking that forkful into my mouth before he changed his mind. I thanked him and that was all I remembered.

Last night was a long night and I was so ready to go home, but before I could, I had to stop at Stephan's apartment. He texted me earlier asking if I could pick up a few things for him when I got off. I know it's a big step for us to move in with each other, but we could save so much more if we were splitting the rent for one place. I do not know the last time he or I have slept in his apartment. He usually goes home to swap out clothes for the following week. We didn't do laundry like we were supposed to last weekend so he didn't have any more clean boxers. I should *accidentally* forget to bring him clean ones from his place. He would kill me, but that would be a good laugh.

I searched in my bag for my set of keys and let myself in. A strong odor hit me as I walked in. I turned on the lights and went on a hunt to find out where it was coming from. It didn't take long to spot the location; the garbage! I didn't even bother to look inside of it, scared to see what may be looking back at me. I tied it up and took it outside. I came back inside, washed my hands, and opened a few windows. I found the bottle of Febreze and sprayed the entire place. When I felt satisfied with the smell, I went into his bedroom to get him some clean clothes. For a man, Stephan has a lot of clothes. Half of these I have not even seen him wear. If we did decide to move in with one another, we would have to put some of these clothes in storage. I picked out a few outfits I know he would wear, grabbed some clean socks and boxers, and put them in his duffle bag.

I was unlocking my car when I remembered that I forgot to close back the windows. I placed the duffle bag in the trunk and closed it as I walked back to the apartment. I closed the windows and locked up behind me.

"Hi, you're Stephan's girlfriend right?"

Startled, I turned around to see who was talking to me. There stood a beautiful Hispanic woman. She could not be a day over thirty.

With a raised eyebrow, "Yes, I am and you are?"

"I'm Gabrielle, his neighbor." She extended a hand.

I hesitated for a bit before extending mine. I knew almost all of Stephan's neighbors, but I never met this one. Her soft silky smooth hands shook mine. Even though I'm secured in our relationship, there was something about her that I just could not trust. Call it my women's intuition if you must, but something was puzzling about her. Maybe her beauty, her soft hands, or her curvy body intimidated me. Hell, it can be all of the above. I wonder why Stephan never told me about her? Knowing him, he knew how I would feel about it. He gave me no reason to doubt his loyalty and commitment to him, but as a human being, you can never be too confident in your significant other, right?

Snapping out of my thoughts and removing my hand from hers, "Nice to meet you, Gabrielle. I've never seen you around here before, are you new to the building?" Call me nosey all you want, but a girl needs to know!

"Not really. My dad became ill a few weeks ago and I have been staying here a lot just to take care of him and help nurse him back to health."

A bit of guilt hit me for thinking my devious thoughts about her when she was just here to take care of her dad. "Who is your dad, if you don't mind me asking?"

"Not at all." She smiled at me. "The neighbor's know my dad as Mr. Stanley"

Again, guilt hit me. Stephan loves Mr. Stanley. "Oh wow, I'm sorry to hear that Mr. Stanley is ill. Stephan has a great relationship with him. We'll be saying a special prayer for him."

"Thank you. My family would appreciate that." She placed her hand on my shoulder, "It was nice to finally meet you. I've heard great things about you." And just like that, she walked away. What did she mean she heard great things about me? From Mr. Stanley or Stephan? I sure hope it was from Mr. Stanley.

I stood there for a few seconds, taking everything in before I headed back to the car. I sat in the car as my mind played tricks on me. It was my insecurities playing with me. Stephan never gave me a reason to doubt him, but I did have my days when I felt like he was too perfect. As I started up the car, visions of him sleeping with her kept popping in my head. I tried to erase the image out of my head, but it would not leave. I know Stephan loves me and I satisfy his needs as much as I can, but he is human and a woman that beautiful, I am sure the thought of her naked has crossed his mind at least once, right? I needed something to distract me, so I turned on my Bluetooth and connected my phone to the car as I let Pandora play some of the newest reggae and dancehall songs. I needed to put myself in a better mindset before I went home.

It didn't take long before the thought of Gabrielle was a distant memory. Before I went home, I stopped at one of my favorite retail therapy stores, Victoria Secret. They were having a 7/$28 sale and I couldn't pass that up. It was a bit crowded for my liking, but I was determined to find my seven pairs of panties. I went downstairs to the *PINK* section and went on a stroll. I ended up with four pairs of boy shorts, two thongs, two cheeky, and one hipster. So much for buying seven. I could not decide between the nine I picked out, so I had to buy them all. While I waited on the line, I got a text from Stephan asking me where I was and I told him I was on line waiting to purchase my items.

Let me guess, you're in Victoria's Secret?

Damn, how did he know? *Ha, how did you know?*

You forgot you signed my email address up to be notified when they have sales?

Oops. I did do that. It was only because he knows how much I love this store and just in case he ever wanted to surprise me with new panties, he would know when they had a sale. A sale means even more panties. See, we both win. *I forgot all about that. Well, do not unsubscribe loll. Where are you?*

Trust me, I'm tempted to lol. I'm packing up and about to leave work.

Ok cool, I'm getting Chick-Fil-A for dinner. Are you ok with that? He had better be ok with that because I was not cooking tonight.

Yup, it's been a while since we had that. You remember what I get from there right?

Good, he's on board. *Yup, I sure do. I'll see you when I get home. Hugs and Kisses.*

Chick-Fil-A was a good drive out, but I have been craving it for a while. I was back home in no time and thankfully our food was still warm.

When I got into the house, Stephan was just getting out of the shower. We spoke briefly as I prepped for my shower. My morning showers are my more intense showers. When I get home from work, I just hope in the shower to feel refreshed. I was showered and dressed in house clothes in less than twenty minutes. I had Chick-Fil-A waiting for me and I refused to let it get cold.

Stephan had the table already set and the cable turned to the *OWN* channel. Tonight was the season finale of *The Haves and the Have Nots*. That was the real reason why I didn't want to cook tonight. We missed last week but recorded it on the DVR. We needed to catch up before the season finale came on.

I watched Stephan as he took a bite into his spicy chicken sandwich. The way the pepper jack cheese was melted on it, made me wish I liked spicy food. I took a bite of my chicken sandwich with Colby jack cheese instead.

"How's your food?" I asked when the show went on commercial.

"Amazing. Like it was made just for me. It was made with love." He chuckled as he threw a waffle fry into his mouth.

"I agree. It's something about how well this Colby jack cheese and chicken sandwich mix. It's so good." I picked up my cup of passion fruit lemonade to wash down all the goodness.

We sat in silence during the show and spoke during the commercials. Tyler Perry did his thing with this show. Stephan and I have been fans since day one. We had about fifteen minutes before next week's episode came on. I got up and cleared away the food.

"Babe, where did you put the bag of clothes that you packed for me?" I heard Stephan call out to me.

Crap. "I forgot it in the trunk of my car. I'll go get it. Let me just throw on some clothes."

I heard him pick up my car keys. "It's fine. I'll get it. Where did you park?"

"Across the street and two cars down."

He came back shortly after with the duffle bag. "You left my duffle bag, but you were sure not to forget your Victoria Secret's bag." He shook his head as he laughed and slapped me on the butt as he walked past me. "Just for that, you better model all those damn panties you bought."

"I'll think about it," I said winking at him.

"Did you check my mailbox for any mail?"

Oops. "No, I forgot. When I got into your apartment, something in your garbage smelt terrible. I had to throw out your garbage and Febreze the place."

"Hmm, what was it in the garbage that had the place smelling like that?"

"Hell if I knew. I wasn't about to set myself up and look in there."

We both laughed as he went through the duffle bag to see what I packed for him. "Thanks again for going to pick these up for me. You got great taste, so I knew you would know what to grab out of my closet."

"You're welcome. Speaking of great taste." *Choose your words wisely, Kris.* "I ran into your new neighbor." Before I could even control it, my eyes rolled at the thought of her.

"My new neighbor? I didn't know we got a new neighbor. What's his name?"

"Oh, it's not a he, it's a she. Her name is Gabrielle."

"I don't know who that is, but what's up with all the eye-rolling and huffing?" He looked at me with a raised eyebrow.

"Hmm, you sure you don't know who that is because she sure knows who you are and knows who I am?" Now my eyebrow was raised.

"Cool it. If I told you I don't know who that is, then trust that I'm telling you the truth." His voice got a little serious and a part of me wondered was he trying to cover something up or was he being truthful.

"Well, she claims that she's Mr. Stanley's daughter and that he's ill. She said she's been there for a little while taking care of him and helping to nurse him back to health." My body language shifted when I remembered that Mr. Stanley is ill.

Stephan's facial expression softened at the mention of Mr. Stanley. "She said he's ill? Did she say exactly what's wrong with him?"

My heart ached at the softness of Steph's voice. He really did care about Mr. Stanley. "No, I didn't want to ask too many questions. I figured you'd call him yourself to see what's wrong."

"I definitely will. I'm surprised Gabe didn't call and tell me. He knows I would have dropped everything to check on his dad. I honestly did not know he had a daughter though. I've only met Gabe and Mr. Stanley has only spoken about him." I saw the confusion written all over his face.

"Well, you know how it goes with some families. Sometimes people don't have that close of a relationship with all their children so they aren't always mentioned. Now that he's sick, maybe they are putting their issues aside. Who knows, but at least he isn't alone. You always disagreed with the fact that he was pushing ninety and living alone while Gabe lives in Florida."

"You're right." Stephan grabbed his phone as he gave Mr. Stanley a call. "No answer." He left a voicemail for Mr. Stanley to give him a callback and wishing him well.

It was time for the season finale of The Haves and the Have Nots. Stephan's mood dropped at the thought of Mr. Stanley being ill. He was the father figure in that neighborhood. I know he felt bad that he hasn't been to his apartment in a while, so no one was able to tell him this. I hope that the show will help take his mind off this for a while. I'm sure he'll be able to speak to Mr. Stanley in the morning. He's probably just resting.

Just as the previews from last week's episode started to play, there was a knock at the door. Stephan and I both looked at each other wondering who it could be.

"Crap. I forgot Latrice texted me earlier asking if she could come over and watch the season finale with us." I gave Stephan the *I'm sorry* look for not telling him as I got up to open the door. "Hey, girl!" I greeted her as she walked in. "You're just in time."

She hugged me as she placed her stuff in the dining room area and joined us on the couch. Stephan and Latrice gave each other acknowledging nods as everyone tuned into the show. Latrice is notorious for always talking through a movie or a show, but she knew how we got when it came to shows we loved. This was one of them. She respected our no talking during the show rules.

As soon as the show went on commercial, she hopped to her feet. "What you guys made for dinner tonight? I'm so hungry."

Stephan looked at me and laughed. Well, at least she made him laugh with her greedy self.

"I didn't cook today. We had Chick-Fil-A for dinner." I knew I was not going to hear the end of this.

"You went all the way to Chick-Fil-A and didn't even save me a chicken sandwich or a waffle fry? You know how much I love that place!"

"I honestly forgot you were coming over. I didn't remember until you rang the bell."

"Wow, some friend you are." I knew she was joking, but I also knew she was disappointed. Latrice did love their food and I wish I had remembered she was coming over.

"I do apologize. I wouldn't intentionally not bring food for you."

"You are free to look in the refrigerator and freezer and help yourself to whatever you find. Just please wash your hands before you do." Stephan chimed in.

"Thanks, Stephan. At least someone cares about me." She gave me the side-eye as she stuck her middle finger at me. She washed her hands and then found her way through my freezer. She settled with tater tots and frozen hot wings. Of course, Stephan's greedy self told her to throw him two wings in the oven too. The show came back on before the oven finished heating, so she had to wait until the following commercial to put her food in the oven.

Latrice was back in her happy place after she ate her wings and tots. Stephan even seemed a little happier too. Food can definitely lift one's mood. It was the final minute of the season finale and we were all sitting at the edge of our seats, wondering why Derrick was crying. It wasn't until he pulled his shirt up and revealed the tattoo on his chest that the uproar in my apartment began. I'm assuming my neighbor was tuned in as well because I heard her yelling too.

"Omgoshhhhhhh, I cannot believe that this whole time Mr. Nice Guy was Hanna's rapist!" Latrice shouted as we all sat in disbelief.

"How can Tyler Perry do me like that? I can't believe this is how he ended it and now we have to wait until the new season to find out what happens!" I was truly hurt. It's so crazy how we react as if these characters are real.

"He did a great job ending it that way. Now that is how you get your viewers to tune in for another season. Baby, check your Twitter account, I want to see what people are saying."

Latrice and I laughed at Stephan. Now all of a sudden he was hooked on Twitter. I did what he asked though. For the next fifteen minutes, I was reading and retweeting people's comments to tonight's show. Stephan took my phone and started posting tweets of his own. I made a mental note to make him his own damn Twitter so he can stay off mine.

We chatted for a bit before Stephan left us in the living room to go watch the game in our bedroom.

"So how are things going with you and Trent?" I asked jumping right into her business. I'm sure if I didn't ask, she would be sure to tell me either way.

"Things are going great that it scares me."

"How so?"

"He's such a gentleman, but still got a little swag to him. Because of his job, he's not calling me 24/7 which I love. You know I like my space. He gives me just that. It's so crazy though because this is the first time in ages that I've been in a man's presence and don't want him to leave. Our conversations are dope, the sex is amazing, he dresses well, good job, girl the list goes on." I watched and listened as her face lit up with excitement as she spoke about all his great qualities.

"Sounds like you're in love," I said half-jokingly.

"I wouldn't say in love. It's way too early for that, but I will say I'm enjoying his company and willing to see where this will go." She opened a bottle of wine and poured us both a glass. "I'm just scared that there's a catch. Like things are too perfect and I'm sure he's got a past or something is going to happen that will bring this all to an end." I watched as the excitement left her face. I can tell she was thinking of all the negative scenarios that could happen.

I took a sip of my wine before adding my two cents in. "Listen, I use to feel the same way with Stephan. I had the same doubts and concerns. My advice to you is to let things flow. Do not speak negativity into the atmosphere. If something does happen or if you find out something then I'll be here to help you deal with it, but don't go creating problems. Speaking from experience, you'll lose out on great moments with him if you're always second-guessing and living in fear of the unknown."

"You're right, Kris. Thank you. I've had my heart locked up ever since things ended with Jackson. I haven't allowed any other man to get close to me, until now. It's something about Trent that's so reassuring." The light was back in her eyes. I'm so happy for my friend. It has been years since she has had anything serious. Jackson really did a number on her; he scarred her. I'm happy to see that she's healing. I need to meet this Trent guy.

"Can't keep that beautiful heart of yours locked up forever. We should do a double date. I'd love to meet him."

"Really? You don't think it's too soon for that?" You can tell she liked the idea but was nervous.

"Girl, the sooner the better. It's not like you're bringing him to meet your family. There's nothing wrong with asking him to join us for dinner one day."

"You're right. I'll run it by him and see what he says. I hope he'll be ok with it. It's been a while since I've been on a double date." My heart warmed at how happy she was. I missed this soft side of my friend.

Latrice and I chatted for a bit before she called her Uber. When I walked into the bedroom, Stephan was already sleeping. I put my bonnet on and joined him.

♥ ♥ ♥

I woke up in a pool of sweat from another bad dream. The clock read 4:29 a.m. Great, I'm sure I won't be able to go back to sleep now. This dream was a bit different though and very disturbing.

It was Mother's Day and Monique and I took our mom to Spa Castle out in Queens. We were having the time of our lives; getting facials, mani and pedis and even sat in the pool while being served drinks. My mom wanted to save the sauna for last. After eating, we sat by the pool area while we digested our foods before heading to the sauna. While in the sauna, Monique forgot to put her phone back in the locker. I took it from her and told her I will put it in mine. I left them in the sauna room as I walked to the lockers. On my way to the lockers, there was this weird looking man. He had on a black trench coat and dress pants. He was sitting by the pool with his shoes on in the water. Thank God, we weren't going back in the pool. I spotted one of the employees and told them about his weird activity. She walked over to him and I headed towards the locker room. On my way back to the sauna, I noticed he was no longer by the pool area. They must have had security escort him out. Seconds later I heard the fire alarm go off. Panic flooded me immediately. I ran to where my mom and sister were so I could make sure we all got out safely. I tried to grab the door handle to the sauna room but seen that it had been broken from the outside. Monique and my mom were banging on the door and trying to push their way through, but the door was jammed. I was looking for anything that could help me unlock the door. I was screaming for help, but no one came. I don't think they could even hear me over the sound of the alarms. I picked up the plant pot and tried to break the glass of the sauna but only the pot broke. I felt so helpless as I heard their cries. Their skin started to blister and I knew it was only a matter of time before it would be too late. Someone must have turned up the temperature in the sauna room, but I couldn't find where it was. I ran looking for help. Just as I was about to scream again, I saw the same man with the trench coat. He looked at me and winked as he headed towards the exit door. I kept running until I saw the firefighters and yelled to get their attention. They headed my way and I explained to them that my mother and sister were locked in the sauna room. One of the firefighters spoke on the radio and told his partners the tools he needed them to bring. I peaked in the room and I could no longer see Monique or my mom. I started crying and screaming and one of the firefighters assured me that they would do everything in their power to get them out of there. Two firefighters came running in with different kinds of tools to get the door open. They immediately went to work on the door. It didn't take them long to pry it open, but by the looks of it, they were too late. When the door opened, Monique and my mom were lying lifeless on the floor. The heat from the sauna ate their skin and they were barely recognizable. I let out a loud cry as one of the paramedics held me in his arms. I woke up right after they were pulling their bodies out.

I didn't bother wake Stephan up. I cried silently in bed for a few minutes until I had enough strength to get up. I walked into the living room and stared at the television. Nothing was on at this time of night. Martin would have been perfect. I settled on cartoons and not before long, I was fast asleep.

CHAPTER 11
STEPHAN

I woke up to an empty side of the bed. It was way too early for Kristen to be gone. I checked my phone to see if she texted me. Nothing. I don't remember her saying she was going to work early today. Confusion filled me as I got out of the bed to see if she was in the bathroom. Nope, not here either. I heard the television playing and that is when I saw her sleeping on the couch. I tapped her lightly and she woke up instantly.

"Everything ok, babe? Why are you sleeping on the couch?" I asked as I rubbed her head. She lifted from the couch and laid her head on my lap.

"I had another bad dream." Sadness filled her eyes and I just held her as she told me all about it.

"Damn, baby. I'm sorry you had a dream like that. That's a tough one to deal with. Why didn't you wake me up?"

"I don't know. I'm just trying to learn how to cope with these dreams without having to be dependent on you or someone else to calm my nerves. This one was one of the scariest though." Her eyes filled with tears and I couldn't help but feel bad that I wasn't there for her when she woke up. How did I sleep past her crying? "I felt so helpless. I can still smell their flesh. It felt so real. I don't know what I'll do if this came true with anyone we love. I wouldn't be able to forgive myself."

"Forgive yourself?" I lifted her head so she could look at me. "You cannot blame yourself for something you have no control over. Yes, it is scary as hell knowing you have these bad dreams and then it ends up happening. However, understand that it is just irony. It's never with the same people you had the dream about, so you cannot say you're the cause of it."

"I know I'm not purposely making these things happen, but I'm scared. I know it's never with the same people that are in my dream, but that's what makes it even scarier. I have no way of warning whom it may involve. It makes me feel even more helpless that I have to sit and wait to see how this will play out. I'm praying that this one won't come true. It was not a pretty sight." The tears that filled her eyes have now escaped. I wiped each of them away as we sat on the couch for a bit in silence. I knew if I didn't get up soon that I'd be late for work, but I needed to make sure she was going to be ok first.

A few minutes later, we got up from the couch and got ourselves ready for work. She turned on her Bluetooth speaker and blasted music as we got ready. I didn't fuss about her song selections this one time. I know she needed this to help clear her mind and put her at ease.

I left the house before her, but she seemed to have been in a better mood. I started up my car, turned on the radio, and listened to the Breakfast Club as I drove to work. They were talking about family reunions and famous dishes that black families make for the reunions. That just reminded me that my family reunion was coming up soon. Traffic was a bit heavy, but I was still doing ok with time. Samantha was already there so I wasn't stressed about being open and ready on time. She and I were always there an hour earlier to make sure everything was ready. I wanted to be there already because today was Friday. Friday's and Monday's seemed to be our busiest days.

I got to work twenty minutes later than I planned, but we had everything set up the night before. All we had to do was unlock the registers and other little things.

"Good morning, Samantha," I said as I walked through the door.

"Happy Friday, Mr. Moore," she said as she continued wiping down the counter.

I made me some coffee before helping her with setup. Minutes later, my employees were rolling in one by one. I am grateful for how dedicated most of them are to their jobs. It is not easy being in customer service. You have to wear a smile every day, even when you are going through it.

There were a few people already waiting outside for us to open the doors. Once my staff was situated and the clock hit eight, I opened the doors and let them in. I stayed in the front to greet some of the regulars as they came in and then went back into my office to finish my paperwork.

It was lunchtime before I knew it. I grabbed my cellphone and didn't realize that it was still on silent. I had thirty-eight unread text messages. My heart dropped, praying that it wasn't Kristen. I let out a huge sigh when I saw that only one of them was from her. The rest were from the group chat with my college boys. I forgot all about us meeting up tonight for drinks. I haven't seen them since January. We try to link up a few times a year, just to stay in touch.

I caught up on all the unread messages and replied that I would be there. We decided to meet at this place in Harlem called Chocolat. I texted Kris back to find out how her day was going and to tell her about tonight. I was almost hesitant about canceling with the guys just to make sure she wasn't alone, but she told me that she and Latrice were going out as well. I guess it worked out for me.

Today was such a busy day and time kept flying by. Before I knew it, it was time to close up. I was telling my staff to have a great weekend as they were clocking out and heading out the door. I still had a few loose ends before I could leave.

"It's Friday night. Don't stay too late, boss." I looked up from my computer to see Samantha standing outside my office door.

"Trust me, I'm not. I should be done here in about fifteen minutes. Any special plans for you this weekend?" I never really pry into my employees' personal life, but the question seemed harmless.

"I'm supposed to be linking up with two of my girlfriends to grab some food and drinks, but I'm beat. Not sure if I'm still going." She worked her ass off today, so I understood her tiredness.

"You're young. Go out and live a little." Damn, I have been around Kristen too much. I'm starting to speak like her. "What I meant was, you worked hard today. You're off this weekend so go out and enjoy yourself. You deserve it."

"I guess you're right. I'm going to go. Thanks for the push. Anything special planned for you and the misses this weekend?" she asked as she leaned on the side of my office door.

"Actually, no. We didn't plan anything, but knowing her, I'm sure we'll be doing something." We didn't do much on the weekends. We usually stay in, clean, and watch movies. The weather is getting nicer though, so I will not be surprised if she asked us to go somewhere.

"You guys are like the perfect couple. I hope I'll be that lucky to find my perfect match."

"There's no such thing as perfect. Trust me, Kris and I go through relationship problems just like everyone else."

"It sure doesn't look like it. You both always seem happy when I see you together. You never come to work upset because of something she did. I don't think I've ever seen you upset." By her facial expression, I can tell she was trying to think of a time that she saw me upset.

"I will say this; she and I have great communication. It was not always that way, but we realized if we were going to make this work that it was a necessity in our relationship. Trust is a big thing for her as well and I had to put in overtime for her to believe that I had her best interest at heart. When you find your soulmate, he will stop at nothing to make sure the relationship is strong and secured. Now it does not mean he will not mess up. We are human, but his mishaps would be so small compared to the red carpets he has rolled out for you, that you won't even stress it."

"Wow, that was deep. You both have been together for years. How do you keep the spark alive and how does she keep it alive for you?" She moved from the door and sat in the seat across from me.

"Every relationship is different. I never stopped doing the things that got her to love me in the beginning. I have taken the time out to get to know her and all the things she liked and did not like. I paid attention to her favorite stores and the things she would buy; her favorite foods, movies that made her happy, her favorite songs, places she liked to visit, and things that are on her bucket list. I made it my duty to always stay on top of what made her smile. I would surprise her with something from her favorite store, bring her to her favorite restaurant, I even took her to a Tamar Braxton concert. That was one of the best nights. I don't think I've ever seen her get so excited. It was as if her inner child was unleashed. It does not always have to be materialistic things. She loves the moments when we are home and I randomly give her a foot massage while we watch one of her favorite movies after eating one of her favorite dishes. Sometimes it is the little moments like that, that matters most to her. Now when it comes to her keeping the spark alive for me, the list goes on. Some of my favorite things are coming home to a clean house and a home-cooked meal. As a man, I do not ask for much or require much but she does go above and beyond to make sure my needs are satisfied. I'm not just talking sexually, I'm talking in general. She always makes sure my snack draw is filled especially when it's football Sundays. When the guys come over, I don't have to worry about her wearing anything inappropriate. If we go out, she carries herself as a woman should, which makes me feel proud to be by her side. She never makes me feel less than a man. Yes, she may not always agree with me, but her pushback is never on a level of disrespect. I love how considerate she is. Remember just a few weeks ago when I got that package? I opened it and there was a new pair of beats headphones. I was just telling her two nights prior that my headphones gave out on me. I never asked her to buy me a pair, nor did she say she was. It's those little things that keep our sparks alive." I picked up my bottle of water and chugged it down. All that talking had my mouth dry.

"Mr. Moore, thank you. I have been through some hard breakups and often feel like there is no hope left, but you just reminded me that there is. You should look into being a relationship therapist as a side job."

"Never lose hope. All of your past relationships are stepping-stones. They are preparing you for your soulmate. There is a certain feeling that you will get that you have never felt with anyone else. It is going to scare you in the beginning because it's a new feeling, but it'll be worth it. As far as me being a relationship therapist, I'll have to pass on that." We both laughed. "I can only speak from experience. My way is not the only way and it will not work for everyone. You can take all the advice I have given you, but you'll realize that you'd have to tweak it for your own relationship."

"You're right. Your advice was on point though and I'm going to let it sink in and marinate on it," she said as she got up from her seat. "Let me get out of here. I have already taken up too much of your time. Thank you for everything."

"My door is always open and I'm always willing to give a listening ear. Have fun tonight, you might meet someone special," I said giving her a friendly wink.

"I'll be sure to tell you Monday morning if I do," she said as she walked out the door.

I made sure I locked up behind her as I finished the work I was doing before she came into my office. I looked at the time and seen that she and I had been talking for almost a half-hour. I needed to hurry up with these documents before I was late to meet up with the fellas. The last one to arrive always had to buy the first round of drinks for everyone. I have yet to be that guy and it wasn't about to start tonight.

♥♥♥

"Can I get seven shots of whiskey?" I cannot believe I was the last one to arrive. Out of all the times we have ever linked up, today was the first day that everyone wanted to be on time. Just my luck.

I gave everyone their shots and took mine. "Cheers to brotherhood." We all clinked shot glasses and took it straight to the head.

"Thanks, Stephan. A shot always hits better when another brother buys it." All the fellas started laughing at Daniel's comment.

"So how has everyone been?" asked Nate. "You have ten seconds to get it all out." This was a ritual for us. We get ten seconds to give a brief rundown on what we have been missing.

"Well, I'll start," Will said. "My wife is pregnant again." Everyone said *damn* at the same time. This is their fifth child. When we did our whip around we weren't allowed to ask any questions until after everyone went.

"I'll go next," Nate said. "Well, you all know my sister passed away a few months ago and my wife and I have been fighting to become my niece's guardians, we finally got approved." The fellas and I all took turns giving him a brotherly dap and hug. Nate is the family man with three kids of his own, and he was doing everything in his power to make sure that he became her legal guardian. He refused to have her put in the system when they were able to take care of her.

"I'm next," Mathew chimed in. "My wife's iPhone was acting up a few weeks ago and she took it to the Apple Store to get it checked out. They ended up wiping it clean and backing it up. When they went to restore her phone, she was getting my messages and hers. Let's just say, she read our group chats and what I sent you guys about the chick I've been messing with." Another *damn* filled the room. I know the fellas were itching to ask questions. I damn sure was.

"My situation ain't that bad, but it isn't the easiest to accept." Daniel got up from the barstool. "So, you all know that my company has been growing tremendously. I was just presented with the opportunity to make it grow even bigger. The only thing is, I'd have to move to Atlanta by the end of July." We all looked at each other. The facial expressions were clear that we were happy about this opportunity for Dan, but weren't too happy about him moving away from us. We gave our congratulations nonetheless, but we were definitely going to revisit this when everyone was done.

"That just brought down the vibes in the room. I guess I'll go next to bring the vibes back up," Lucas said. "Sharon and I have been going strong and I think I'm ready to pop the question."

"Bout damn time!" Trent said. We all agreed. They have been together for over seven years and even have a two-year-old son together. He should've been asked her.

"My turn. Kristen and I talked about moving into her apartment together, and even though I am over there ninety percent of the time, I still like that I have my own place. I mean, it would be nice for us to save more with paying rent for just one apartment, but I also would rather it be an apartment we got together instead of me moving in with her. It just doesn't sit right with my ego." The head nods I got let me know that I was not wrong for feeling the way I felt. I love staying by Kris' place. Even though I'm there most of the time, it didn't make me feel like less of a man because I still had my own spot.

"I guess I'm the last to go," Trent said as he took a sip of his drink. "I think I've fallen for someone I had a one-night stand with." By the look on everyone's faces, this was going to be an interesting story.

"There's a lot that was said at the table and we need to tackle it all. Let's just go in the order that we went," Nate said.

"Fine. I started so we can tackle my situation," Will said.

"So baby number five. Damn, brother. When will it end?" Trent joked.

"I remember when she was pregnant with Amari, we agreed that we wouldn't have anymore."

"You guys don't believe in condoms?" Matthew added.

"Word or birth control fool?" Trent jumped back in.

"I'm married. We have not used condoms since before we were engaged. She is on birth control though."

"So how the hell she gets pregnant if she's on birth control? Trent asked.

"They say its ninety-nine percent effective. I guess that one percent was a strong one," Will laughed. "The only thing negative about it is that she's been having difficulties with this pregnancy because she got pregnant while on birth control. The doctor tried to break it down to me, but the women's reproductive system is complicated. We were not planning to have another kid, but the thought of possibly losing this child because of all these complications has us both stressed out. I try to help her stay positive because added stress isn't good either, but it's hard man, it's hard." He tried to hide his emotions, but I could see the worry in his face.

"That's a tough one. I do hope and pray that it works out for you guys. Please let us know if there is anything we can do," I said as we all picked up our drinks to cheer to a healthy pregnancy and baby.

"And cheers to this time being a girl. All you've been making are boys," Mathew added to the cheer.

"Amen to that!" Will said as we took a sip.

"I guess I'm next," Nate said. "Well, it was a long and drawn-out process of becoming the legal guardians of my niece. They only provided us with temporary guardianship in the beginning, but after filling out hundreds of documents and having all these house visits to ensure my home was a safe environment, they finally gave us the approval notice. She does not know yet. My wife and I are going to tell her on Sunday. We are having a big Sunday dinner at the house to celebrate the great news." Everyone gave Nate their congratulations. "I honestly couldn't have done it without the help of Trent though. They have you sign so many documents and I won't lie some of those words had me confused. Trent is one hell of a lawyer though. He helped us fill out the documents and understand what we were signing." Everyone clinked glasses with Trent and Nate and took another sip. I had like one more sip left before I needed to order another drink.

"Mathew, your dumb ass is next. I told you a long time ago to get a Galaxy and leave that iPhone alone. The iPhone is for men who don't cheat like Stephan's ass," Trent said while everyone else laughed.

"Man, I've been meaning to switch my phone, but I was waiting until my contract was up so I wouldn't have to pay full price. I really fucked up this time."

"You damn sure did," I chimed in. "But don't listen to Trent's ass, iPhones are not for men who don't cheat. You shouldn't even be condoning his cheating ass," I said directing my comment to Trent. "We've been telling you for the longest that if you weren't happy in your marriage then you two should just separate."

"Well, I'm guessing this time she has had enough. I have not been to our apartment in almost two weeks. I have been staying between my parents and the other chick's house. When I want my alone time, I'll stay at a hotel or sleep in my office."

"Are you going to go back and try to work things out?" Lucas asked.

"I tried, but she's not trying to hear it. I even sent flowers to her job and she sent me a video of her throwing it in the garbage."

"Damn, she's over your shit," Daniel said laughing.

"Tell me about it. I can't even blame her," Mathew said as he shrugged his shoulders.

"Let me know when you're ready to file for divorce. I'll be sure to represent her in court," Trent said as we all busted out laughing.

"You ain't shit, bro. I won't even be surprised if she calls you asking how much she can get out of me if she divorces my ass," Mathew said.

"And I'll make sure I can get her every dime. No one told you not to sign a prenup. That's the type of shit that Stephan will do because he loves too hard," Trent said adding into the equation yet again.

"I think you're jealous of my relationship. Kris and I are always in your mouth. You want my life or something?" I asked as I sipped the last bit of my drink before ordering another one. That had all the guys in an uproar. Trent is always calling me out when it comes to how I am with my relationship with Kristen. He doesn't believe that a man can be faithful to one woman for the rest of his life.

"You got it, bro. My bad. I'm not even going to go there with you tonight," Trent said as he tipped his drink my way.

"Next up, Daniel," Mathew said. He was clearly trying to break the awkwardness.

"Yes, so fellas, I may be breaking away from New York soon." Daniel owned a clothing company with his cousin. He sold many special occasion clothing. You can walk into his store and to the left, you would feel like you just walked into Brooklyn and to the right, you would feel like you walked into Hollywood. I guess that is why his store is called *From Tims 2 Shoes*. "My cousin Derrick and I are debating who would be best to move out there. Both of us haven't started a family yet or have anything too serious going on out here, so it could be any one of us."

"I'm proud of you, brother. When will you know if it's you or your cousin going?" Lucas asked.

"We are making our final decision by next week Friday. I honestly have my eye on a place out there already. The house is dope!"

"Damn, this is really happening. Well, let us know if the decision is you. We gotta throw you a bomb ass going away party. Strippers and everything," Mathew said getting more excited than he should.

"And this is why your wife done kicked you out of your house. Your ass always looking for an opportunity to be around some fresh meat," Daniel said as we all laughed and shook our heads. "On a serious note though. Trent, if you don't mind I'd love it if you could look over the paperwork they sent me for the new location."

"My pleasure. Just send it to me when you get in. I'll look it over this weekend for you."

We all ordered another drink as we cheered to Daniel and his new store.

I looked down at my watch and it was already midnight. Damn, it did not even feel like we had been out that long. I texted Kris to make sure she was ok and she told me she was still out with Latrice. I told her to be careful and I would check in with her in a few.

"Lucas, it's your turn. Let's hear about this engagement you're planning," Daniel said passing the attention off to Lucas.

"Yea, fellas. I think it's time. We've been through more than enough for me to know that she's the one."

"Congrats in advance, bro. When are you going to pop the question?" Mathew asked.

"She's graduating with her Masters in a few weeks and her family is throwing a big party for it. I was thinking since everyone is going to be there that it would be the perfect time. I already got her dad's blessings."

"Dope. All the best on that. Marriage is a beautiful thing. One of the best decisions I made in life," Will said as we all cheered to Lucas.

"Stephan, it's your turn, my brother," Lucas said.

"I already gave you guys most of the rundown. Kristen and I have had several conversations on moving in with each other. I have no problem with it, but as I said earlier, I'd feel better knowing this was something we got together rather than me moving into her place."

"It's your ego and I understand it. Have you guys tried applying for those lottery apartments?" Trent asked.

"What's lottery apartments?" I guess I was the only one who did not know about it by the looks the fellas gave me. Trent explained to me how the process goes and even showed me some of the apartments he applied for.

"I'm going to put Kristen on to that. We'll definitely be applying. Thanks, man."

"Brand new apartments for an affordable price, hell yea you better apply," Daniel chimed in.

"Alright, the moment you've all been waiting for, it's my turn brothers," Trent said as he dramatically chugged down the rest of his beer and slammed it on the table. "Bartender another round please." I couldn't help but shake my head at how dramatic he is. "Ok, all jokes aside, one of my partners at the firm decided we should go to a bar one day a few weeks back. We ended up kicking it with these two fine ass women. We were all talking and my boy notices that one of them had a wedding ring on her finger. So he questions her about it and she ends up telling us that she just found out that her husband is gay!"

"How the hell she found that out?" Lucas asked the question that I wanted the answer to as well. Leave it to Trent to have the craziest stories.

"She said she had some type of fraudulent charges on her bank card and when the bank was trying to dispute the charges she said were fraudulent, they gave her the name to some gay bar and told her that after investigating that this charge wasn't fraudulent. She ends up going to the gay bar and showing one of the bartenders a picture of her husband. The bartender confirmed that her husband is a regular there." We all had astonishing looks on our faces. I can only imagine how embarrassed she must have been. "So my boy gives her his business card and tells her that he's a lawyer and if she decided to file for divorce to give him a call. We drank a few more drinks before the girls said they had enough. They ended up calling an Uber, but not before I got her friend's number. He and I sat at the bar for a few minutes and I ended up texting the friend to make sure she was good. Next thing I know we were outside her hotel room. She and her friend were both there together. It gets better. We inside the hotel room, we drunk, they drunk, everybody drunk. The girls start making out with each other and next thing I knew I was banging shorty back out. We woke up the next morning and went our separate ways."

"My man!" Daniel said as he gave Trent a pound. "You and I need to go out before I leave for ATL. Hopefully, you'd bring me some of your good luck."

"You mentioned that you've fallen for her. I'm taking it that you guys have kept in contact after your mini orgy party?" Mathew asked.

"Yea we have. It's like we are working backward. I already got the goods, but we have taken the time out to get to know each other. Funny thing is, I never take women who I sleep with on the first night serious, but it's something about her. Earlier she texted and asked if I would be ok with a double date with her best friend and her man. My initial answer would've been hell no, but I said sure."

"Damn, bro. She's changing you. I need to get her an award," Lucas joked.

"Real talk! Who would've thought this day would come that someone would tame your wild ass," I added.

"I don't know, brothers. It's something about this one. She different," Trent said as he drunk his beer.

"Well do we get a name or get to see a pic of her?" Daniel asked.

"Nope. I'm not trying to jinx it. When I figure out where this is going, then I'll let you guys in on your request," Trent said sounding serious and drunk at the same time.

"Respect," Mathew said as we all cheered on the possibility of someone taming Trent's wild ass.

We ordered another round of drinks as we drank and talked about every and anything. I was too busy arguing with Lucas about the Golden State Warriors and the Raptors that I didn't realize that Trent was trying to give me the warning sign that someone was staring me down. It was not until she approached me that I put two and two together.

"Hi, Stephan," she said as she brushed her breasts against me while she placed her glass on the bar table.

"Hello, do I know you?" I asked while looking up from her breast. Damn, she was beautiful. I definitely would have remembered a face like hers.

"I'm Gabrielle, but my friends call me Gabby. I'm Stanley's daughter." And just that quickly I remembered the conversation I had with Kristen. Shit, Kristen! Here I am looking at this woman, admiring her beauty as if I don't have a lady at home. This has to be my last drink.

"Oh, nice to meet you. My girlfriend told me that you guys met the other day." I heard the guys laugh at the way I said "girlfriend". I did not mean to drag it out in a hesitant way.

"Yes, we met outside of your apartment," she said as she asked the bartender to pour her another round of whatever she was drinking.

"I've never met you before though, so how do you know who I am and who she was?"

"My dad has a picture of you guys from a BBQ a few years back. Before he got ill we were talking about you and some of the others he has built a relationship within the neighborhood," she said as she sipped her drink and twirled her tongue around her straw. I felt a little twitch in my pants and knew it was time to go home. This girl is trouble and even though I don't believe in cheating, the thoughts I'm having alone will get me in trouble.

"I've tried calling him a few times but haven't gotten through to him. If it's ok I would love to stop by and see him." All negative thoughts left my mind as I thought about how sick Mr. Stanley is.

"He would love that. His memory is going in and out as he's going through Alzheimer's, but I know he still remembers you." She patted me on the shoulder as she pushed her chair closer to me. "Funny thing is, he can tell you everything that happened last summer, but he doesn't remember where he placed his phone the other day. By now the battery is dead and I still haven't been able to find it."

"That makes sense. Well, I'm glad he has you by his side. I was surprised that Gabe didn't call me to check on him, but I see why. He's in good hands." I smiled innocently at her.

"Gabe should be coming down in about a week or so. We are going to be rotating with who stays with him. I will tell Gabe to reach out to you when he gets here. I'm sure he would love some positive company." Her hand touched my knee this time, but she didn't keep it there for long.

"I appreciate it. Thank you for keeping me in the loop. I'll make it my duty to swing by before this weekend is over." I chugged down the rest of my drink and glanced over at the fellas. They were acting as if they weren't eavesdropping.

"Well let me get back to the house. I only stepped out to grab a few drinks while he slept." She got up from the seat after finishing her drink.

"It was nice meeting you. And again, thank you for keeping me in the loop." She smiled back at me as she paid her tab, grabbed her purse, and left.

"If Kristen would've seen how you were drooling over that chick, she would've had you by the balls," Trent said as everyone laughed.

"I was not drooling. Look, there's nothing wrong with admiring a beautiful woman." I tried to defend myself, but I'm not sure if I sounded convincing enough.

"Right! Tell me anything. I guess good guys do cheat," Mathew said as everyone laughed again.

"I will never cheat on Kristen. I have self-control. If I didn't then I guarantee you that I would've got more than just a hello from her tonight." I wasn't always the good guy and they knew it.

"That is true. Do you guys remember how Stephan use to be back in college? He was worse than Trent," Lucas said laughing.

"Now that's a damn lie. Ain't nobody worse than hoe ass Trent," Daniel added in.

"Thanks, Daniel. I am far from Trent. I've had my fair share of women, but I've respected them unlike my brother here." I glanced over to Trent giving him that *you know it's true* look. He didn't even fight me on it. We all just laughed and agreed. "Well before I get myself into any trouble tonight, I'm going home to my woman."

We all got up to close out our tabs. We were all waiting for the bartender to come back with our cards and receipts. When he came to our side of the bar table, he told us that one of our cards declined. I was almost positive that it was not my card, but with all these scammers around, you can never be too sure. When the bartender called out the name on the card, I was grateful that it was not me, but I felt bad for Mathew. We all knew he has been going through it and I know it must not be cheap living out of hotels and other people's houses. Trent did not hesitate on putting Mathews tab on his card. Trent can be a real ass at times, but he did have a big heart for those he cared for.

Mathew looked at Trent with defeat and embarrassment written all over his face. "Don't worry about it, brother. I got you." Trent patted Mathew on his back as we all headed for the door.

"Where are you staying tonight?" Lucas asked Mathew as we all walked to the corner.

"I was going to stay at a hotel, but by the looks of it, I damn sure don't have the funds for it. I guess I'll go stay at my mom and pops crib."

"Listen, I'm barely at my apartment. You can stay there for tonight and I'll come by in the morning and see what we can work out," I said to Mathew.

"Are you sure?" he asked with gratefulness in his voice.

"Am I not my brother's keeper? I wouldn't have it any other way," I said as I gave Mathew a brotherly pound.

We all said our goodbyes as I drove Mathew to my apartment. It was almost three in the morning and traffic was a bit heavy for this time of night. I felt my eyes closing a few times when I was stuck at the light. I had to open the windows and turn up the music a bit to keep me awake. Mathew on the other hand was knocked out. This is why I don't like driving on the nights we hang out. I would have taken an Uber to work this morning if I remembered.

We finally arrived at my apartment. I had to nudge Mathew a few times to get him to wake up. There was no way I was carrying a grown-ass drunk man. I unlocked the front door and led him to my bedroom. As soon as he saw the bed, he went headfirst into it. I can't believe how drunk he was. Shit, I was drunk too, but not that bad. I had to take his shoes off so he wouldn't dirty my sheets. I don't like sitting on my bed with outside clothes on, but I damn sure wasn't about to undress him. Taking his shoes off was good enough for me.

I felt a little lightheaded as I tried to make my way back to the front door. I decided to listen to my body and sit on the couch for a minute. My eyes felt heavy again and I knew the smartest thing to do was to close them for a second. Before I did, I sent a text to Kris letting her know I was at my apartment. She was probably asleep by now so I didn't bother to wait for a response.

♥ ♥ ♥

The sun was shining so bright through my living room window that it woke me up. I looked at my watch and the time read 7:38 a.m. So much for me just resting my eyes for a second. I got up to check on Mathew and he was still knocked out. I went back into the living room and seen that Kristen texted me back saying ok and for me to be careful. She sent that four minutes after I texted her. She must have been waiting up for me.

I went into my bathroom and took a quick shower. I almost walked out naked but remembered that Mathew was here. I wrapped my towel around my waist and quietly walked into my bedroom to look for something to wear. I found some clean clothes and dressed in the living room. I texted Mathew and told him he could stay as long as he liked. I doubt there was food in the fridge to eat, but I'm sure he could find something in the cabinets. I told him that the door was auto-lock so all he had to do was make sure he pushed it closed properly.

I closed the door behind me and made a mental note to come back later to visit Mr. Stanley. It was too early to be popping up unannounced at his house. I hopped in my car and drove to Dunkin Donuts to get Kris and me a breakfast sandwich. I woke up starving. I bought the two for five dollar's bacon, egg and cheese on a croissant for me and turkey sausage, egg and cheese on a croissant for her. I had to go back inside and order again because I forgot to get hash browns and orange juice. Usually, the cashier would ask if I wanted hash browns with my order, but she didn't. She must be new. I took a bite out of one of my sandwiches as I waited for our hash browns. I texted Kris and told her I was coming home with breakfast. She texted back and said great because she was starving and was about to cook breakfast.

I was home ten minutes later and Kristen gave me the quickest kiss as she grabbed the Dunkin Donuts bag from my hand. I guess we both woke up needing food. We barely said two words to each other as we tore into our sandwiches.

After we ate, we sat and talked about our night. I gave her a brief rundown of how the guys were. I couldn't fill her in completely, that's against guy code. She told me that she and Latrice went out to eat, then to the movies to see Men in Black: International. I'm surprised she didn't drag Latrice to see the Avenger's End Game before it finally left the theatre. We saw it twice together and she has seen it again with Monique. I thought I was a die-hard Avengers fan, but Kris had me beat. After the movies, she and Latrice went to 7-Eleven to get snacks and came back to the apartment. Monique came over after her shift and the three of them hung out until about four in the morning. I thought she was still up because she was waiting up for me, I guess that was not the case.

We were cuddled up on the couch watching the Fresh Prince of Bel-Air. Not before long, we were both asleep. Good food will do that to you.

The vibration of my phone made me jump out of my sleep. I looked at my phone and it was Mathew. I looked at the time and it was 11:11 a.m.

"Hey, Mat, how you feeling?" I asked as I answered the phone.

"Umm, can you please come back to the apartment? It's kind of urgent." Mathew can be a bit dramatic sometimes. I'm sure he broke something.

"Mat, what happened? Did you flood my toilet or something?" I asked laughing into the phone.

"There was a fire. They had us all evacuate the building. They won't let us back inside. I'm standing outside with no shoes on my feet." My heart dropped immediately.

"A fire, in my building? Is anyone hurt?" I popped up off the couch, which woke Kristen up in the process.

She asked me what was wrong. I told her what Mathew told me. I put my shoes on as she ran and quickly got dressed. I sat in my car as I waited for her to get in. Before hanging up with Mathew, he told me that he wasn't sure which apartment was on fire. There was too much smoke to see where it was coming from. I was relieved to know that he was ok though, but I needed to get there ASAP.

Kristen and I drove in silence as I sped through the busy streets. As we got closer, I saw the smoke filling the sky. Again, my heart dropped as I prayed that no one was hurt. I double-parked my car as I ran out of the car with Kristen right behind me. I found Mathew across the street from my apartment with the rest of my neighbors.

"Any word yet?" I asked as I approached Mathew.

"Hey, no nothing yet. They just calmed the fire down."

"Damn, I can't believe this." I scanned around looking for a neighbor who lived in my building to see if anyone could tell me something.

"Hi, Ms. Young. Do you know what apartment the fire came from or what caused it?" I asked as I spotted my neighbor who lives on the floor underneath me.

"No, sweetheart, I don't. Many of the neighbors are not even home so I cannot even tell. But I do pray no one is hurt."

"Steph, isn't that the chick from last night?" Mathew asked as he spotted Gabrielle running towards the building. One of the firefighters caught her before she could enter.

"It sure is. That's Gabrielle," I said as I crossed the street to find out what was going on.

"Gabrielle!" I called out for her.

She dropped her bags as she ran towards me. "Is my father across the street with you?" she asked as she looked over my shoulder in search of him.

"No. I just got here a few minutes ago." I walked with her to the chief firefighter and asked if he could tell us which apartment it was. When he said apartment 3B, Gabrielle almost dropped to the floor as she began to cry. I caught her just in time.

"Her father lives in that apartment, do you know if he's ok?" I was scared for what his response may be, so I made sure I held on to Gabrielle a little tighter.

Before he could respond, the firefighters were coming out of the building.

I don't know what was worse, finding out that Mr. Stanley died in the fire or that his body was burnt so bad that he was no longer recognizable. When the firefighters told us the news, I could barely hold myself up, as my knees got weak. Kristen came from across the street just as they were explaining how bad the fire was. Thankfully, the neighbors whose apartment is directly next to Mr. Stanley was not home. According to the firefighters, they would have had a hard time getting out alive.

Gabrielle explained to police officers that she went to the store to grab a few things to make for breakfast. She said she woke up and saw Mr. Stanley in the kitchen trying to make grits, but he did not realize that he was boiling salt and not grits. She said that she sat him in front of the television and told him to sit there until she got back. She was only going two blocks to the supermarket. She didn't think anything of it because she wouldn't be gone for long. She ended up having trouble with her debit card and got stuck on hold with the bank as they tried to figure out what the issue was. She told the police that when she was walking back to the apartment she saw all the fire trucks and ran to the building. The firefighters were honest and told us that it was not evident as to what caused the fire and they would have to wait for further investigation.

It felt like hours later when the coroners finally arrived. Seeing the coroners roll out Mr. Stanley's body in a body bag made me sick to my stomach. His body was burnt so badly. We all knew he was the only one in the apartment, so whether we could identify the body or not, the reality was, Mr. Stanley was not coming back.

CHAPTER 12

STEPHAN

I tossed and turned all night. Today was the funeral for Mr. Stanley and I dreaded every minute of it. I could not get the images that clouded my head. I hate that he had to die this way and alone at that. Gabe and I have been in communication since the death of his father. It was clear that he and Gabrielle did not have a great relationship because I felt like the middleman when it came to handling the funeral arrangements. When Gabe found out about the death of his father, it took him a few days to get to New York from Florida. He claimed he had to secure somethings his father made him promise to do when he died. I did not bother to dig any further into his family business. All he asked was that I did not let Gabrielle make any final decisions until he got there. How was I supposed to do that, only God knew. Good thing was, Gabrielle wanted the extra support and did not mind me tagging along. I did feel bad though because while we were picking out the funeral arrangements, I was sending pictures to Gabe for his approval. I was able to convince Gabrielle on the things Gabe liked without her knowing he had any input. I hated not fully knowing what the issues were between them, but by his tone whenever we spoke, I knew it was serious. It was only a matter of time until the truth would be revealed.

The funeral started at three o'clock. It was only nine in the morning, but I had a few things to take care of before the funeral. Gabe asked me to go with him to check over the final arrangements before the rest of his family arrived. This was going to be a no casket funeral for obvious reasons. Gabe had a customized quilt made to put over the table that held his father's ashes. He had everyone who loved Mr. Stanley send him kind words about his father and had them printed out on the quilt along with some of his best photos printed on it.

I pulled up to the Paper Factory hotel where Gabe was staying and waited for him to get into the car.

"Good morning," he said as he sat down and put his seatbelt on.

"Morning, Gabe. How did you sleep?"

"Sleep? I don't think I know what that feels like anymore." It was evident that his statement was true.

"Hopefully when this is all over you'll be able to rest a bit and put your mind at ease." I was trying to be hopeful, but I knew how death took a toll on people.

"I sure hope so. I hope my family does not act a fool in there. You know how black families get at funerals." We both laughed knowing how true that is.

♥ ♥ ♥

I dropped Gabe back off to the hotel and made my way back uptown. I picked up my tux before heading to the house. Hopefully, Kris was done with the bathroom so I could just hop in and get ready.

Parking was not on my side today. I circled the block numerous times until I decided to park a block and a half away from the apartment. I'm not sure if I'll be wearing this suit jacket today. For it to be the first week of June, it was hot. Summer wasn't due for a few more weeks.

I opened the door to our apartment and placed my suit on the couch. I walked into our bedroom and saw Kristen laying down on her side of the bed. She had on the same house clothes I saw her in when I left this morning. I looked at my watch to make sure I was not bugging. It was 1:17 p.m. The service starts at three, she knows how long it takes her to get ready, so why is she not out of bed?

"Hey, Kris. Why are you still in bed? You do know the service starts at three right?" I asked trying to control how annoyed I felt.

"Yea I know. I decided that I don't want to go?" She was laying down facing the opposite of our bedroom door so she could not see how annoyed I was.

"What do you mean you're not going? You know how much Mr. Stanley meant to me." This was a terrible time for her to be selfish. I needed her support to get through this.

"When you left, I got up, took my clothes out, and ironed it. I started cleaning the apartment and you know I always go into deep thought when I'm cleaning, especially when my music is on. I couldn't help but think about how responsible I am for his death. Just days before he died I had that dream about my mom and Monique being burnt in the sauna and now look!" Tears started streaming down her face. I was so caught up in my feelings about his death that it didn't hit me until now that she was dealing with it for her own reasons.

"His death is beyond unfortunate, but you have to stop blaming yourself for these coincidental things that you have no control over." I stripped out of my outside clothes as I sat at the edge of our bed and placed her feet into my lap.

"I can't help it. It's starting to take a toll on me." She buried her face into the pillow and cried. My heart ached for her and I wish there was something I could do to not make her feel responsible. I can't lie though, this is starting to become creepy.

"I can't force you to come to the funeral just like I can't force you to believe that you're not responsible for any of this. What I do want you to know is that even though I would love to have you by my side, I understand why you don't want to go and I won't hold it against you for not going." I got up from the bed and kissed her on her forehead as I gathered my stuff for my shower.

I turned on Pandora and switched to the Chris Brown station as I turned the water on and stepped in. I needed some good tunes to uplift my spirits. Not only was I not excited about going to this funeral, now I had to go alone. Kristen needed help but I wasn't sure who to reach out to without making it seem like my woman was crazy.

It only took a few minutes and the base from my speakers to put me in a relaxed mood. I was sliding and gliding down my shower floor as I danced along to some of the newest hits. You can always count on Pandora to keep you up to date with today's music. I was jamming along to a song I didn't know when Kris opened the shower door and scared me half to death. She thought it was the funniest thing but I didn't.

She stepped into the shower with me and began to lather up her washcloth. We didn't exchange words, just showered together, and enjoyed the music. I turned to face the showerhead to let the water rinse off all the soap. I felt her arms wrap around me as she laid her head on my back. We stayed in that position for a few seconds before I turned around to face her.

"I changed my mind. I'm going to go. You need the support and I need to accept what has happened." A tear slid down her face as I wiped it away.

"I love you." The words left my mouth without even thinking. I didn't know what else to say.

She leaned up to kiss me and I accepted her invitation. We kissed passionately as the water continued to beat down my back, splashing her occasionally. It's something about the way we kiss that gets me going every time. She looked down and smirked as she saw how excited he was.

"Let me take care of that," she said as she licked her lips. She took him into her hands and did as she said; took care of him.

By the time we got out of the shower, it was 2:20 p.m. We were going to be late. Thankfully, she already knew what she was wearing. That would have taken another hour that we didn't have.

It didn't take me long to dry off and lotion. I had on my boxer briefs, socks, and t-shirt as I watched Kristen look for her "good" black bra. Maybe if she didn't have so many bras and panties in the draw she'd have an easier time finding what she needed. I wouldn't dare say that to her though.

We were both dressed moments later. Thankfully Kris didn't have major plans for her hair. That would've taken us all day. Instead, she settled on a low slicked back bun. It's the simple things she does that are the most beautiful to me.

By the time we were seated in my car, it was 2:57 p.m. That means we had three minutes to get to the funeral home. Not happening.

We got there in twenty-two minutes. I was thankful for valet parking. Kris held my hand as we walked into the funeral home. There were a few funerals happening today. We searched for the room with his name on it. As we entered, I scanned the room and saw a few people from our building and neighborhood. The rest I didn't know. I spotted Gabe and he motioned for me to sit in the row behind him. I was not planning to sit that close to the front. I felt my body freeze as I walked down the aisle. Kris gave my hand a squeeze to reassure me that everything was going to be ok.

I can honestly say that the service went better than I expected. I did shed a few tears but quickly wiped them away before anyone saw it. When it was time to share our greatest memories of Mr. Stanley, Kristen walked up with me for support. I felt myself get choked up a few times but managed to get through.

After the service, the immediate family and close friends went to Mr. Stanley's sister's house in Long Island. It felt like such a long day and I just wanted to go home. When I told Gabe that I wasn't going, his facial expression showed pure sadness. How could I have not changed my mind after that? Kristen volunteered to drive us there and told him we would follow right behind.

It felt like forever to reach Long Island. You would think since the funeral took place in Long Island City that getting to Long Island wouldn't be bad, negative! I learned today how far the two areas are from each other. I want to know who named these places and did not think to make them close to one another.

We pulled up into this huge driveway and I could not stop staring at how beautiful just the outside of the house was. I can only imagine what the inside looked like. Kristen parked the car behind Gabe's car. Gabe motioned for us to follow him to the back of the house.

"Now this house is what you call goals!" Kristen said as she and I both stood in awe.

She wasn't lying. It was beautiful. "I agree, baby. I agree." I was at a loss for words.

This white and grey house was beyond beautiful. You can tell this was a three-family house. It was too huge to be anything less. Gabe gave us a tour of the outside of the house first. In the front of the house was freshly trimmed grass surrounded by beautiful plants. You can tell his aunt Elise took pride in her garden. She had many different flowers and each of them had their own section. Kristen grew up learning how to plant at a young age, so she was schooling us on the flowers that were there. I learned what sedums, petunias, geraniums, and other flowers I never heard of were called. I saw the joy in her eyes as she snapped pictures of the garden and sent them to her mom.

We walked through the long driveway to the back of the house where all the music, food, and people were. Their backyard was even bigger than I expected. The weather was beautiful for an outdoor celebration of life. Rain or shine, they could have anything outside. They had this beautiful pergola built in the back. Tables and chairs were set underneath it. People were just starting to trickle in and grab seats as they waited for the food to be brought out.

The music was playing and everyone was mixing and mingling. For such an unfortunate situation, it was great to see everyone conversing and celebrating life. Tomorrow is not promised to any of us, so we must cherish these moments.

Kristen and I were sitting at one of the tables eating when Gabrielle walked into the backyard. I noticed the stares she got at the funeral home, but how they stared at her now was more intense. What was the issue? I wish I could read everyone's thoughts so I can put it all together. Kristen and I both looked at each other with confused looks on our faces. She shrugged and kept eating. I decided to do the same but was still attentive to everyone's body language.

She went online to get some food. She awkwardly stood by the gate that separated the cars from the back yard. Some people were still staring at her while others tried to ignore the fact that she was there.

Gabe walked out of the house moments later and as soon as he noticed her, he walked back into the house. His aunt Elise came out seconds later. People started to make things awkward now. Everyone was looking from Elise to Gabrielle. Elise motioned for her to come into the house. They were in the house for a while when the rest of the family finally went back to doing what they were doing before she came.

Kris and I joined in on a card game of Spades. She and I were on the same team while Lisa and Carl played against us. Lisa is Elise's oldest daughter and Carl is her husband.

We were playing our third round. Kris and I won the first round, Lisa and Carl won the second, and now we were about to see who was breaking the tie. We were in the lead and I knew we were about to win, but just as we were shuffling the deck there was a commotion in the house. Leslie, Lisa's younger sister ran into the house. Lisa excused herself from the table and did the same.

"It never fails," Carl said as he shook his head and took a swig of his beer.

"Everything ok?" I asked.

"Just family drama. It's like this at every family function when Gabrielle pops up. Good thing she doesn't know about all the family functions." Lisa and Carl have been married for seven years. You can tell by his voice that he has experienced this before. I wasn't the nosy type, but I wanted clarity on this situation.

"Is she not welcomed here?" I could not think of a better question to pry him out of more information. Kristen was usually the one that's good at that, not me. But knowing her, I know she probably thought it was best if the men spoke.

"Hell no! She has caused a lot of damage to that family. She's very toxic. If you don't know her, you'll think she's this innocent thing, but she can't be trusted. If only you knew what she has put this family through," *Well shit, Carl. That's what I'm trying to figure out.* I wish I had the balls to say that. Instead, I just nodded.

The arguing went on for a few minutes before Gabrielle exited the house with Lisa on her tail yelling and screaming after her. I couldn't hear everything she was saying over the music, but some things were clear as day. I heard when Lisa yelled out that she probably killed him on purpose. It didn't take a rock scientist to figure out who she was talking about. I understood that families had issues, mine sure did, but damn I hated that this was happening now.

Gabrielle hopped in her car and drove off. Lisa walked back into the house and was in there for a few minutes before coming back to our table.

"I'm sorry about that guys. This is not how our family functions usually are." Carl gave her that *yea ok* look. She laughed and said, "Well only when she pops up."

"No need to apologize. Is everyone ok though?" Oh, now Kristen wanted to talk. Wait until we get in the car.

"Yea, now that she's gone everyone should be fine, for now," Lisa said. "Let's pick up where we left off at, shall we?"

We continued playing spades and of course, Kris and I won. We decided to start heading out. We said our goodbyes and I told Gabe I would give him a call tomorrow.

Since Kris drove us here, I drove us back home. This part of Long Island wasn't too far from Brooklyn. It didn't take us long to get home as it did driving from Queens.

When we got home, Kris jumped in the shower and I did the same when she was done. It was 9:15 p.m. by the time we got home and a little after ten by the time we finished showering. I was grateful that tomorrow was Saturday and we both were off. We decided to stay up and watch a movie while eating chocolate chip cookie dough ice cream. We scrolled through Movies on Demand for something funny to watch. Lifting our spirits was needed after the day we had. After scrolling for a bit, we decided on Bringing Down the House starring Queen Latifah and Steve Martin.

Halfway into the movie, Kristen got a text on her phone from Latrice.

"Shit, babe. I forgot to ask you if you were busy tomorrow night?" she asked.

I looked at my calendar. "Nope, nothing saved on my calendar. Why wassup?"

"Latrice wanted us to double date. I told you she met a new guy and wants us to meet him."

"Why can't you just be the third wheel? She never minds being the third wheel when we go out."

She reached over and punched me in my arm. "I will not be anyone's third wheel, so thank you in advance for coming." She blew me a kiss as she rubbed my arm where she punched me.

I just looked at her and shook my head. I guess I was going on a double date. *Great.*

She texted Latrice back and told her we were down for going.

When she finished sending her text, I motioned for her to come lay on my side of the couch. We continued to watch the movie until the movie started watching us. I knew it wouldn't be long before we both knocked out on the couch.

The time read 1:07 a.m. when I woke up. I woke Kris up and led her to the bed. Sleeping on the couch the whole night would have had both of our bodies aching. I would rather sleep in our bed and get the proper rest we needed.

CHAPTER 13
KRISTEN

I don't remember how I got into bed. According to Steph, he woke me up at one in the morning and told me to follow him. I must have been tired. Stephan got up about fifteen minutes ago to go for a morning job. He asked me to join him, but he knows jogging is not my thing. I would rather walk on the treadmill while watching my shows on my phone. While he went for a jog, I decided to start breakfast. It was 9:17 a.m. and he'll be gone for about thirty minutes. I had a few things I wanted to get done before we had to meet up with Latrice and her new boo.

Scanning the fridge, I realized going food shopping needed to be on tomorrow's to-do list. I pulled out the eggs, grabbed the waffles from out the freezer, and found the turkey bacon. I decided to be healthy by taking out some spinach. I bought spinach last week and haven't opened it. It was expiring in two days. It needed to be used. I preheated the oven as I washed my pot to make the turkey bacon.

By the time Stephan got back from jogging, I was making the eggs.

"Smells good in here, baby," he said as he walked through the door. He kissed me on the cheek and slapped my butt as he headed for the shower.

When he got out of the shower, breakfast was done and waiting for him at the table. With limited supplies in our refrigerator and freezer, I was able to whip up some spinach egg and feta cheese omelets, waffles, and turkey bacon. Orange juice was waiting for him as well.

He finally made his way to the table as we said our grace and dug in.

"Damn, baby. I can't lie, I was a little skeptical about having spinach in my omelet but this taste damn good," he said while putting another forkful in his mouth.

"I've seen people do that a lot on Instagram, but as you said, I've been skeptical too. I didn't want my spinach to spoil so I decided to give it a try," I said pleased that he liked it. It did taste good.

"Good choice. What's on your agenda today?" he asked.

"Well, I need to wash my hair and give it a good treatment. I want to sweep and mop as well. Laundry needs to get done too and the bathroom needs to be cleaned a bit. I want to get it all out the way so that tomorrow all I have to do is go food shopping and cook dinner."

"Sounds like you got your hands full. What time are we supposed to be linking up with Latrice again?"

"She made reservations for 7:30 p.m. at the Cheesecake Factory by Queens Center Mall," I said.

"Ok cool. Let me check how long that drive is," he said as he pulled out his phone and typed in the address. "It's about a thirty-minute ride, so that means we need to be out by 6:50 p.m. the latest just in case we hit traffic."

"Sounds good to me."

"Anything I can help with? I don't want you drained from doing all these household duties," he asked.

I couldn't help but smile at him. I just love me some Stephan. There are different kinds of men in this world. Men who expect women to do all of these household duties and men who appreciate a woman for doing it, but will also do his part and help. The good thing about Stephan is that he was raised right. His mom may not be the best cook but she made sure her house was always clean. Stephan picked up his cooking skills from his dad and his cleaning skills from his mom.

"The option is yours, you can either sweep for me or sort the clothes so I can start the laundry." *Watch he choose to sweep*. He hated sorting clothes.

"I'll sweep." I laughed at how fast he responded. I knew him all too well.

While he swept the apartment, I was in our bedroom sorting the laundry. He turned on the speakers and started playing DJ Khaled's new album, Father of Asahd. I went into the bathroom and placed Ajax, Lysol, and Bleach in the tub. I will scrub it out later.

"What you laughing about?" he asked startling me.

"Just the other day someone posted something on Twitter about how black people clean their bathroom. I can't remember verbatim, but it was something like how black people put cleaning supplies in their bathtub and let it soak like they are marinating chicken." We both busted out laughing.

"It's so true! You definitely do that and my mom always did that when I was growing up. I hated those days when I had somewhere to go and the bathtub was 'marinating'."

"Listen, when that bathtub gets a good soaking, that tub be looking brand new," I said.

"You're right. Trust me, I am not complaining. I love it when the bathroom has that clean look."

"You and I both."

He went back to sweeping and I went back to sorting clothes. Doing laundry for two people can become a lot when it isn't done frequently. We had to get into the routine of doing it every other weekend. Stephan bought us a washer and dryer about a year ago and it was the greatest investment ever. We had the one where the washer sat on top of the dryer. I hated driving to the laundromat to wash our clothes and having to fight for a dryer. It took Stephan one time to witness how real it got in the laundromat for him to say never again. I came home the next day and my washer and dryer were being delivered and installed. I was not complaining at all. I never stepped foot into that laundromat since.

I finished sorting our clothes and decided to start with our undergarments and nightclothes. While that was washing, I grabbed my hair products and began washing my hair. I put my homemade treatment in and put on my shower cap. It has been a few weeks since I have given myself a treatment so I added a few extra drops of Jamaican Black Castor Oil to my homemade treatment. It does not have the greatest smell, but it does wonders on my hair. Peppermint and Jojoba oil helps mask the smell of it along with other natural products I mix in.

My first set of clothes finished washing just in time. I threw them in the dryer along with some gain sheets. Stephan was straightening up our bedroom while I went in and grabbed our bed sheets, bath towel, and washcloths for washing. I threw those in the washer and prepared to mop the floors. Investing in a Swiffer Wet Jet was the best decision I have made. It cut my mopping time in half and still gave my floors the same great results compared to my regular mop. I poured Fabuloso, bleach, and water into the bottle I used for mopping. The Swiffer comes with its own liquid cleaner, but I save that for when I mop the floors a second time.

I walked into our bedroom as I waited for the floors to dry. The room smelt like powder. I loved laundry day. I taught Stephan to put powder on the mattress before putting on clean bedsheets. It gave the room a pleasant scent and made lying in bed even more relaxing because of the welcoming scent of baby powder. I sat on the chair we had in the room. I wouldn't dare lay in bed with my clean sheets without taking a shower. I smelt like bleach, Fabuloso, and Gain.

After mopping the floors a second time, I took out the clothes from the dryer and put the bedroom and bath sheets in. Our work clothes were the last to wash. I was doing better on time than I expected. While the clothes were washing and drying, I washed the treatment out of my hair while Stephan folded the dry clothes.

I put my leave-in conditioner from Shea Moisture in my hair and let it sit in and air dry a bit while I cleaned the bathroom. I had no clue what I was going to do with my hair. I decided to take a shower after I was cleaning.

I was laying down in bed on Instagram and YouTube as I looked up quick natural hairstyles to do. It just hit five o'clock and whatever style I was going to do could not be something that needed time to set in. I finally found a hairstyle that was quick and yet still elegant for tonight. I grabbed my blow dryer and heat protectant and gave my hair a light blow dry. I placed Eco Style on my edges as I styled my hair in a pompadour and pinned up the back. It was 5:35 p.m. when I finished my hair. Grabbing my silk scarf, I tied down my hair so it can have my hair looking even sleeker. This scarf is not coming off until it's time to leave.

Stephan and I agreed to be that corny couple who matched their outfits. It was my request actually, but he was ok with it. I decided to keep it cute and simple. We were both going to wear black and white. I had these new black jeans from Fashion Nova, my white tank top bodysuit, and my black blazer. My red shoes and red purse were going to give it a little pop. Stephan pulled out his black fitted jeans, a white-collar shirt, and some all-black shoes. I could not wait to see him dressed.

We only had a little time to get ready, so while Stephan ironed, I was applying my makeup. We were going out to eat, so I didn't want to do too much, but I couldn't help but put on my red lipstick. I was in love with Rihanna's beauty line. Tonight I was wearing her Uncensored (Perfect Universal Red) Stunna Lip Paint.

My makeup was done and my purse was packed. I had about fifteen minutes to get dressed before we had to leave. The hardest part was done, so fifteen minutes was more than enough time. After getting dressed, I looked myself over in the mirror with pure approval. *Damn, I look good.* Stephan walked up behind me as we stared at each other through the mirror. We looked damn good together.

"You look handsome, baby."

"And you look beautiful, my love," he said as he pulled me into his arms.

"Don't start, Steph," I said as I felt his hand gripping my butt.

He winked at me and said, "Just feeling on my lady. No harm in that."

"Yea ok and I know exactly what that leads to," I said moving from his grip.

He pulled me back to him and kissed me deeply. I'm surprised my lipstick didn't get all over his lips. I need more lipstick like this.

I felt him unsnap the button to my jeans and I stood there and just looked at him. I couldn't help but shake my head.

"Babe, this can wait until we get back home. We are going to be late."

"You know Latrice is never on time. I'll make it quick," he said winking at me again.

He led me to our bed and undressed me waist down as he bent me over the bed. Before entering me, he played with my clit a bit to help get my juices flowing. I heard myself moaning as he touched all the right places. I lifted my tank top and squeezed my breast. This lasted for a few minutes until I felt the head of his penis open me up. He started with slow strokes and then picked up the pace. I didn't want this feeling to end. We were going to be late.

♥ ♥ ♥

We found parking a block away and walked hand in hand to the Cheesecake Factory. To my surprise, Latrice and her date were already there. This was a change for her. Their backs were facing us as we approached the bar.

"Hey, girl," I said as we approached the bar table.

She turned around at the sound of my voice. "Hey, Kris!" She got up from her seat and hugged me.

"No way!" Latrice and I both looked at Stephan to see what the problem was.

Latrice's date got up and gave Stephan a brotherly hug.

"You two know each other?" Latrice and I said in unison and then looked at each other and started laughing.

"Do we! We went to college together," Latrice's date said as he extended his hand to mine. "I'm Trent and you must be the lovely Kristen that Stephan always talks about," he said as he showed the prettiest pearly whites I've ever seen.

"Trent? The Trent?" I said looking from him to Stephan.

"Yes, baby, *the* Trent," Stephan said as he gave Trent a look that only they understood.

"Wow. I've heard a lot about you as well. It's nice to finally meet you," I said smiling back.

I need to find out who his dentist is. My teeth are white, but he had me beat.

"Well, I'm happy that everyone knows each other and of

each other. Now can we grab our table, I'm starving," Latrice said.

"You're always starving," Stephan and I said in unison as everyone laughed, even the people beside us.

Latrice walked ahead to let the host know that we were ready to be seated. The host directed us to our seats. Latrice and I sat on the inside as the men sat on the outside of our table.

It felt great knowing that the person that Latrice has met was one of Stephan's closest friends. I've met most of his college friends, but Trent. I've only said hello to him over the phone.

I'm sure that everyone who walked past us thought the four of us been friends for decades. Our laughs, the vibes, the energy, everything was spot on. Nothing felt forced or dragged out. Trent is the perfect balance for Latrice. He has a wild side just like her, but because of his profession, you can tell he knows when to use it and when to lose it.

The rest of the dinner went on too perfectly that none of us wanted the night to end. We couldn't stay at the restaurant because people were waiting to be seated. The waiter kept coming back to our tables asking if we needed anything else. I caught the hint first and told the rest that we have outstayed our welcome.

Trent paid for the tab. He insisted and gave Stephan a look that I am assuming meant do not fight with me. We thanked him for paying and we all headed for the door.

"It's so beautiful outside. I don't want the night to end," I said giving Stephan a pouty look.

"Neither do I, babe," Lattice said to Trent matching my look.

The guys looked at each other and laughed.

"How about we drive back to Brooklyn, hit the liquor store, and have a game night. Couples edition. We haven't done that in a while," I said, sounding like an excited kid about to go to the candy store.

The guys looked at each other again and both gave each other that look that I don't understand.

"Sure, babe. Whatever you want," Stephan said to me.

Latrice and I decided to drive Stephan's car back to Brooklyn and Stephan rode with Trent. I needed some girl chat with her. Some alone time without the men. We had to discuss dinner and everything. I'm sure the guys would appreciate it as well.

"Girl, you need to spill all the tea you know about him," Lattice said. She wasted no time jumping into it as we buckled up in the car.

"Honestly, I don't know much. I do know he and Stephan are close. It's funny because Trent is you in our group."

"What you mean by that?" she asked.

"Meaning. You know in our circle, you're the daredevil type. You're always up for a challenge. You are the one that goes after what you want. Well according to the little that Steph shares with me about his boys, Trent is the wild one and the go-getter. He's the one who lives life on the edge. I must say though, he does have good balance because he knows how to put on his professional voice when it's needed." I have heard how articulate he is when he is in business mode.

"That is true. I think that's what drew me to him and what scares me about him as well. I see a lot of me in him, but then when that business side kicks in, I'm like damn, he's a great catch."

"I agree. I think he is a good balance for you. Not only do I think he would challenge you into wanting more out of life, but you can learn a lot from him. No offense. He still has his wild side, but he pulls it out when it's appropriate. Your wild side has no hiding place." I know my words hit her a bit hard, but she knows it is all out of love. "I just want what's best for you friend."

"I know you do and I love how open and honest you are with me."

"It wouldn't be me if I weren't," I said glancing at her before focusing back on the road. "So how do you feel things are going between you two?"

"Honestly, things are going great. I love how he is passionate about his work. You know I dislike a man who sits at home all day and doesn't have anything going for themselves. Our conversations are always great. Even if it's just five minutes of us checking in with one another. He is pushing me to step out of my comfort zone. The other day we were at his house and he asked me if I planned on working at the shop forever. He asked me what my long term goals were. And I must admit, it made me open my eyes and realize that I don't have any long term goals for myself."

"Well, are you ok with working at that shop forever?" I asked.

"Not at all. It's something I'm good at and love to do, but paying booth rent for the rest of my life isn't it."

"So what are your next steps to ensure that you're not doing that forever?" I asked.

"I love doing hair and that is something I don't mind doing for the rest of my life, but I rather have my own shop. I would rather charge other people for booth rent. There's so much I would do if I had my own shop," she said.

"Like what? Enlighten me."

"Well for starters, when school is about to start, I'd love to have a day where kids can come and get their hair done for free. Have a Mother's Day special. I would have male barbers there as well so that on Father's Day, the men can get a special too. Discounted prices for birthdays. I have so many ideas. I just want to give back to our community. There's not a lot of people doing that nowadays. It sure did not exist when we were growing up. I want to help break that cycle."

I couldn't help but to smile and feel proud. Everyone knows Latrice to be the loud and ghetto one out of the bunch, but I knew her on a deeper level. She has always been a big advocate of giving back. She still participated in feeding the homeless on Thanksgiving Day. Always donating for toy drives. She really does have a passion for it. We didn't come from much and she had less than I did, so it warmed my heart to see her wanting to make a change.

"I must say, I can see you accomplish all of that and more! You know I will always be your biggest supporter and when you are ready, I will be there to help you get this off the ground. When it comes to the financial aspect of opening your own shop, you should meet with Stephan one on one. Now that you and Trent are in a relationship, he can be your legal eye when it comes to contracts, agreements, etc. And when you need help designing your shop, you know I got that creative eye," I said winking at her.

"I love you so much, Kris. No one believes in me the way that you do," she said teary-eyed.

"You know I love you too. You got this, girl."

I believed it in my heart that she could do everything that she had her mind set on. She may have her wild ways, but she has it in her to be a great businesswoman. Having Trent around is just an added bonus. She's going to do great. I know it.

CHAPTER 14
STEPHAN

Trent and I hopped into his BMW as he started up the car to drive us back to Brooklyn.

"I can't believe the woman you were talking about the night we all hung out was Latrice. Who would have known that the two wildest people I know are dating? The irony!" I couldn't help but laugh.

"Man listen, it's all new to me. You know me best and you know I'm not into women who are just like me, but there's something about her that made me want to see where this could go," he said as he pulled out of the parking spot.

"You sure it wasn't the sex?" I asked.

"Positive. You know I have never had a problem getting my needs taken care of. I think that is what intrigued me more; knowing that sex was not what kept me entertained with her. Now don't get me wrong, she's great at what she does, but it's more than that this time." He stopped at a red light and looked at me. The look in his eyes showed how truthful he was being.

"I respect it. You know I have been telling you for ages to settle down and leave that fast life to the young ones. So if Latrice is the one to make that happen, then I'm all for it," I said meaning every word.

"I think she is. I know it's still early to be so sure, but this feeling is new and I like it."

"Well just promise me one thing," I said looking at him.

"What's that?" he asked as he glanced at me.

"That you won't hurt her. Latrice may be a tough cookie, but she has been through a lot. When she hurts, so does Kris and I can't be having you messing with my happy home."

"Trust me, nothing in me wants to be that guy anymore. I haven't even returned any text messages or phone calls from my regulars," he said.

"Damn, ok now I know it's serious. Bout damn time," I said as I gave him a pound.

We were in Brooklyn in no time. We parked outside the liquor store as we waited for the women to reach. I don't know how we beat them here when they pulled off before us.

About ten minutes passed by and they still weren't here. I ended up calling Kris to make sure they were ok and she told me they stopped at Rite Aid to grab some snacks. I told her it would have been nice if they called and said that. After she apologized, I told her to meet us back at the apartment, and Trent and I would just grab the drinks.

You would have thought we were about to have a party with all the liquor we just bought. We bought Jack, New Amsterdam, Pineapple Cîroc, and Malibu. The Jack was for us men and the rest were for the women to choose from. We grabbed some cranberry, orange, and pineapple juice. I don't drink like that so the ladies are going to have to be the bartenders tonight. I don't know what goes well with what.

Parking wasn't bad tonight. We grabbed the bags and headed into the apartment. The ladies were already inside and stuffing their faces with Dorito's. I placed the bags down on the counter, washed my hands, and took a handful of Dorito's. Kris knows snacks are my weakness. I hope she bought me some Pringles.

As if she read my mind, "Babe, I got you Pringles, it's sitting by the counter where the microwave is."

I kissed her on the forehead. "You love me," I said winking at her.

"Of course I do," she said winking back.

"Ugh, I hope we don't get like that," Latrice said to Trent. They both looked at us and started laughing.

"Oh trust, it's bound to happen. Just wait!" Kris said as she got up and kissed me.

"Nope!" Trent and Latrice both said at the same time.

Kris and I both looked at each other and started laughing. "See, it's starting already," Kris said as we all laughed.

"Anywho! What are we playing tonight?" Latrice asked.

Kris got up and went to where we kept our board games. "We have cards, Uno, Trouble, Taboo, Battle of the Sexes, Black Card Revoked, Dominoes, and Family Feud."

"Let's play Dominoes. I haven't given someone six love in a long time," Trent said.

"I don't know how to play Dominoes and what the hell is six love?" asked Latrice.

"Don't worry, baby. I'll teach you," Trent said.

"Oh boy, that means we're about to hear his fake ass Jamaican accent as he slams down dominoes on my table," I said.

"You're just afraid to get your ass beat again. Last time we played, it was Will and I against you and Daniel. We beat y'all something terrible," Trent boasted.

"Ain't my fault you've been playing since you were like five years old. I grew up with southern parents, they don't know anything about playing dominoes," I said.

"Don't worry, baby, we've been practicing. We got this!" Kris said as she massaged my shoulders. She's damn right, we have been practicing. After that night when they beat us in the game of dominoes, I ordered some dominoes off Amazon. I was determined to get my practice in before the next time I had to play against him.

Trent explained the rules to Latrice as Kris and I listened in for more knowledge. This game, when played correctly, really is a mind game. It has a lot to do with being able to read everyone else's hand without having the ability to see what their holding. Based on what they put down and what they pass on, you can kind of figure out who has what. I have not quite mastered it, but I feel more confident than the last time.

My hands started to cramp up from holding the dominoes pieces. I don't know how people did it. Kris and I weren't winning, but we sure as hell wasn't allowing them to give us six love. Every time they would get close, we would end up winning the next round and having to start over from one.

A knock at the door startled us all. I looked at the clock and it was 11:17 p.m. We all looked at each other, not sure who it could be.

"Relax, it's just my sister and her husband," Kristen said as she got up and went to the door.

"Hey, family!" Monique said as she and Carl entered the apartment.

"Hey, sis!" I said as I got up to greet her. I pulled her into a bear hug and squeezed her.

I gave Carl a brotherly hug. "It's been a while."

"It has been. It's very rare when Mo and I get the same night off."

Carl is an EMT worker. They both work very hectic schedules. Sometimes they even go days without sleeping in the same bed at the same time. Kris and Mo's mom lives with them so she can help take care of the twins. I don't know how they do it. That lifestyle is not for me.

"Well, well, well look who it is!" We all looked at Monique to see who she was talking to. Following her eyes, she was staring at Trent.

"Wait, you two know each other?" I asked puzzled.

"Do we?" They both said in unison.

"This world is too freaking small for me," Latrice said. I didn't know whether to laugh or be concerned about how they knew each other.

"Anyone care to share how you two know each other?" I asked breaking the silence.

"Well you know I'm a criminal lawyer. Mrs. King has put away many of my clients. Let's just say, they haven't spent that much time behind bars because I'm that good of a lawyer," Trent said sounding every bit of cocky.

"No, let's just say this idiot has let some of the most dangerous drug dealers back out on the street," Monique said shaking her head at him.

"Don't call the man an idiot, baby. He's just doing his job. Somebody has to do it," Carl said while rubbing Mo's arms.

"Yes, Monique, listen to your husband," Trent said.

"Stay in your lane, sir," Carl said giving Trent a warning sign.

I think it's time to end this conversation before things go left. "Hey Carl, you drink Jack right?" I didn't even let him answer before I continued, "Let me pour you a double shot so you can catch up with us."

Kristen got my clue and fixed Monique a drink. "Here, sis. Drink this."

It didn't take long for the vibes in the room to pick back up. We were all drinking, laughing, and having a great time. We decided to retire the game of dominoes. Trent and Latrice were not giving us six love tonight. We decided to play Taboo. Men against women. I wish Kris and I were on the same team. No one has ever beat us when we played together. I just hope these men weren't too drunk to get the hints.

It was my turn. I picked up my card as the ladies flipped over the sand timer. My first word was *Pillow*. The words I can't say are *head, sleep, soft, bed,* and *blanket.* Damn, this is going to be hard.

"Ok, so you use this to rest on. Sometimes you have to double up on it for more comfort..."

"A couch!" Trent yelled out with pure confidence.

"No dumb ass! How are you supposed to double up on a couch!" I couldn't help but laugh at his comment and how confident he felt.

"Time is running out!" Kristen yelled.

"Ok, ok, ummm, when you close your eyes to go night-night you lay down on it. It's small and rectangular..."

"A pillow!" Carl called out.

"Yes!" I screamed as I grabbed another card. There wasn't much time left so hopefully, they can get this one.

The next card made me wish that Kris was on my team. She would have gotten this in no time. My next word was *Candle.* The words I cannot say are *light, flame, burn, fire,* and *window.*

"Ok. Ladies like to go to this store to buy it because it makes the house smell good…"

"Perfume!" Carl shouts out.

I'm playing with a bunch of idiots! "No not make them smell good. It makes the house smell good. If you get 3-wick it's better."

"Oh, I know!" Trent says.

"What is it?" Carl asked.

"A cand…"

"Time!" the women screamed in unison as Latrice presses the buzzer.

"You idiot! Why didn't you just call it out?" I asked as I put the two cards to the side.

"Good try, babe. I would've gotten that one," Kris said as she picked up the deck of cards and prepared for her turn to go.

"Ok ladies, y'all ready?" The ladies had their game faces on as they waited for me to flip the sand timer. This ought to be good. "Ok, it's not spring, fall, or summer, so it's?"

"Winter!" They both shouted in unison.

"Yes! Ok, next one. If I don't cook enough blank I won't have enough to take for lunch tomorrow."

"Food!" Monique yells out.

"Nope. I can only cook this at night. If I cook it in the morning it would be considered breakfast."

"Dinner!" Latrice yelled out.

"Yes, ok next one. Latrice was always afraid of these when we were younger. She would run from them at birthday parties."

"Clowns!" Monique said.

"Shit, I'm still afraid of them," Latrice said as we all laughed.

"Yes, ok next one. Barney made a song out of this. Blank blank go away, come again..."

"Rain!" Monique and Latrice both yelled in unison.

"Yes! Ok..."

"Time!" I yelled out as Carl pressed the buzzer. Damn my baby is good at this.

"How much we got?" Latrice asked.

"We got four!" Kristen said excitedly.

We played this game for about another hour or so and of course, the women beat us by a lot. I could not even be mad. We had such a great time laughing and yelling at each other.

Everyone stayed for a bit longer. We ate all the snacks that the women bought. Monique and Carl left first. They wanted to have some alone time before the twins woke up. I wasn't mad at that. Latrice and Trent left about ten minutes after.

"And then there were two," Kristen said.

I pulled her into a tight embrace and kissed her on her forehead. She lifted her head and kissed me on my lips. That kiss was passionate and I didn't want it to end, but she pulled away from me and started cleaning up. I helped her with the dishes as she straightened the table. I finished washing out the glasses while she was sweeping up little crumbs from off the floor. When she placed the broom back in the closet, I grabbed her from behind and pulled her into me.

"I wish I could just stay like this forever," I said as I rocked back and forth with her in my arms.

"I would give anything just to have this feeling last forever," she said as she followed my rhythm.

Turning her to face me, I lifted her chin as I kissed her just as passionately as she kissed me minutes before. I led her to our bedroom where I dimmed the lights.

"Take everything off." My voice was demanding, yet filled with lust. She did as she was told. "Good girl." She reached towards the buckle on my pants, but I removed her hands. "I'm taking care of you right now. Don't worry, you'll have time to repay me," I said. If her cheeks could turn red, right now would have been that time.

I had her lay down with her feet planted on the bed. "Open up." Obeying my rules, I started my kisses from the bottom. Starting from her feet, to her ankles, her calves, licking my way up her thighs, and stopping as I reached her opening. I felt her body tense up as a soft moan escaped her. Instead of diving right in, I decided to love on her a little longer. Skipping past her love box, I started kissing on her stomach, her belly button, and back to her mouth. The heat her body was giving off made me know she was ready for me to give her body my full attention. Leaving her mouth, I made my way to her breast. The double d's belonged to me and only me. I gave them both equal attention. Hearing her soft moans as I circled my tongue around each nipple only aroused me even more. I needed to hear her moan a little louder before I gave her what I knew she wanted. Sucking each breast, not too rough but not too gentle, I got the moans I was looking for. Slowly making my way back to her love box, I started playing with it before I let my tongue take over. Her moans and her hand on my head let me know I was doing something right. Knowing how she likes it, I placed two fingers inside while my tongue still sucked on her clit. Her hips moved with the motion of my fingers. Feeling her ride my fingers and face, I knew it was only a matter of time before she was going to cum. As much as I would love for this moment to last forever, I knew I wouldn't be able to hold out much longer either. I was rock hard and needed to release.

"Baby, I'm about to cum." I felt her muscles wrap around my fingers and knew she was near. I picked up my pace, sucked a little harder, and dug my fingers a little deeper. Seconds later I felt her unfold as she cried out to me. Bingo! My turn now.

I let her catch her breath for a few seconds. I needed to feel her, be inside her. "Bend over." She did as I said with no hesitation. Just how I liked it, she arched her back as she positioned herself for me to enter. I took my time entering her. I had to. It felt too good with just the head entering her love box. Her muscles clenched as I felt her vagina wrap around my whole penis. If her muscles don't loosen up, I'm not going to last long. As if her vagina read my mind, she started to loosen up and I was able to slide in a little easier and deeper. I don't know if it's the way she moans, the way she feels wrapped around me, or a combination of it all, but it just makes this moment so much better. Holding on to the headboard for support, I pounded my way into her. Smacking her ass occasionally, loving the way it jiggled with each thrust. I needed to see her expression, have her look me in my eyes as I give her my all. I turned her onto her back without missing a beat. I placed her legs on my shoulder, giving her my best strokes. "God, I love you." The words escaped my mouth and I didn't care because I meant it. "I love you too," she said and it only made me want her more. Digging deeper, I found her spot and didn't stop until I felt her legs begin to shake. I can feel her toes curling against my shoulder blades as she's about to cum. I can't help but pick up the pace. I need to feel her unfold. Her muscles tighten around me and in an instant, I feel myself about to cum too. "Cum with me, baby." Those were the last words I said before both of our bodies exploded.

Her body went limp as I collapsed next to her. It took us both a minute to get up and clean ourselves off. I was already back in bed when Kristen came and joined me. She snuggled up in my arms as we watched our usual reruns of Martin. It didn't take long before I felt her breathing getting heavier. She was out for the count.

CHAPTER 15
KRISTEN

"No ma, I'm not sure why it happens or what the cause of it is," I said to my mom over the phone. I was driving to work when she called to check in on me. As usual, we always end up talking about my dreams. She always asks the same questions as if she's about to get a different answer.

"I just wish I knew how to help you. Ever since you had that dream about us being trapped in the sauna, it hasn't been sitting well with me." *Of course, mom No one wants to hear that someone had a dream about them dying.* I didn't dare say that to her though.

"Trust me, mom. I wish I could stop dreaming all together."

"Have you had any other dreams since the sauna one?" she asked concerned.

"I did. About two weeks ago, Stephan and I hosted a game night at our house. That day was filled with so much laughter and fun times. That same night I ended up having a terrible dream. I woke up scared and angry. Scared because again I knew something was going to happen but I never know whom it's going to happen with. I was angry because for it to have been such a great day, it ended up being shitty. Sorry, mom. I didn't mean to curse."

"It's ok, honey. What was this dream about?"

"I had a dream that we were having a family beach day. Everyone was there. You, me, Monique, Carl, the twins, Steph, Latrice and her brother's kids, Trent, and a few others I can't remember. We were all having the time of our lives. Some of us were playing volleyball, while the others were lounging around. The kids were in the water enjoying the waves. Long story short, Laurence's oldest son starts screaming for us. We all look up and the waves are pushing Madison deeper into the water. Stephan is the first one to get there and he's trying to get to her as the waves keep pushing her further. Monique is screaming for the lifeguard to help save her child as we all are running into the water. You grabbed the other kids and got them out of the water. There was another guy who was already in the water who was trying to get to Madison as well. The waves pushed him back. We knew which direction the waves pulled them but we could no longer see her. The lifeguard got further than Stephan and was deep into the water and then he disappeared too. We saw his head peak out of the water and it looked like he had Madison in his arms, but it wasn't clear. Morgan started crying hysterically. Her cries scared us all. I wasn't sure if it was her twin senses that were telling her that her sister wasn't ok or just her going through the motions of what was happening. Monique ran over to comfort Morgan and I ended up waking up right there." I felt my heart tightening as I was retelling my dream and had to remind myself to breathe.

"Kris, these dreams are not healthy! I really wish you would seek help."

"I know, mom. Trust me I know. School is over in a few weeks, I'll make that my top priority this summer."

"I sure hope you do."

I switched topics and spoke with her a few minutes more before I had to walk into the school building.

♥ ♥ ♥

"Ok class, before you pack up for gym, my seniors, please remember that your final payment for your senior dues was due last week. Your senior trip is next week so if your final payment is not in, you won't be able to attend."

"Ms. Johnson, can you please call my mom and remind her? I have been telling her and she keeps brushing it off. Maybe if she hears it from you, she'll know how serious it is," Anthony asked.

"Sure thing. I'll give her a call while you guys are at gym. Leave all of your homework on the table and I will come by and collect it. Matter of fact, Jason, can you collect all of the homework please?"

"Of course," he said as he got up from his seat.

As they were packing up, I made a quick to-do list for me to do while I was on prep.

Call Anthony's mom
Grade Social Studies homework
Check-in with Stephan about our weekend getaway

I walked the class over to the gym and happily handed them over to Mr. Greene. "They are all yours," I said giving him a tap on the shoulder.

"You sure you don't want to hold onto them for a little longer?" he asked with pleading eyes.

"Nope. Enjoy!" I said as I walked back to my classroom.

I put Pandora on and began checking their social studies homework. It made me happy that my kids did their homework and for the most part, everything was correct. It could be that it's now June in a few days and they know this last report card determines whether they move on or not. Speaking of moving on, I just remembered that I had to call Anthony's mom. Next year isn't going to be the same. Most of my kids are graduating this year. Anthony, Octavia, Malcolm, Samiyah, and Jason were all going to be leaving me. I wonder what my new incoming students would be like? I hope they have great personalities like the ones I have now.

I dialed Anthony's mom and she picked up on the second ring, "Hola?"

"Hi, Miriam. It's Ms. Johnson."

"Oh, Ms. Johnson, how are you? Anthony in trouble?" I love how strong her accent is. I have to stop myself from mimicking her accent when I talk to her. I don't want her to think that I'm making fun of her. I don't know why us black people feel we have to put on this accent when we speak to people with strong Spanish accents.

"No, no, he's fine. I was calling because his last payment for his senior dues was due last week."

"He told me but I don't have the money for it right now. I worked overtime just so I can pay for his senior dues, but one of the workers stole from my boss and now none of us are getting paid until they say who it was."

"Miriam, you do know it's illegal for your employer to

withhold your money for reasons like that?"

"Yes, Ms. Johnson I do know, but we can't do anything about it. We are all undocumented and getting paid under the table. I can't believe I just told you that, please don't say anything. I can't afford for anyone to find out and risk losing my job."

"You have nothing to worry about. I won't say a thing."

"Thank you so much. As soon as I get the money I will pay off his balance. Do you think the school will allow him to still attend his senior trip, prom, and everything else if my payment is late?"

"Unfortunately, the school has to pay these vendors so the money had to be in by last week. They were generous enough to push it to this week. I'm not sure if they'll push it any further since the senior trip is next week."

"Anthony is never going to forgive me for this. I'm such a terrible mother."

My heart broke when I heard her crying over the phone. "Miriam, you are a great mother. You are one of the most supportive and active parents I've ever met while working here. Listen, I will pay his balance and this will be our little secret. Anthony doesn't need to know it was me."

"Ms. Johnson, I couldn't have you do that. You do enough for these kids already."

"From 8 a.m.-2:40 p.m., these are my kids too. Anthony deserves nothing but the best, so it's my pleasure to be able to help out whenever I can."

"You are heaven-sent. God bless you, Ms. Johnson. Thank you so much!"

"No worries, Miriam. Take care."

I ended the conversation with her and called the main office to find out what his balance was; $127. I had about twenty-five minutes before the kids had to be picked up from the gym. I went to the bank, withdrew the money, and went to Payomatic to get a money order. I walked into the main office and gave it to the secretary. I'm sure she'd put two and two together, but she knew just like I knew how hard some of our kids have it.

When I got back to the fourth floor, I saw Octavia in the hallway crying and Mr. Greene standing between the gym doors asking her what was wrong. I walked over to them to see what was going on.

"Octavia, what's wrong sweetie?" I asked as I crouched down to her level. I looked at Mr. Greene and gave him the look that asked what happened? He shrugged his shoulders and I mouthed to him *I got her*. It took a few seconds to convince her to walk back with me to the classroom.

When we got into the classroom, I closed the door behind us.

"What's going on?" I asked as I sat down next to her at one of the desks.

She put her head down and continued to cry. I walked to the front of the class and grabbed my box of Kleenex. I pulled two and handed it to her.

"When you're ready to talk, I'm right here."

It took her a few moments, but she dried her tears and began to speak. "I'm afraid my family and I are going to get deported."

I wasn't expecting that. "Why do you think you're going to get deported?"

She handed me her phone and showed me the recent news that Trump will be deporting people who are here illegally. I truly hate that this man is now in office. This is a sensitive topic and one I have to do more research on and cover in class for social studies. In the meantime, I am going to need help from the school support team.

"I'm going to help you as much as I can to ensure that this won't be the case for you and your family," I said as I patted her back.

"That's not all, Ms. Johnson," she said as tears continued to pour down her face. My sister texted me and said that our aunt and uncle were just taken. Someone reported that they were working at the diner illegally and they raided it. What is going to happen to my cousins? They don't even know what's happening." I held her as she cried into my arms. My heart broke and I felt helpless. I didn't know much about this and how I could be of any help. All I knew was that I had to do something.

After a few minutes of letting her cry in my arms, an idea hit me. "Do you mind if I reach out to Mr. Jones and Ms. Santana?" Mr. Jones is the school's guidance counselor and Ms. Santana is the school social worker.

"Are you sure they can help? I don't want this to make matters worse," she said as she wiped away her tears.

"You'll be in the best hands with them. They have more resources and connections than I do. I would not recommend them if I did not think they would be of great help. Do you trust me?"

"Ms. Johnson, you know I do."

"Great. So let's get you the help you need."

I called Mr. Jones' office and he said he needed a few minutes, but he will meet us down at Ms. Santana's office. I asked Mr. Green if he could hold on to my students for a few extra minutes while I took Octavia downstairs.

Mr. Jones must have already called Ms. Santana because when we walked through the door, she already had Octavia's file on her desk. Mr. Jones joined us a few minutes after. Octavia and I sat in silence for a bit as they discussed possible resources. After a while, they told me they'll take over and that they'll keep me updated. Octavia stayed downstairs with them and answered questions. I said a silent prayer as I walked back upstairs. Based on what I gathered from what they were discussing, she was in the perfect hands.

The rest of the day flew by and I was grateful that it did. I was ready to head home to unwind. Stephan had a staff meeting after work so he wouldn't be home until later. That gave me time to go food shopping for dinner and finalize our weekend trip.

The supermarket was more crowded than I expected. My watch read 4:15 p.m. I guess everyone was trying to get things for dinner. Today has been a busy day for both Steph and me, so we weren't able to discuss dinner options. I guess tonight's choice is all on me.

I walked through each aisle and still had no idea what to make. I pulled out my phone and checked my saved images on Instagram. I'm always bookmarking things and I'm sure I have a few food images that can help me decide. It took me less than five minutes to decide what to cook for dinner. Seafood! I picked up some jumbo shrimps and asked the guy in the seafood department for a couple of pieces of whiting fillets. I grabbed my seasonings for the seafood, two boxes of Goya yellow rice, some olives to throw in the rice, corn on the cob, and string beans. I think that would be enough. My stomach growled at just the thought of eating. Before getting on the line, I picked up some of Stephan's favorite snacks, some fruits for us to grab and go for the week, and a couple of other little things we needed for the house.

I was home in no time. Before I started working on dinner, I stripped out of my work clothes, took a quick shower, and threw on a pair of leggings and a t-shirt. Stephan should be home around seven o'clock, which means I have a little less than two hours to have dinner ready. Before washing and cleaning my seafood, I closed my bedroom door and put on a pot of water. My grandmother taught me to put cinnamon sticks into a pot of boiling water when frying fish. I hated how the scent of seafood stuck to our clothes in the house. Boiling cinnamon sticks masked the smell of seafood.

Dinner was coming along great and the house smelled amazing. I pulled out my MacBook while the food was finishing and started looking into our weekend getaway. This weekend was Memorial Day weekend and thank God Stephan and I was both off the following Monday. I had to decide whether or not it made sense to leave from Friday afternoon, come back Sunday, and rest on Monday. Then there was the option of resting on Friday after work, leaving Saturday and coming back on Monday. It all depends on the pricing and if rooms were available. I grabbed my notebook and a pen to write down the options, pricing, and any other comparisons I found while searching.

After searching for a while, I decided that the Harrah's hotel in Atlantic City was our best option. It was going to cost a pretty penny, but we expected it since it was a holiday weekend. Steph and I haven't been away in a while, it was needed for both of us. I decided to splurge a bit and book the hotel from Friday until Monday. We can leave at a decent time on Monday to beat traffic and still be home at a reasonable hour.

As soon as I entered my payment information and clicked submit, my phone lit up, alerting me that I made a purchase over five hundred dollars. Ouch! Stephan would be paying for everything else that weekend. I did my part. Speaking of Stephan, I heard him put the keys through the door. I got up to check on my fish. Dinner should be done in a few minutes.

"Smells good in here, baby," he said as he walked in and kissed me on my forehead. "What made you decide on seafood tonight? This is usually a weekend dish for us."

"We didn't get to discuss dinner today so I was walking around the supermarket clueless. Thank God for Instagram and all the foods I save to my bookmark. I saw a picture of seafood from Bed-Stuy Fish Fry and decided to cook some seafood tonight. Now that I think of it, I could've just went to Bed-Stuy Fish Fry on Utica and picked up dinner from them instead of cooking."

"But I love your cooking and I love coming home to watch you cook," he said as he slid his arm around my waist and pulled me in for a kiss.

"Now that's the kind of greeting I was waiting for," I said kissing him back.

"There's a lot more where that came from," he said as he kissed me again.

"Well, that will have to wait until after dinner, which is almost finished so get situated."

It still amazes me how much he could make my body tingle just by his touch. I had to stop myself from staring at him as he walked towards our bedroom.

Dinner was ready a few minutes after. I set the table for us and poured out our drinks.

"Babe, the food is ready!"

"I'm coming!" he called back as I heard his footsteps coming my way.

After saying our grace, we dug in. Silence filled the room for a few minutes as we both enjoyed my home-cooked meal.

"So how was your day?" I asked breaking the silence.

"Beyond busy. I could not wait to get out of there. How was yours? We barely got to speak today."

"Mine was busy as well. A lot happened." I filled Stephan in on my day and it felt good getting it off my chest. I felt useless not being able to help Octavia the way I would have loved to, but the comforting words of Stephan made me feel a bit better. He reminded me that I could have just listened to her and never said anything to the counselor and social worker. He was right, this wasn't my field of expertise, and handing it off to the experts was one of the best things I could've done for her. I have to trust that God will work things out for her and her family.

Dinner was done, dishes were washed, our weekend getaway was officially booked and planned and all that was left to do was to relax. Stephan and I were lounging on the couch eating a cup of cookie dough ice cream. We decided on making tonight a movie night. I scanned the On Demand movie channel as we searched for a good movie to watch. After a few scrolls, we decided to watch *What Men Want* starring Taraji P. Henson. We were supposed to have watched it in the movies when it first released but never got to. Now was our time.

CHAPTER 16
KRISTEN

Friday was finally here and Stephan was waiting for me to get off from work so we can start our weekend getaway. I didn't drive today because I knew he'd be picking me up straight from work and we'd be making our way to Atlantic City. I have been excited all day for this moment. The day dragged of course, but I was determined not to let that bring down my energy. I waited at the clock for 2:45 p.m. to hit so I can clock out. It wasn't like me to be one of the first teachers to leave, but today I wasted no time. The staff in the main office laughed at me as I impatiently waited for the long hand to make its way around the clock. They thought I was just eager to get home and get away from my students. I will gladly let them believe that. They did not need to know that I was eager to start my weekend vacation with the best thing that has happened to me. I'm not answering any emails this weekend or grading any papers or homework. This weekend was going to be about Stephan and me. I even gave Monique and Latrice a heads up that I would have limited access to my phone this weekend. I want it to be all about us. Even though we live together, we haven't had this much alone time in a while.

It was officially 2:45 p.m. as I slid my card through the time clock. I grabbed my bags and headed towards the exit. Right on time, Stephan was double-parked and waiting for me.

"Hey there, handsome," I said as I threw my bags in the back seat and hopped in the front.

"Hey, beautiful. How was your day?" he asked after I leaned in and kissed him.

"It was boring and dragged! I could not wait to get out of there. How was your day?"

The rest of the car ride was great and relaxing. Stephan filled me in on his day and I gave him the latest updates on my kids. Midday traffic was a bit heavier than usual, but as long as we were heading in the right direction, I didn't care.

"I got some fun stuff planned for us this weekend," Stephan said as he handed me my food from the McDonald's drive-through we stopped at.

"Like what? I thought this weekend was supposed to be us relaxing and just enjoying each other's company?" I was a bit confused by this 'fun stuff'. I chose Harrah's hotel so we didn't have to leave it. They had everything included. The pool, Jacuzzi's, restaurants, gambling, and parties. You name it, they had it.

"Just wait and see. I promise it's nothing big. We are going to get a lot of needed relaxation time, but I also want to have some fun while we are there as well. Can you just trust me on this?" He looked at me with pleading eyes and I gave in.

"Yes, I'll trust you."

CHAPTER 17
STEPHAN

Kristen did not seem too happy when I told her I had some fun stuff planned for her. I know this trip is supposed to be a mini getaway with us relaxing and enjoying each other's company, and I promise it will be just that. I just wanted to spice up some things while we were here.

As we approached the front desk to check-in, I noticed that they now have kiosk machines for easy check-ins. That just made my first surprise workout even better. I convinced Kristen to wait on the line to get our casino cards registered as I got us checked in.

I was finished checking in just in time to meet her on the casino card line. We have been here before, but of course, neither of us knew where our reward cards were. We gave them our identification cards and they were able to print out new cards for us.

We grabbed our luggage as we headed toward the Waterfront Tower elevators.

"Babe, why are we heading to this elevator? Our room is located on the Coastal Tower side." She looked at me with pure confusion and I couldn't help but laugh inside.

"You said you trust me right?" I challenged her.

"I do, but..."

"No buts allowed. Let's go," I said as we continued walking towards the elevator.

When we arrived on our floor, I was anxious to see how she would react.

"Would you like to do the honors?" I asked her while holding the room key between my two fingers.

She didn't hesitate in taking the room key from me and opening our room door.

"Oh my gosh! Steph, this is beautiful!" She turned to face me with tears threatening to leave her eyes. I couldn't lie, this room was even more beautiful in person than in the pictures.

We took a tour of the suite together and the deeper we walked into the room, the more in awe we were. My favorite was the pool table that was set up in the living room area. She loved how huge and spacious the bathroom was. They even had a Jacuzzi in it. The view was beyond amazing and the bedroom was huge! We were going to have a great time here.

"How did you pull this off? Wait, scratch that, how can we even afford this? Did you rob a bank? Oh Lord, my baby done robbed his own bank!" I couldn't help but laugh at how dramatic she was being.

"I did not rob a bank, silly. Let's just say, it's good knowing people in high places. I was able to pull a few strings for us to get this room. Check your account in a few business days. You should see a refund from what you paid for the other room."

One of my long-term clients has a partnership with this hotel and when we spoke about my weekend plans, he insisted that I rented out this suite. When I looked at the price and nearly choked on my sprite, I had to respectfully decline. That's when he told me about his partnership. When he logged in with his account information and his discounts were applied, I could not believe how dirt-cheap I got this room for. I refused to tell Kristen all of this, I needed her to bask in the moment. I couldn't help but enjoy the feeling of how happy she was thinking that I had to jump through hoops to book this room for us. I'll tell her the truth one day, just not today.

"This room is beyond beautiful. Thank you so much for this, baby." She leaned up and kissed me.

"Anything for you," I said kissing her back.

"Now what shall we do first?" she asked as she continued to roam the suite.

"Well there's a few things we can get into before the night is over, but there's one thing I've been dying to do since we walked into this room."

"Oh, yea? What's that?" she asked.

"I can show you better than I can tell you." I led her to the lounge area and pushed her onto the pool table.

"Babe!" She squealed. "What if the table breaks? Let's just go to the bed."

She tried to get up but I pushed her back down.

"Shhh, it won't break. Just trust me and let's enjoy this moment."

We went from the pool table, the loveseat, the bed, and ended in the Jacuzzi. Let's just say that I'm going to owe my client a huge thank you gift.

It was after nine and we were contemplating where we should have dinner. We finally decided on *AC Burger*. Everything we needed including the restaurants was all inside of this huge hotel. I put on a pair of pants and a T-shirt and Kris put on a pair of leggings and one of those long cardigans that she loved.

There wasn't much of a line to wait on to get inside. We were seated in less than five minutes. The issue was deciding on what to eat from the menu. Everything on it sounded so good. By the third time the waiter came over, we were ready to order. I ordered the Cheesesteak with waffle fries and Kristen ordered the sweet chili tenders and tater tots with melted cheese. I knew she was going to order that. She is so predictable; her love for tater tots is real.

"I'm so happy we finally pulled through with this plan and made it happen!" she said.

The excitement written all over her face made me happy as well that we were able to take advantage of this weekend. Living together is one thing, but it's important as a couple for us to do things like this when we get the opportunity to.

"It's been way too long since we've been away. Even if it's just for the weekend."

"Agreed. I wish we could do things like this more often," she said as her mouth formed into a pout.

"We can, it doesn't always have to be a plane ride

somewhere. We can discuss possible places another time, but there are nearby getaways we can do once in a while."

"Yes, I've always wanted for us to take a trip to the Poconos, but that's a trip that needs to be planned well in advance because I want us to rent a cabin and I want it to be like a couples retreat."

"You've been watching too many of those Tyler Perry movies. But yes, that does sound like a fun getaway."

"It will be, trust me. Now that Latrice has an official man, I can finally plan a trip for us to do together. I've wanted to do a group trip for the longest, but it never felt right doing it without her."

"I get it. I'm sure she would have felt some type of way if you did plan one and she didn't get an invite."

"She would've gotten an invite, but I know she would've turned it down because she was never that serious with any of her previous partners."

The food came just in time. Everything smelled so good. We both could not wait to dive in. First, grace.

"Your chicken tenders look nice and crispy," I said damn near drooling over her plate and mine.

"Here take a bite greedy and don't ask for another!" She dipped the tender in ranch dressing before feeding it to me. I was right; this tender was amazing!

"Mmm," we both said at the same time. Her enjoyment was from the tater tots she just tasted. Wait until she tasted those tenders! I should have ordered that for myself.

"This is so good!" she said as she finally took a bite of her tenders.

"It really is. You want to take a bite of my cheesesteak?" I asked as I held it for her to bite.

"Eww. No thanks. I can smell the onions all over it. You did that on purpose!" The pout on her face was back and I couldn't but laugh at how cute she looked when she did that.

"I forgot to tell her no onions. Well, more for me!" I bit into my sandwich. It was good and well seasoned. It didn't compare to her tenders though. We'll definitely have to eat from here again so I can order it for myself.

"Selfish! Don't ask to taste nothing else off my plate," she said giving me the side-eye.

"That's fine. I usually just take what I want." And just like that, I stole a tater tot just to get under her skin. She tried to knock it from my fork with her fork, but I was too fast for her. That tater tot was good. We are definitely coming back here.

Dinner was great. We left stuffed and satisfied. Instead of going back to the hotel room, we decided to roam the place and walk off our fullness. We walked through the casino but left after a few minutes. There were too many smokers there and it was filling our lungs. Second-hand smoking was not for me. After walking for a bit, we remembered that there were two different parts of the casino. One was for smoking and another section for nonsmoking. This place was huge.

"I want to play the penny machines for a bit," she said. She interlocked her fingers with mine as we went to the machines.

"Knock yourself out. Don't go betting our rent money though," I said jokingly.

We both sat next to each other and each put ten dollars into our machines. It did not take me long to lose my whole ten-dollar bill. I refused to put any more money into that machine. I just sat and watched Kristen win and lose back her money over and over again. She ended up cashing out $32.15 and I ended up cashing out my pride.

We played a few more machines. Tonight must be her lucky night. She has been losing money and gaining back double of what she put in. After losing my money in three different machines, I decided to stop playing. I ordered drinks and watched her addiction rise.

"I can't believe I won this much! $479!" she said excitedly as we went to cash out her money.

"Are you sharing your wins or what?" I asked while giving her the side-eye.

"Nope, you didn't help me win, so you don't get no parts of this."

"That's fine. Lunch on you tomorrow then."

"I guess I can do that," she said winking at me as she counted her cash. "Let's go check out the ice cream spot." She grabbed my hand and pulled me in that direction.

On the way to the ice cream spot, I spotted the sports center area. They didn't have this the last time we were here. They had a big area full of leather lounge chairs. There were multiple games on. I had to sit and watch for a few. Kristen followed my lead and didn't complain, thankfully. She knew either my love for sports would have led us here eventually or she wanted to test out how comfortable those chairs were herself. Either way, I was grateful.

I didn't want to be inconsiderate of our time together. "Let's go see what kind of ice cream they have."

The ice cream spot had too many options. Good thing I wasn't hungry because it would've made my decision even harder. Kristen ordered a scoop of chocolate chip cookie dough and a scoop of red velvet ice cream. I decided on pistachio and rocky road. All this ice cream and all these flavors, our stomachs were bound to be rumbling before the night was over. Kristen was more lactose intolerant than I was. My poor nose tonight is going to suffer.

With our ice creams in hand, we toured the rest of the hotel. We got to see the indoor pool and Jacuzzi through the glass windows. This place was bigger than I remembered. We couldn't go in because the pool area was closed. One of the workers said that they were prepping for a party tonight. I looked at Kris to see if she wanted to attend, but she had that tired lazy look on her face. He assured us that there was another pool party tomorrow and that Saturdays were usually the biggest nights. He said Ja Rule would be there performing on Sunday. We'll definitely be in attendance for that.

On our way back to our rooms, we spotted the other eating places, the gift shops, and all the other couples and families that were there.

"Next time we come, we should bring Latrice and Mo with

their significant others. Make this a couple's trip," she said as excitement filled her face.

"You'd have to arrange that, but I think that would be fun. I'm sure the fellas would love the sports center area on the other side. I can picture it now, you ladies going to get massages while we sit back and watch whatever game is on."

"Yes! I'm going to plan when we get back. This place is too beautiful not to enjoy with the girls."

"Whatever makes you happy, babe."

Back in our hotel room, we sat in the lounge area with the big screen TV and ate the rest of our ice cream. We were snuggled up on the couch, watching Think Like a Man Too. Every time we watched this movie together, the wedding questions would always come; *could you see us having a wedding in Vegas? Do you think we would have a lot of people at our wedding? I already know what colors I want for my wedding, but what colors did you have in mind? What kind of food should we serve?*

Of course, I want to marry her one day, but the wedding planning was going to be all on her. I trust her judgment. I'm sure she'd want it to be perfect, so for the most part, I'll just be agreeing with whatever she wants. The only thing I told her that I want to have an input on was the food and cake.

I must have fallen asleep shortly after the movie started. When I woke up the couples were all in jail. I probably would have slept through the night if Kristen's farts didn't wake me up. This was going to be a fun night.

CHAPTER 18
KRISTEN

Steph and I must've been tired because we both fell asleep on the couch. When I woke up, the clock read 1:10 a.m. I woke him up as well and guided him to the king-sized bed. I don't know what mattress company this was from, but it was the most comfortable mattress I've ever laid on. Before I knew it, I was in a deep sleep.

The sun was shining brightly through our hotel window. I'm glad I remembered to pack my bath bombs from Lush. I was going to enjoy a nice warm bath while he slept. I got the water to the perfect temperature, turned off the lights, and slid into the tub. I had my air pods in so I could enjoy some smooth R&B without waking him. The warmness from the water and the aroma and colors from the bath bomb relaxed my body instantly. It's not every day I get to enjoy a warm bubble bath. I was going to take advantage of this moment. I closed my eyes as I let the smoothness of Jhene Aiko's voice take me to another place.

I didn't want to get out even though the wrinkles in my hands and toes told me that it was time to. I convinced myself that five more minutes wouldn't hurt. Besides, I was on vacation. It was only right that I get to pamper myself and get some self-care time in. Closing my eyes, I leaned back and enjoyed my last few minutes of warmth and relaxation.

"I see you started the party without me," Stephan said as he walked into the bathroom, scaring me half to death.

"Yup. You were sleeping. I didn't want to wake you. But the party is over now, I'm about to get out," I said as I started draining the water.

"Damn, guess I got bad timing then."

"Oh hush, it's not like you take baths anyway.'

"That's true, but I wouldn't pass up any opportunity to get wet with you," he said, as he started undressing.

"Why are you taking off your clothes, Mr. Moore?"

"Well, Ms. Johnson, if you must know, I'm about to take a shower. And since you just finished taking a bath, I know you're about to shower as well. Why not kill two birds with one stone? Besides, we are helping the hotel save water if we shower together." He gave me the naughtiest look ever.

"You and I both know damn well that you don't care about their water bill. Good try," I said as I washed the rest of the water and bubbles down the drain. I turned on the showerhead as I rinsed off. I turned to grab my washcloth and bar soap just as Stephan stepped into the shower with me. "Watch where you're poking that thing," I said while looking down at his package.

"You don't like it when I do this?" He poked me again.

"This is why I shower alone. You don't know how to act."

"Sounds like I need to be punished," he said as he wrapped his arms around me from behind.

I allowed myself to sink back into his arms. Between the

warm water and his warm embrace, I didn't want this moment to end. He started singing Sweet Lady by Tyrese in my ear. I rarely get to hear him sing and when he does it makes me melt instantly. Stephan has such a beautiful voice, but he never thought to pursue anything with it. I allowed myself to live in the moment and soak it all in. We swayed slowly back and forth, as he continued to sing.

Turning me to face him he said, "I don't think you truly understand how much I love you. I wake up to you every morning and thank God for you. Even when we get into our little arguments, I know we'll get past it. I know it sounds cliché, but I can't see myself with anyone else. You complete me, you make me whole and I'm forever grateful to have you as my soulmate."

If I didn't know any better and giving the circumstances of us being in the shower, I would've thought he was about to propose to me. Part of me wishes that was what was happening. His words not only made the tears form in my eyes, but I felt how genuine it was.

"I'm not sure where that came from, but I loved every bit of it. You show me daily how much you love me. That is something that I never second-guess. But hearing it right now feels amazing. I thank God for you on a daily as well. There is no place I'd rather be than right here with you. My love for you will never dry out."

"You'll still love me even when I'm old and gray?" he asked while drying my tears.

"I'll still love you when your old, gray, and with sagging balls." We both busted out laughing.

He pulled me into him for a long and passionate kiss. It was only a matter of time before his hands started roaming my body. I knew what this was going to lead to and I was more than ready to enjoy it.

♥♥♥

After our shower, we were dressed in our bathing suits and heading down to the pool area. I had on a one-piece black and white bathing suit with a white cover-up. Stephan had on black trunks with white lines at the side and a white tank top. While we were in the elevator, I took a few selfies of us. We don't get moments like this often, so I was pleased to see that he was willing to match with me and take pictures.

The indoor pool area was huge and beautiful. The temperature was perfect, not too hot and not too cold. Since we were both hungry, we decided to sit at the bar first and order food. We decided on getting quesadillas. I ordered the shrimp quesadilla and he got the buffalo chicken one. When the food arrived, both of our mouths were watering. As usual, he just had to take a bite of mine. He knows I don't like spicy food so I didn't even bother to taste his. The buffalo sauce was so strong that it burnt my nose. I wouldn't dare set myself up for that. We sat by the bar side, stuffed and satisfied. We had the best bartender; he kept refilling our drinks and said it was on the house. Stephan tipped him well as a thank you from us. Our bartender was a great conversationalist. We spoke about everything from New York to New Jersey, politics, food, cars, work, family, etc. Stephan entertained him more than I did. I'm not sure if he was flirting with Stephan or me. Maybe it was the both of us, who knows. For free drinks, he could flirt all he wanted.

After we said our goodbyes and promised to be back

tomorrow, we decided to join in on the volleyball game that a few adults were starting up in the pool. One of the staff members were setting up the net inside the pool as the rest chose which team they would be on. It ended up being guys versus girls.

"I hope you're ready to get that ass beat," Stephan said.

"Loser pays for dinner tonight," I said.

"Deal."

When we finally found two empty lounge chairs, I pulled out my phone and seen that it was almost three o'clock. We must have been playing for almost two hours. Time does fly when you're having fun. It was even more fun because the women won and now Stephan has to pay for dinner.

I found a comfortable spot to lay down as I grabbed my book out of my bag. I decided to catch up on reading while Stephan caught up on work emails. Even though we were on a mini getaway, he still had to stay in the know with what was going on. While he did that, I flipped through the pages of my new favorite James Patterson book, *Liar Liar*. It was the third part of a series. The suspense always had me on the edge of my seat. I secretly wanted Stephan to take his time in checking in with work so I can enjoy a few pages before we got into our next activity, whatever that may be.

God must have been on my side because Steph received a phone call from work and it sounded important. That means even more reading time while he figured out whatever was going on. People never understood how I could be a teacher and love to read as much as I do. They would often ask me how I could love reading when I have to read lesson plans and grade work all day. My response is usually the same, the reading I do for work is to help me keep my lights on and pay my rent on time. The reading I do on my own time is for my enjoyment. Reading has become one of my favorite hobbies. The irony is that I hated reading as I child. You could not get me to read even the title of an article.

I'm not sure how much time has passed, but my stomach grumbled just as Stephan asked me if I wanted to get something to eat. He must have read my mind or heard my stomach. We decided on going to AC Burger again. The line was a bit longer this time, but we weren't in a rush to go anywhere so we decided to wait. Stephan asked me if I was ok with waiting in line without him. He had to take a call from Samantha and he couldn't discuss people's personal information in the ears of strangers. He already warned me that there were going to be moments where he had to check in with work. It didn't bother me because I know how important his job is.

The line was moving faster than I expected. I texted Stephan to tell him that we had one more person ahead of us. I could see him from where I was standing but he wasn't looking in my direction. He looked at his phone and texted me back that he'll be over there in two minutes. Before I could even respond, the host asked me if I was dining alone.

"No. Table for two, please. He's right over there, walking this way," I said as I pointed Stephan out.

"Make that a table for four please." I damned near jumped out of my skin when I felt someone breathing down my neck.

I turned around to face the familiar voice. Latrice was standing behind me with Trent by her side.

"I hope you don't mind us crashing your getaway. Stephan thought it would be fun for us to join you guys," Latrice said as she hugged me.

"Oh really. He sure didn't run that suggestion by me." I did not mean for it to come out the way that it did. I always love being around Latrice, but this was supposed to be our getaway from everyone. If I wanted to share this long overdue mini-vacation with everyone then I would have invited her myself and told Monique to come as well.

Stephan's facial expression read that he was sorry that he did not tell me ahead of time. He greeted them as we walked to our tables. He grabbed my hand and squeezed it while planting a kiss on my cheek. I know he can tell that I am a bit disappointed but I know his intentions were good. I decided to just let it be as I squeezed his hand back.

Dinner was going great. Steph and I filled them in on all the foods we had and what we enjoyed the most. We ended up ordering way too much food for the table, but luckily we have a fridge and a microwave in our suite. No food will be wasted on my watch.

Latrice and I left Stephan at the table as we walked to the bar to order milkshakes to go. We could've very well ordered it from our tables, but I know Latrice too well by now. When she suggested that we go make a to-go order, I knew she wanted to talk privately.

"So, are you that disappointed that Stephan invited us to come?"

"I won't lie, I wasn't expecting to spend my mini-vacation with you and Trent, but I'm kind of happy now that you're here."

"We were hesitant on whether we should come or not especially when I found out that you didn't know and for it to be a surprise. I know how you feel about surprises, but Stephan was very persuasive and felt it would be good for me to be here just in case he had any moments where he had to get things done for work."

"I get it and I appreciate him for thinking about me and not wanting me to be alone. So far, it's only for a few minutes here and there. Nothing too major," I told her as we thanked the lady who made our milkshakes. We grabbed the milkshakes and headed back to the guys.

I was appreciative of Trice wanting to make sure I was ok that they were there. This was supposed to be our little mini romantic getaway that I won for the bet we made watching Power. Having my best friend here does not mean it still cannot be romantic. It's not like they are sharing a room with us. We will still have our alone time, I hope.

We made it back to the table and decided to all head back to the suite to play some games and drink. We made a stop at the liquor store that was inside Harrah's and purchased liquor, snacks, and mixers. Trent slid a pack of condoms on the counter, but only I noticed. When he saw the smirk on my face, we both silently laughed.

Back in our room, Latrice and Trent were amazed at how huge and beautiful our suite was. I could not help but be in amaze with them. Steph went all out to make sure I was enjoying myself this vacation. How can I even be mad at him for inviting them when he has gone above and beyond to make sure I was satisfied. It's one thing to tell Latrice how beautiful this room is, but for her to witness it in person is so much better.

After they toured every part of the suite, it was time for the games to begin. Latrice and I prepared the drinks as the guy's set up the first game, 5 Second Rule.

We started playing couple against couple and ended playing girls against guys. Latrice and Trent beat us in the couples round, but Latrice and I beat the guys by thirteen points. She and I together are undefeated. Trent hasn't been around the both of us long enough to know that we never lose when she and I are on the same team. It's so much easier to win guessing games when you know each other like the back of your hand.

Next game, Taboo. The men were not ok with us being on the same team again after we beat them. We agreed to switch it up and make it fun. Trent and I were on the same team now and Trice and Steph were now partners. We won the first round but they slaughtered us the last two rounds. Every time your team lost, you had to take a shot. I needed Trice back on my team. All these shots were adding up and I didn't want to have a bad hangover tomorrow.

We decided to move on to the final game, Black Card Revoked. Now that I think of it, Stephan had this vacation planned out. He and I couldn't play some of these games by ourselves. I mean we could, but it damn sure wouldn't have been this fun. He knew exactly what he was doing when he told me to pack our games.

Black Card Revoked didn't require us to be in partners, so

it was every man for themselves. It was Trent's idea for us to take a shot for every question we got wrong. Before the game began, we ate our leftovers and drunk a ton of water to soak up as much liquor as possible. I enforced that request. Everyone swore up and down that they wouldn't get too drunk and that they knew their black card game was strong. I was not taking any chances.

Not even ten minutes into the game and Latrice already had taken three shots. I knew what I was doing when I made everyone eat. Every shot she took was followed by water. No one was getting sick on my watch, fingers crossed. I can't lie, some of these questions had me lost. Stephan's question had us all lost for a bit and forced us to think. The question was, *In what state did Rosa Parks sit in the back of the bus?* The answer is *Montgomery, Alabama.* The other choices also sounded real country, which had us stuck. Stephan looked at me for help and I told him just because I teach history does not mean I know all the answers. Let's just say Stephan had to take that shot. I made that mental note of the answer just in case we played this game again and that question came to me.

Thankfully, my question was funny and easy, *Jerome was a playa from where?* Everyone knows how much I love Martin. There's not one episode I haven't seen. I had to put on my Jerome accent and answered, "From the Himalayas!" We had such a good laugh with that one.

We noticed after twenty minutes of playing that we forgot to keep score. After agreeing that we have all taken one shot too many, we continued to play without the drinks. Saving this game for last was a great choice. The tears of laughter that filled the room was going down in our history book.

It was after two in the morning when we finally decided we

have played enough. Trice helped me pack up the games while the guys discarded the drinks and food we devoured. We sat on the comfy couches and talked for a few minutes before we called it a night.

I was beat! Steph stripped down to his boxers and jumped into bed. I joined him after tying down my hair. I wasn't that drunk to not remember what I would look like in the morning if I didn't.

I snuggled up close to Stephan as he scrolled the television looking for something to watch. We finally decided on watching Transformers. It didn't take long for Transformers to be watching us. He fell asleep first and it didn't take me long to follow right after.

CHAPTER 19
STEPHAN

It was Sunday already. Kristen was still asleep when I woke up. As much as we drunk yesterday, I am sure she's going to wake up with a hangover. While she slept, I went downstairs to grab us some breakfast. I could've just ordered room service, but if she woke up with a pounding headache as I did, then Advil was going to be needed. I'm sure room service doesn't provide that. It was our last full day here before we had to head back home tomorrow. I would hate for it to be ruined because we all drunk too much last night.

I texted Trent to tell him that I was picking up some Advil and if he needed any then he could come by our room to get some. Just as I pushed the sent button, I saw him and Latrice sitting by the pool lounge area. I walked up to them and caught the end of their conversation. They were laughing at some of the questions we had from last night's game of Black Card Revoked. Here I am thinking that they were going to wake up with the biggest hangovers and they are sitting right here perfectly fine. So perfectly fine that they started laughing at how terrible I looked. To my defense, they are heavy drinkers. I barely drink and if I do drink, it's usually just a beer.

I left them there still laughing at me. Instead of ordering something heavy and greasy from the bar, I decided to head to the café and get us both a turkey bacon, egg, and cheese sandwich. I grabbed two bottles of orange juice, crackers, and peanuts. I'm not sure what the perfect food is for hangovers so I'm hoping this will do. After paying for our food and drinks, I headed to the convenience store they had and purchased four packets of Advil. Hotels know how to get your money. Back in NY, these packets are a dollar each. Here they are charging $2.25 each. They are lucky it is needed or else I would have left it right on the counter.

When I got back into the room, Kris wasn't in the bed. I opened the bathroom door carefully, hoping I wouldn't find her face buried in the toilet. Instead, she was in the shower singing her life away to some gospel song. I opened the glass door and she jumped. I asked her was she ok and she said she was fine. She said she got my text that I went out to get us food and decided to get her shower out of the way so she can be comfy when she eats.

Usually, I would have just joined her in the shower but seeing how fine she was and how regular Trent and Trice looked had me feeling less of a man. Was I really the only one who had a hangover? I closed back the shower door and did my walk of shame back to bed. I was so concerned about how sick she was going to feel when she woke up that it didn't hit me how sick I was already feeling. The room felt like it was spinning. I just needed to lay down for a bit.

I decided to close my eyes until the room stopped spinning. My stomach felt so uneasy. I was sure at any given moment that I was going to throw up everything I ate in the last twenty-four hours. I accidentally left the bags of everything I bought on the nightstand by Kris' side of the bed. The way my head was feeling, I was not going to be able to reach the bag. If only I had the powers that Matilda had, I would make that bag come to me.

I'm not sure how long my eyes were closed for, but Kristen woke me up out of my sleep when she came out of the bathroom with her gospel music blasting. If looks could kill. I didn't even have the strength to give her a mean look. The slightest movement of my head had the room spinning again.

She walked over to me and asked what was wrong. With my eyes closed, I explained to her everything I was feeling. After all the words left my lips, I was disappointed in myself. I sounded like a little bitch. It was time for me to man up, get my breakfast, pop those pills, and go on with my day.

In the midst of me giving myself a pep talk to get up and get out of the bed, the room started spinning faster and a wave of nausea hit me. I guess I'll be the biggest bitch today. I was not moving out of the bed. Kristen saw how defeated I looked and brought the bag to me. She was my Matilda. I took a few bites of my sandwich, popped two pills, and washed it down with orange juice. Kristen turned off the lights, lowered the television, and let me have my moment of weakness.

My body wouldn't allow me to pretend that I was ok, so I stopped fighting it and decided to nap it off. Before I closed my eyes completely, I told Kris that I booked us both a couple's massage for ten, but I doubt I would be up and ready for it. She told me that I should just cancel it and she would stay in with me. The thought sounded great, but I would feel even worse knowing she spent our last full day in bed watching over me. After a lot of convincing, she called Latrice and asked if she would like to join her. Lucky for her, Trent had some documents he needed to catch up on and would use that time to do so. We agreed that we would all link up for a late lunch. Once I knew she was taken care of, it was lights out for me.

I woke up feeling much better than I did when I first laid

down. The lights were still turned off in the room and all that was on was the television. Kris wasn't back yet. I looked at the clock on the nightstand and it read 3:47 p.m. I can't believe I slept for that many hours. I checked my phone to see if I had a missed call or text from Kris, and I did.

Hey, babe. You were still knocked out when I got back to the room from my massage. BTW, it was amazing! Thank you so much for that. Wish you were there to enjoy it with me. Trice and I decided to sit by the poolside. Come join us when you wake. Love you, lata!

I took my time getting out of bed and showering. I searched inside my suitcase for a shirt and some shorts to throw on. After being semi satisfied with my look, I placed my hotel room card in my wallet and went to go meet them.

I spotted Trent before I spotted the ladies. Thank God they told him to come too. I don't know if I'd be able to handle Kris and Trice by myself. They were so engrossed in deep conversation that they didn't even see me until I sat at the edge of Kris' lounge chair.

"Look who it is, the walking dead," Latrice said. Of course, she would be the one to start with me.

"Leave him alone!" Kris laughs as she leans in to kiss me and pulls me up towards her.

"Fine! Thanks for the massage, brother. It was great seeing how sexy your woman looked as a strong man massages every muscle in her body," Latrice says.

"She's kidding, Steph," Kris says as she rubs my arm up and down. "No strong man was massaging my body. We both had women masseuse."

I didn't say anything. I just sat there and placed Kristen's feet into my lap, giving them a gentle massage.

It didn't take long for things to return to normal. Trent and I started talking about sports and the ladies spoke about whatever piqued their interest.

After everyone witnessed the embarrassing sound of my stomach growling, we all decided to grab something to eat. On the way out of the pool area, we spotted a huge poster out hanging from one of the glass windows. Ja Rule was going to be performing here tonight. The ladies went inside to find out how to get tickets to the pool party/concert that was happening. They explained that the advanced tickets were sold out. They suggested we get there before ten because the lines get long. Plus, if we wanted a spot closer to the stage then getting their early was our best bet. Little did they know, I already got advanced tickets for us, thanks to my connections.

We decided on grabbing a large pie of extra cheese pizza with half pepperoni and half BBQ chicken. We also got two orders of wings. One with mild sauce and the other with chili sauce. Both cooked well done.

By the time we got back to the suite to eat all this goodness, it was almost six o'clock. Knowing Latrice and Kristen, it was going to take them a while to get ready, so we didn't waste any time eating. We chatted for a bit before Latrice and Trent left for their rooms.

Kristen decided she wanted to take a nap before she had to get ready. I told her I would wake her up around eight-thirty. Her taking a nap was perfect for me. It gave me enough time to get something's situated before we had to head to the concert tonight.

CHAPTER 20
KRISTEN

The bad thing about taking a good nap is when someone wakes you up. I was having a good dream for once and Stephan had to ruin it. Yes, I told him to wake me up around 8:30 p.m., but I wish he could have read my mind and seen that I needed at least ten to fifteen more minutes. I'm going to be highly pissed if this concert isn't worth breaking my nap.

What I should have thought about before I decided to take my nap was what I am going to wear. Of course, like most women, I overpacked. Yet I still have no clue what I want to put on. I laid down in bed for a few minutes, just trying to think about what was in my luggage.

I pulled out two dresses. My red dress from *Fashion Nova* and my black dress from *Pretty Little Thing*. Stephan was adamant that I pack these two dresses, so of course to make our last night special; I'll be wearing one of them. I laid out both dresses on the couch and pulled out my black shoes to wear with my red dress and my royal blue pumps to wear with my black dress. I had to get my duffel bag out of the closet so I could retrieve my black clutch and royal blue wristlet. I knew I overpacked, but this was way too many clothes for a quick weekend trip.

My hair! Now I'm regretting Steph waking me up at 8:30 p.m. It should have been 8 p.m. Good thing I washed my hair last night. I've had it in medium twist and pulled back into a bun. My hair should be fully dry and stretched. That's if I decided to go with wearing my curls out.

After showering, I sat at the edge of the bed and watched Stephan get dressed while I put on my lotion. We decided to color coordinate and our best option was my black dress. He put on his black straight jeans, black dressy shoes, and a sexy button-down blue shirt. I decided to keep my makeup somewhat lite and simple. The only thing I did that was a little extra was my blue lip and blue eye shadow. I had to do something to make the blue pop out a bit. As for my hair, since I went with my off the shoulder black dress, the best option is my famous half up and half down hairstyle. Instead of putting the top half in a bun, I pulled it into a high ponytail and let my curls up top and in the back hang loose.

After taking pictures in our full-length mirror, Steph and I were ready to go. It's not every day we get to dress up and step out. I am praying that tonight is a great fun night. Steph may not want to drink due to how bad his hangover was, but I sure am! We get to go to a concert and not have to drive to get there or drive to go back home? Oh, I am definitely taking advantage. Latrice told me that she and Trent were already downstairs waiting in line. I am really starting to like their relationship. Trice is never on time to anything and I am pretty sure I have Trent to thank for us not having to wait on her tonight. By the time we spotted them, it was 10:07 p.m. The staff from earlier were not lying. People were out here lined up.

"I hope they let us in. It seems like it's going to be pretty packed," I said as I leaned in to kiss them both on the cheek.

"I do too. It will be a shame to have gotten dressed up just to miss this concert," Latrice said.

We stood in line for a good ten minutes before one of the

workers made an announcement, "If you have tickets please step forward and have your IDs out. Everyone else will need to remain on the line."

"Good thing these heels are comfortable," I said.

"Now, baby, you should know your man got us tickets," Stephan said as he reached into his back pocket and pulled out four tickets.

If I wasn't scared of getting kicked out, I would've screamed much louder than I did. Stephan went out of his way to make this mini-vacation a great one. Tonight, he will know how grateful I am. Snapping me out of my nasty thoughts, he took my hand and led us to the line for those who have tickets. Latrice and Trent were right behind us.

We were on the line for less than five minutes before we were making our way to the front of the stage. The way they turned the pool area into a concert scene was beautiful. The stage was lit with bright lights and the DJ was playing some good ole old school music. According to the flyer, the concert should be starting at eleven. We had a little less than thirty minutes before Ja Rule hit the stage.

"You ladies want something to drink from the bar? We can't all go because we have to hold our spots," Trent asked.

"We can go and you guys stay here," Latrice said as she grabbed my hand and led the way. "We know what you both drink, we got this!"

"I want something good to drink tonight," I said as we reached the bar and tried to get to the attention of one of the bartenders.

"Same, but I want something girly, nothing strong. This is going to be a night that I need to remember."

"Since when do you care about remembering a night? Where is my best friend, I don't recognize this woman in front of me," I said jokingly.

"Well, it's not every night that I get to be on a quick getaway with my bestie, her man, and my new one. Plus, this is Ja Rule, you know I love him. I already freed up my memory on my phone because I have to record his performances."

I guess she was right, tonight was special. I hope he performs my favorite song, *Put it On Me*. I think I would lose my cool if Vita and Lil' Mo came out to perform with him. Just the thought of it has my anxiety through the roof. Latrice must have been reading my mind because she asked me the same thing. We would look like some grown-ass groupies if they performed that song. How could he not though? It's like one of his biggest hits! Stephan and I always perform that song when we go to Karaoke. All of our friends know that is our signature song.

We decided on ordering two Amaretto Sours for us and two Jack and Cokes for the guys. I tried not to spill our drinks while we walked back to the guys. It was jammed pack in here. While walking, I saw someone who looked just like Monique. If I didn't have two drinks in my hand I would've snapped a picture of her. They say everyone has a lookalike and I just found hers. She would have loved being at this concert but would not have loved how crowded it was. She is always on edge when it comes to large crowds. I guess that comes with the job. It was about five minutes left before the concert was expected to begin.

Eleven o'clock on the dot, the DJ cut the music and introduced Ja Rule. He came out rapping to *Holla Holla*. The crowd went crazy when we all joined in and screamed 'It's Murder!' You would think after all these years that we would forget the lyrics, nope! He performed hit after hit. I thought we ladies were going crazy, but these grown-ass men in the crowd were making more noise than us.

The concert was going great! I was sweating like crazy and I'm sure my curls weren't popping like they were when I first left the suite. Right on cue, they broke for a quick intermission. The guys saved our spots as Trice and I rushed to the bathroom to freshen up. I needed to beat the lines and get back so I wouldn't miss a second of the concert.

Just like I thought, my curls, or lack thereof, is proof that I have been sweating. I decided to put water in my hands and comb through my curls to wake them up a bit. At first, I was going to leave it as is, but after Latrice's reminder that I did not want to be caught looking crazy in any pics or videos the camera crew was taking, I decided to fix myself up. We had a spot right in front of the stage, I'm sure we'd be caught in plenty of pictures. Thank God, I put my travel size bottle of Eco Style gel in my bag. That plus the water will have my curls looking good as new.

We got back to our spots just in time. I only spotted Trent though. I asked him where Stephan went, and he said he went to the bathroom. Just as I turned around to see if I saw him, he was right behind me, wrapping his arms around me. God, I just love this man. I leaned back against him and enjoyed his touch. That special moment didn't last long because Ja Rule came back out with Ashanti singing, *Always On Time*. I leaped out of Stephan's arms and started singing along as if I was the one performing on stage. By the time their performance was over, I was already in my flats that I packed in my bag. I tried to keep it cute and classy, but the heels were slowing me down from really jamming out.

It's like God heard my plea. We just finished rocking out to *Down Ass Bitch* and then I heard it. My song! The way I started screaming, I am pretty sure I won't have a voice tomorrow. Stephan and I looked at each other and got right into character. I didn't realize that one of the cameramen had his attention focused on us until Latrice tapped me and showed that we were on the big screen and people were cheering for us. Stephan turned me back to face him as he continued. I was nervous now that eyes were on us, but after looking into his eyes, the nervousness started to disappear.

The music stopped way before the song was even finished and we all stopped singing and looked at the DJ. The disappointment was written all over my face. How can you not play the full song? Ja Rule spoke into the mic and said that he couldn't continue performing knowing that he was faced with competition from a random couple in the crowd. My heart dropped instantly. I didn't know our little performance was going to get him upset. He asked his security guards to escort us out. I was in so much shock that I didn't even know what to say. They got to us in seconds and pulled us from our spots. Stephan looked at me with regret-filled eyes. As we were walking, I realized we weren't walking to the exit, we were heading toward the stage. My heart dropped all over again. What the hell was going on? I looked back at Stephan and those regret-filled eyes were now filled with excitement.

Ja Rule spoke into his mic and said it wouldn't be a real concert unless he showed how much his fans still love his songs. We were handed two mics and the music started all over again. Now I wish I would've had something stronger than a damn Amaretto Sour. How the hell am I going to perform in front of hundreds of people sober? Stephan looked like a kid that just won a year supply of candy. For that look alone, I had to do it, and just like that, we were back in character.

The crowd was loving us. My adrenaline was pumping! Ja Rule let us sing the majority of the song by ourselves then they all joined in. Having Vita and Lil' Mo standing next to me had my knees weak! Thank God, I had on my flats. If I would've had on my heels, I'm sure I would've fallen flat on my face by now. At the end of the song they gave us hugs and we thanked them for this amazing experience. It was the last song of the night and as Ja Rule stood on stage with all the other artists, he gave them all shout outs and thanked all of us fans for coming out. Stephan and I started to walk towards the exit of the stage. Then Ja did something I wasn't expecting. He called Stephan by his name. How did he find out his name that quickly? Did he know mine? I wanted to feel special too.

"Where are you guys going so quickly? Stay up here with us for a bit." We turned around and headed back to the middle of the stage. "You know it won't be a Rule concert if I didn't do something special for my fans." My poor heart is probably going to fail me soon with the number of times it has dropped tonight. What did Rule have up his sleeve? Shit, I hope he's giving us a free car or something. "It's not every day that you get to see beautiful couples who you are evidently in love. It's also very rare to find a man nowadays who will go the distance just to prove to the woman he loves just how much he loves her. It is my honor to make tonight happen for you both. Family, come join us."

If clueless was a person, I'd be her. I didn't know what was going on. Everyone turned to the stairs of the stage and at that very moment, the tears started to stream down my face. There was Monique, Carl, Latrice and Trent. I turned around as I heard Stephan's voice on the mic singing to *All of Me* by John Legend. He grabbed my hand as he sang to me. He wasn't singing to anyone but me. His eyes were glued on me! Emotions filled me as the tears continued to fall. This beautiful man standing before me is singing to me and giving me all of him.

As he sang the last few words of the song, he got down on one knee and held my hand. I felt how nervous he was as his hand trembled in mine.

"The love I have for you is unexplainable. Not a day goes by that I don't thank God that you are the woman that I get to wake up to every morning. You are my peace in the midst of a storm. You are my rock and my strength. Life is worth living because I know I have you by my side. I can't and don't want to picture what life would be like without you. I love you beyond measure. You are more than just my soulmate; you are my best friend, my confidant, my whole world. Kristen Simone Johnson, will you do the honors of being my wife?"

"I would want nothing more than to be your wife. Yes! Yes, I will!"

The crowd started screaming and cheering. I can't believe I am engaged! I knew it was going to happen one day, but no way in hell did I know it would be like this. I felt all eyes on us as Stephan got off his knee and his lips met mine. The fireworks that exploded inside of me was like nothing I have felt before.

I felt a pair of hands touch my shoulders. When I turned around, I was staring into the eyes of my sister. So it was

Monique who I saw earlier. I couldn't hide my excitement as I hugged her as tight as I could. Latrice joined in on our hug and we welcomed her with open arms. We pulled out of our hug as they admired my ring. I didn't even get a chance to admire it myself. I looked down at it for the first time and instantly fell in love with my engagement ring. Stephan knows how much I love hearts and I told him when we first got serious that if he ever proposed that I would want a heart-shaped ring. He listened and remembered!

As the six of us sat at AC Burger and waited for our food, I couldn't stop smiling. The most important people to me are here, celebrating this beautiful moment with me! How can I not be smiling at a time like this?

Our food came and I don't know if it was because I was hungry, excited or both, but my meal tasted extra good. Like the chef knew I just got engaged and made it with extra love. Either way, I'm grateful. Stephan wanted us to all go to this fancy restaurant to celebrate, but I wanted those chili tenders and tater tots again. They all laughed at me for being this dressed up and wanting to go to a burger spot. Once I got my food and they tasted my chili tenders, no one had anything else to say. Monique ended up ordering a batch for the table. Funny how the tables have turned.

We ended off our last night with another game night. This time was even more fun because we had more players, Monique and Carl.

After saying our goodbyes to our guests, it was time for me to say hello to my fiancé. He needed to be shown just how happy he has made me tonight. I tied my hair into a bun and showed him how much he was appreciated for everything he has done to make tonight beyond special.

CHAPTER 21

KRISTEN
PROM NIGHT

My principal went all out with renting this cruise ship for prom night. The kids looked beautiful and the staff stepped out. It felt like it was our prom too. A photographer was waiting to take pictures as each student loaded the ship. They had a beautiful black and gold backdrop. After we accounted for each student, the staff took a couple of pictures in front of the backdrop. I asked one of my coworkers to take a few photos of me on my phone. No point on waiting for the photographer to take weeks to send us these photos.

We had a female DJ and she was killin' it. She was playing all the tunes. The school staff was standing around watching the students dance and pulling apart those who were dancing a little too close. Occasionally, the Dj would play something a little old school and a few of us would step onto the dance floor to show the students how it's really done. They had their phones out recording and enjoying every moment of it. It felt good hearing them cheering us on. The kids were showing off the new school dances and we tried to keep up with them. I haven't danced and sweated like that in a long time. I headed to the bar to grab a non-alcoholic drink. I ended up ordering a kid-friendly Shirley Temple, which was amazing! Assistant Principal Boyd joined me at the bar and ordered the same. We sipped on our drinks and ate the mini appetizers that were at the table next to the bar. From boneless hot wings to cheeseburger sliders and then pizza skins, I was full! The appetizers were unlimited, and they kept bringing out more and more. Sitting so close to the appetizer table was the wrong thing for me to do. I had to make sure I stopped eating soon so I can have a little room for when they served dinner.

A.P. Boyd spotted my engagement ring and wanted every detail of my engagement night. Reliving that moment and having to tell every detail made my heart feel so full all over again. Boyd and I have a great school relationship, but when we all came back from school after our extended weekend, there was so much stuff to get done that I didn't have time to sit in her office and share the news. The excitement was written all over her face as she hugged and congratulated me. She ordered us another kid-friendly Shirley Temple so we could toast to my engagement.

We sat at the bar for about another twenty minutes before we rejoined the kids on the dance floor. I needed to move around to help me digest all this food. Thank God, I put on Spanx under my dress. With all the food I ate, I am sure people would have thought that I was pregnant. I cannot have that rumor spreading around.

We had about an hour left before we docked back to the city. I stuffed myself again with dinner. I went with the stuffed chicken, garlic roasted potatoes, and broccoli. I was full halfway through my plate, but it was so damn good that I couldn't stop eating. I would rest my fork for a few minutes and then go back to eating. Stephan would be so disappointed if he saw how much I forced this food down. Good thing he was not here.

I don't know how these kids have so much energy. I was full and my feet were hurting. They asked me to join them back on the dance floor, but I needed to sit and digest for a little longer. Mr. Stevens, the art teacher, A.P. Boyd, and Mr. Greene, the gym teacher were seated at the same table as me. Again, I had to share the details of the night of my engagement. Greene gave me a high five and Stevens hugged me. We then started talking about all the memories we shared with our soon to be eighth-grade graduates. Laughing at all the memories made my cheeks hurt. Greene and Stevens had it worse than I did. They met with all students. I only had my self-contained kids. Greene shared a story of him having to break up a fight in the gym between two of the students, Amanda and Francisco. He stated that Francisco threw a ball and it accidentally hit Amanda on the butt. Instead of apologizing, he laughed. He said before he knew it, Amanda had Francisco by the hair and was dragging him around the whole gym. Amanda is about four feet and five inches tall, so to imagine her pulling Francisco, who is about five feet tall around, is something I wish I could have seen.

Stevens shared a story about one of the roughest kids in the school, Adam. Adam went to the bathroom one day and came back to finish his art project only to find that his paper and paint supplies were missing. Now what puzzled me is that everyone knows that Adam is the last one you should want to play with. Adam asked Mr. Stevens if he knew what happened with his stuff and Stevens told him no. He asked the whole class, they also said no. Stevens asked that whoever took it to put it back to avoid getting detention. Adam sat at his seat quietly for a few minutes waiting to see who would return his stuff. After a few minutes of waiting, he grabbed a new bottle of red paint and started pouring paint on everyone's projects. No one came forward nor tried to stop him. After failed attempts of asking Adam to stop and trying to get the bottle, he had to call Boyd to remove him. After he was removed from the class, Stevens asked the class who took it. After a few seconds of silence, David admitted that he took it, but that the class decided to do it. They all admitted that they were tired of Adam thinking that he can bully everyone, and nothing be done to him. Stevens explained it to Boyd later that day and both were proud that the class stood up as a collective. No punishment was given besides having to redo their project.

After a few more laughable stories, I excused myself and went to find a bathroom. The bathrooms on the top floor were filled with my girls taking selfies and looking in the mirror. I ended up going to the bathroom on the lower level. The cleanliness in it was proof that the kids didn't know this bathroom was here.

On my way back to the staircase that leads to the dance floor, I spotted some of the workers running with a bucket of water. I was going to mind my business, but that small voice in my head was telling me to go and find out what they were up to. I followed behind them and spotted the problem. There was a leak coming in and they were using the buckets to pour the water back into the ocean. My heart dropped immediately.

"What's going on here?" My voice sounded just as nervous as I felt.

"Ma'am, please return to the party. We've got this under control," the manager said to me as calmly as possible, but I still heard the worry in his voice.

"No, if my kids' safety is at risk, then I need to know what's going on."

"Fine. We have a broken fire suppression," the manager said while scooping water into the buckets. "We aren't that far back to the dock. If we can keep the water to a minimum, then we should be fine."

The word *should* did not sit well with me. I pulled my hair into a bun and began helping them scoop the water into buckets while some of the others dumped the water back into the ocean. It felt like the more water we poured out, the more came in. The water was barely touching the surface when I first got here and now it was up to my ankles. We needed more hands to stop this water flow. The five of us will not be enough.

"I'll be back with more help." I ran upstairs and told my colleagues what was happening. Jones, Greene, Stevens, and Boyd ran back downstairs with me as Boyd directed the rest of her staff to stay with the kids.

By the time we got back downstairs, the water had risen again. It was a little above my ankles now.

"Holy shit!" Mr. Green said as the water turned the bottom of his light grey slacks into dark grey.

"Well, Greene, it looks like we have to put your gym drills to use. Let's see how fast you can dump water. Let's go, people, we will not have another Titanic. Not on my watch!" I love A.P. Boyd for her boldness and sacrifice for our kids.

We all fell in line and got to work. We had a little less than an hour or so before we docked. At the rate of this water flow, I was worried that an hour may be too long. Even with the pace that we are going, it may not be enough.

Everyone was quiet for the moment. We were all focused on our task, getting as much water as we could out. Ten minutes into throwing the water back into the ocean, I decided it would be smart to take my shoes off. Every time I slipped, more water poured out of my bucket. That wasn't helping.

"Ms. Johnson, what's happening here?" Leave it to one of my students to be the one to find us.

"Nothing, Anthony. We are just helping the crew clean up a little water spill." I tried to sound as calm as possible.

"Looks to me like we're gonna sink and y'all trying not to tell us that we all are about to die!"

"No one is going to die, Anthony. But I do need you to promise that you'll go back upstairs and pretend that you didn't see what is going on down here," Ms. Boyd said.

"Now, Ms. Boyd, you've always told me that lying won't get me nowhere in life, and now you're asking me to lie to my friends? I don't know if I can do that. How would I ever be able to look at myself?" Anthony said sarcastically.

Even though nothing about this moment was funny, I had to admit that his sarcasm calmed my nerves for the moment.

"We don't want you to lie, Anthony. It's more like stretching the truth," I explained.

"We just need you to go back upstairs and enjoy the rest of your time," Ms. Boyd chimed in.

"But what do I get out of keeping this very big secret?" Anthony asked mischievously.

"You get to keep my foot out of your behind," I whispered in his ear. I wouldn't dare let anyone hear me say that and I knew Anthony well enough to know he wouldn't repeat my playful threat.

"Well, in that case, I'll leave you all alone. It looks like you're going to need some extra hands though," Anthony said as he pointed to all the water that was now up to our shins.

We were all so focused on trying to kick him out, that we stopped dumping the water. It felt like all the work we just put in was for nothing.

Anthony was finally gone, but I wasn't so sure how long he'd keep this a secret. Sooner than later, these kids would find out about this flood. The only way off the ship was to past through this floor. At this rate, there won't be a dry foot getting off. I just hope we can keep this quiet until it's time for us to exit. There's no telling how these kids would react if they found out what was happening.

♥ ♥ ♥

We were less than five minutes out and weren't able to get much water out. The water was still at shin level but that was the best we could do with the little bit of help we had.

The ship safely docked, but the hard part was going to be getting these kids out. Ms. Boyd went upstairs a few minutes ago to give them the heads up and set some order. The kids were lined up in single form and waiting for instructions on when they could come down and exit. So far, everyone was calm.

Clearance finally came in and we were able to start letting the kids off. I went upstairs to let Ms. Boyd know. She assigned two of the teachers to lead the students off along with Mr. Jones. Mr. Greene was responsible for the middle of the line with two other staff and Boyd and I had the back, making sure we were the last ones to exit.

As we were making our way to the back of the line, I heard the screams of some of our kids. It was coming from the front of the line. I ran to where the screams were coming from as one of the students told me what happened. The ramp was wet from water trying to escape and one of the kids slipped and fell. The ramp didn't feel sturdy at all and was swaying side to side. The other students panicked and started running off the ship. Thankfully one of them screamed out, which caught Mr. Jones' attention. The student that fell, Emma, was still on the ground and everyone was either running around her or stepping on her to get off. Mr. Jones ran to her and helped her up, but was accidentally pushed by one of the students who was running off. As he was trying to catch his fall, he went backward and was now hanging from the ramp.

I ran as fast as I could and assisted the other crewmember and one of the teachers on trying to pull him up. The other teacher was trying to calm the kids down as she tried to hurry them off the boat. The ramp wasn't as wide as we needed it to be. It felt like there was no way we could get these kids off and pull him up at the same time without there being another major accident. Mr. Greene was finally here and took my spot in trying to pull Mr. Jones up. I held the rest of the kids back while they tended to Jones. This wasn't an easy task. Jones is about six feet three inches and around three hundred and twenty pounds. Greene is only five feet nine inches and one hundred and ninety pounds. Even with three people, they were struggling to pull him up. The kids were screaming and even though we were trying to calm them down, I was scared too. If Jones dropped, it would not only be hard to pull him out but also even harder just to find him. He'd be buried under the ship.

After many attempts, they were able to pull him up and back onto the ramp. The attending staff helped him off as the rest of us proceeded with getting the rest of the students off the ship. I gave firm instructions while we were waiting to move quickly but in a single line. No pushing or shoving was allowed. They saw what happened with Mr. Jones, so the firmness in my voice and what they already witnessed was enough for them to follow my instructions.

Thankfully, the parents were all in the waiting area and not by the loading dock. I can't even begin to imagine the panic on their faces if they had to witness this. After calming everyone down as best she could, Boyd led the line from the loading dock to the waiting area. Since she was in charge, she said she had to be the one to inform the parents of what had happened.

They didn't take the news well but was appreciative that we did the best we could to keep their kids safe. Boyd rode with Emma's family to the hospital to get her checked out. She had bruises all over her body from the kids stepping all over her to get off the boat. They had to be sure that nothing was broken.

Stefan was there waiting for me. He looked horrified when Boyd was telling everyone what happened. I buried my face into his chest as he held me tight. The tears threatened to fall but I couldn't allow myself to unfold in front of my kids. We waited until all the kids were gone before we hopped in the car and drove home. As soon as he closed the car door behind me, the tears fell. I wanted to get out of there as fast as I could and Stephan did just that.

I got an email shortly after I got home. It was from Boyd and it was addressed to the whole middle school; staff, students, and parents. She was apologizing for the way the night ended. Taking complete responsibility for what happened. I don't know why she was blaming herself, this wasn't something she could've prevented. She did say she already put in the request for substitute teachers for tomorrow if any of us staff needed to take the day and that any students who'd like to stay home wouldn't be penalized. Stephan told me I should take the day and that he would stay home with me as well. I told him that I would see how I felt in the morning and take it from there.

♥ ♥ ♥

I woke up the next morning with a splitting headache. I was tempted to stay home, but I wanted to be there for any of my kids who showed up. I rolled myself out of bed and got ready for work. I looked exactly how I felt. I showered and put my hair in a ponytail. I put on my black stretchy slacks, a mustard color blouse, and my black moccasins. I was presentable and comfortable. If there was ever a day that I didn't care about how I looked, today was that day.

Good thing I did decide to come to work. Octavia, Malcolm, and Anthony were all in the yard waiting for morning entry. I waved to them before I headed inside. The secretary in the main office told me that Ms. Boyd was out this morning and would be coming later. I hope everything went ok at the hospital last night.

Since I had a few minutes to spare before I had to collect my students, I decided to set my classroom up a bit differently. I wasn't in any mood to teach and I'm sure my students weren't in any mood to listen to me talk for hours. I just want today to be a relaxing day for us all. I'm not sure what they'd vote on doing, but we will be winging today.

When they walked into the classroom and seen how it was

set up, they all turned around and looked at me.

"Who stole something, Ms. Johnson?" Adam asked.

"What makes you think something was stolen?" I asked.

"Because the last time the tables were set this way, you went ham on us because one of the iPad's were missing," Anthony chimed in.

"Nothing is missing. I just wanted to do things a little differently today. So have a seat and we'll discuss what that means," I said to the class.

They all hesitantly made their way to their desk. I couldn't help but laugh to myself as I remembered the last time I had the tables set this way. One of the iPad's went missing and I needed to look everyone in the eye as I questioned the class. I was furious. I trusted my kids, so I never thought I needed to double-check that they placed it back in the cart. It wasn't until they went to lunch and I went to charge the iPad cart that I saw one was missing. Waiting forty-five minutes until they were finished with lunch and recess felt like I was waiting for hours. I looked high and low and couldn't find it. The iPad's have trackers on it, so I knew we would get it back, but I didn't want to go through that whole process. Plus, they would get the youth officers involved because it would be considered theft. When they finally got upstairs, I had the chairs set in a U shape, ready to interrogate every one of them. I had them sit at their assigned seat. They looked back and forth at each other, wondering why the classroom setup and why my face looked the way that it did.

I started my questioning by saying, "I'm really disappointed that one of you would disrespect me. I've been nothing but loving and fair to every one of you. Not only did you mess up things with me, but you also made things worse for your classmates. Now I have to be extra strict and limit your accessibilities in my room. I'm going to give you thirty seconds to come clean and hand over the device. The stolen iPad needs to be on my desk at that time. After the thirty seconds, school safety will be alerted and then it's out of my hands." Before I could even start my timer, Anthony raised his hand. I allowed him to speak, and that is when he reminded me that one of the teachers had it. Ms. Leonard sent one of her students over to borrow an iPad during first period. Pure embarrassment was written all over my face. I couldn't believe that I forgot all about it and made such a fool out of myself. Some of my students forgave me for accusing them, but Anthony and Malcolm milked it. I was giving out donuts and extra credit that whole week!

This time was different though. I wanted them to have a semi-free day. I explained to them that we were going to have a ten to fifteen pow-wow session. Just to check everyone's energy and mental state. After we would pull out the laptops and they were free to access any approved websites and do as they pleased. We were also going to pull out some board and card games and play a few group activities and then for lunch, I was taking them out for pizza. We would grab some snacks from the store and end the afternoon with whatever movie they vote on. They all agreed with the order of our events and that is exactly how the day went.

I got home and Stephan was already preparing dinner. I don't think people know how much of a blessing it is to have a man that can cook and loves to do it. We get so caught up in the stereotype that women are supposed to always cook for the men, that we forget that it's a partnership. I kissed him hello and prepared for a shower. My headache from this morning was gone and the smoothness from today had me feeling even better. A shower and a good home-cooked meal were going to put me in an even better mood.

By the time I got out of the shower, the table was set. I quickly dressed and joined him at the table. Salmon, shrimps, yellow rice, broccoli, corn, biscuits, and my fine fiancé were waiting for me. I felt myself doing the happy dance when I saw all the food on the table.

We spoke about our day as we dug our forks in and enjoyed this delicious dinner that he prepared. I poured me a glass of Barefoot Moscato and poured him his Jack. Since tomorrow was Saturday and we both didn't have to work, I made sure to pour a little extra in our glasses. That Barefoot had me feeling tingly inside. Tonight was going to be a night to remember.

CHAPTER 22

KRISTEN
TWO MONTHS LATER

It felt like it was yesterday that I was hugging my students goodbye and congratulating them on graduating, but here we are in August. This is my last month off before I have to start mentally preparing to go back to work. I was unpacking our suitcases while waiting for Latrice to come over with breakfast.

"About time you got here," I said as I opened the door for her.

"Girl, if you would've seen the line! I almost walked out and went to the Mc Donald's drive-thru for our breakfast," she said as she handed me the bag of food and headed to the sink to wash her hands.

"I'm glad you waited because I had my mouth set on these pancakes. Mc Donald's pancakes are good, but they have nothing on Ihop!"

"You got that right!" she said as we high fived each other. "So tell me all about your vacation. I want to know every detail, so don't even think about having amnesia right now."

"Girl! It was truly amazing. I won't lie, I was skeptical in the beginning. I told you that his parents booked it as an engagement gift, so there wasn't much detail that we knew. All we knew was when we were leaving and where we had to be at designated times. They booked a four-day cruise to the

Bahamas. We had to fly to Miami and boarded the ship from there. It was a Carnival Cruise ship. Girl, it was huge and beautiful! Next year, we need to plan for all of us to go." I got excited all over again just thinking about the amount of fun we had and how much more fun we would have next year with everyone there.

"You weren't scared to get back on another boat though, after going through what you went through with your students on prom night?" Latrice asked me.

"You sound like my mom. She loved the fact that his parents wanted to do something nice for us but hated the fact of me having to relive that memory. But, honestly, I was fine. I think I was too excited about going to the Bahamas and knowing that Stephan was with me put me at ease."

"That's good. Not to be a buzz kill though, but did you ever look into getting help?" Latrice asked.

"Get help with what?" I felt my forehead crease as I looked at her with confusion.

"About why you have these scary-ass dreams that come true in some form. I thought this last one would have been enough to land you in someone's chair or examination table. You had that dream where the kids were caught in the waves and you guys had to run and rescue them. All the water kept pushing Madison back and it took multiple people to try and save her. Then you go on this boat with your students and you guys end up with a flood. The guidance counselor could have lost his life if you all didn't step in and pull him up. Sounds to me that you had yet another dream that ended up coming true in some way. You know what, I take it back, I think what should've made you seek help is when you had that dream that your mom and Mo got burned alive in that sauna room and then Stephan's neighbor ends up dying in his apartment because of a fire. If you don't see how crazy these dreams and coincidences are, then I don't know what else to tell you."

I was trying to read her facial expression. Part of me felt like she was more scared for me than I was for myself.

"Now you sound like Stephan. I love how much you guys worry about my mental state. Trust me, this isn't easy to go through, but I'm also scared to seek help. I don't think normal people go through this on a regular, and the last thing I need is for someone to think I need psychiatric help. Every time I picture myself seeking help, I see myself being judged and blamed for everything that has happened. I guess I'm just scared." I think this was the first time that I admitted how scared I was to seek help and to potentially be looked at as a mental disaster.

"It's ok to be scared. Shit, I am scared for you. However, you have to understand that I will be here every step of the way. You have a huge support system, let us be here for you." Latrice got up and hugged me as the tears fell down my face. I blame myself all the time for all the things that have happened, and I know seeking help can guide me into forgiving myself. We talked a little more about how I was feeling about it and it felt good to get it off my chest. This was a weight I've been carrying for too long and it felt good to release some of it.

"Now enough of this sadness, let's get back to your vacation!" Latrice said switching the topic and mood.

"Yes! So, after we boarded the ship, we checked into our room and waited for our luggage to be delivered. We had a copy of the itinerary and started planning what we wanted to get into. Now that I think about it, I think Stephan knew more than he told me. While we were planning, he told me that when we land in the Bahamas, we need to be one of the first ones off the boat. He said we had a full two days planned and needed to make sure we stayed on schedule. He let me plan all of the activities on the ship and he took care of everything off the ship. Needless to say, I had the easiest job.

On day one, we went touring the cruise ship, ate at the burger joint, and had a nice dinner. Now before you go judging, we ate a lot on the ship. The food was all included, so every time food became available, we took advantage of it. We grabbed some ice cream from the ice cream machine and relaxed in the Jacuzzi before we decided to go to our rooms and call it a night. The next morning, we were up bright and early and one of the first ones at the breakfast table. We had everything that could fit on our plates. We both walked away with two plates each. Our plates were filled with eggs, pancakes, waffles, sausages, bacon, grits, hash browns, toast. We had it all! We headed back to our room and got ready. The ship already docked, but we had to wait for them to announce that we can exit the ship. When we finally got off the ship, we were directed to a bus that was taking us to swim with the dolphins."

"You went swimming with the dolphins?" The excitement was all over Latrice's face as she waited for me to continue.

"That same look on your face was my face times ten! I was the only one on the bus that didn't know that's where we were heading. It's funny how this engagement trip was for both of us, but yet Stephan was still full of surprises. We had so much fun swimming with the dolphins." I showed Latrice the pictures we took.

"We went to the beach afterward and rented a Cabana. We had enough fun in the water with the dolphins, so we deiced to just relax and take in the sun. Our server, Denise, was so dope and friendly. She kept bringing us different tropical drinks to try. When we got the bill, I was expecting it to be crazy high, but she only charged us for two drinks. When Stephan asked her why she said she overheard us talking about how much we were enjoying our newly engaged vacation and thought she would help make it even better. We gave her a very nice tip. She hugged us and then apologized for it, but I told her it was more than ok as long as she didn't hug Stephan longer than she hugged me. We all laughed and then Stephan and I said our goodbyes as we headed back to the ship. We showered and changed, as we got ready for dinner. The chef's special for the night was sriracha shrimp and honey-glazed salmon. I don't know what extra loving he put into the food, but girl it was amazing! I had the itis after, but I wanted to go to the comedy night. I got us tickets before we went to dinner, so after dinner, we went straight there to grab good seats. The comedian had us laughing all night! He even made jokes about people in the audience and I was praying the whole time that he didn't say anything about me. Thank God that he didn't because I don't know if I would've had the same positive attitude as the people in the audience. You know I don't like being put on the spot. Anyway, so we left when it ended and walked around the cruise ship, taking more pictures and touring again. We made our ice cream cones and headed to the top floor. We stood by the front of the ship and enjoyed the view. It was dark outside, but the little light that was there showed how beautiful the waves looked. It was a little after midnight before we headed to our rooms. I wish we could have stayed out there longer, but according to Stephan, we had another busy day the next day.

He wasn't lying when he said we had a busy day ahead. We

were up bright and early and back online for our breakfast. We didn't grab as much as we did the morning before because he said this activity wouldn't be best on a full stomach. Girl, before I could even register what was happening, I was signing my name on a paper and being instructed on how to ride a Jet Ski. Now you know it's on my bucket list, but Trice I was scared shitless! I had no time to mentally prepare myself. My anxiety was through the roof and Stephan's ass kept laughing at me the whole time telling me I was going to be fine. He finally convinced me to get on and I decided to put my big girl panties on and ride my own instead of riding with him."

"Oh, girl. You were being extra brave! I'm surprised your scary ass didn't hop on the back of his Jet Ski and held on to your Hercules," Latrice said as she started laughing.

I couldn't help but laugh with her because she was absolutely right. I would have felt much safer holding on to him versus riding by myself.

"Alright, bitch, stop laughing or you won't hear the rest of the story."

"Ok continue," she said as she repositioned herself in the chair.

"So, after we are given the basic instructions on how to operate the Jet Ski, the instructor takes us out onto the water, and we follow his lead. I was finally getting the hang of it when he took us into the deeper parts of the water. That is when I felt my anxiety slowly rising. Stephan kept shouting out that I was doing good and to keep going. The instructor told us that we needed to speed up a bit when we hit the big waves. I was speeding now and trying to keep up with the instructor, but the waves were picking up. One big wave came and I tried to accelerate but I didn't get it up to speed fast enough and there I was falling over. I hit the water and knew I was going to die. I had a life vest on but I was panicking too much that I was still going underwater. I was kicking and screaming. I saw Stephan trying to make his way towards me. The panic on his face made me panic even more. Then I thought I saw a shark and girl, I started going crazy. The instructor was trying to get me to calm down so that he can help me back up. Stephan pulled up beside me. He was trying to instruct me on how to get back on the Jet Ski. I felt like every time I got a grip on the Jet Ski, the water pressure was pulling me back down. The instructor told me how to do it and I finally got one leg on. I went to swing the other leg over and boom I fell backward right back into the water. They thought I panicked the first time; this time was worse. I was fighting to stay above water. Stephan jumped off his Jet Ski this time and came to my rescue while the instructor had me hop on the back of his. I guess he was tired of trying to save me. I didn't care though. I was just happy that he let me ride back on the back of his. Now if you want to compare that dream that I had of us at the beach to anything that happened in real life, it would be this. I felt like I was Madison in the dream. The fact that Stephan and the instructor both had to come to save me and pull me out of the water. I didn't drown, but I now know what a near-death experience feels like. After he got us back to the meeting point, I was over it. I just wanted to get back on the ship and eat my feelings away and that's exactly what we did. After showering, we walked around the food court area and grabbed a little bit of everything that looked appealing to us. I got a burger with fries. Stephan got pizza. Then we split a plate of mango jerk chicken tacos. Stuffed was an understatement of how we felt. I felt bad for wasting half my burger, but there was no way I was not tasting those tacos. They were truly amazing! We went back to our rooms and took a nap. That night was the captain's night. Which meant we had to dress in our best for dinner. I wasn't really hungry when we woke up, but I was looking forward to getting dressed up. I brought a burgundy dress that hit the floor and had a high split up my right thigh. Stephan had on a burgundy button-down shirt, black slacks, and burgundy shoes. You couldn't tell us that we weren't dressed to impress that night." I showed Latrice the pictures we took on our phones plus the professional pictures that were printed.

"Damn, y'all really stepped out! I can't wait to see how you look on your wedding day. This dress is a tease! The cut, the length, the way it hugs your body, girl you were killin' it!" I knew I looked good in that dress but hearing Latrice pay me those compliments had me smiling extra hard and feeling even better about myself.

"Thank you, Trice! To make that night even better, it was a competition night. I won best dressed and Stephan won best hair. You know he takes pride in his locs and girl were the women drooling over him because of it. My gift was a hundred dollar Amazon gift card and Stephan got a haircare package. We gratefully took our gifts and put them in the room. I got us tickets to a late-night performance they were having. We got there a few minutes early to get good seats. It was so amazing. The crew from the cruise put on different performances. Girl, these people were talented! They had voices for days and their choreography was on point. I wish I could've shown you, but they wouldn't let us record. They made that very clear in the beginning. The next day we were at sea, so we had no choice but to stay on the ship. It was a fun calm day. We ate as usual. They had a pool party that was so dope. We danced to old school music and jammed to the new school. They had a dope DJ. We ended up playing pool games with two couples we met earlier and then left them for some downtime in the Jacuzzi. We got out, ate again, walked around for a bit, and then went back to our rooms to take a nap. We woke up and got ready for our last dinner on the ship. I had this amazing chicken Marsala and Stephan had this buttery steak. I don't know who the chef was for that night, but I wish I did because I needed to know how he made the steak so damn juicy. If it were part of the all you can eat, they would've had no steak left for anyone else. We walked around for a bit after dinner before heading back to our room and packing. The last morning, we showered, got dressed, and headed to our favorite breakfast line. It was our last chance to be fat and greedy so we grabbed everything that looked worth trying. The rest of the morning, we were on the line waiting to exit the ship and head to the airport. This was a trip to remember. When we got back yesterday, we were so drained that we didn't even bother to unpack, plus he had to return to work today so we just chilled for the rest of the night. I told him I would unpack for us and wash the clothes. We have his family reunion next weekend so I have no choice but to get these clothes in order. But yea, girl, that was our vacation," I said as I picked up my last turkey sausage and ate it.

"I can't even lie, I am jealous! I wish I were there to make those memories. We are going next year. I am so happy for you though. This is the vacation that you needed. We crashed your other mini-vacation, but it was for a great reason," Latrice said as she winked at my engagement ring.

"You guys definitely crashed my mini-vacation, but I wouldn't have traded that for the world! That was the happiest night of my life and I'm so happy I had you and Mo there with me."

"Agreed. I'm happy he asked us to be there. I would've still been ecstatic for you if you called me to tell me you got engaged, but to be there to witness it, now that's a memory I'm happy to have," Latrice said as her eyes began to water.

"You better not cry!"

"I'm not crying, it's my allergies acting up," she said as we both started laughing, knowing damn well she has no allergies.

"All seriousness, Trice. I think Trent has turned you into a softie. I don't think I've ever seen you this emotional."

"I can't even lie, he really has. We were watching The Avengers, Infinity War the other night and it got to the part where Thanos was making everyone disappear and Spiderman started fading away and was telling Mr. Stark/Iron Man that he didn't want to go and was holding onto him for dear life. Girl, the waterworks that flooded my face! Trent looked at me like I was crazy. I've watched that movie multiple times and never cried." Her eyes started to tear as she played that specific part on her phone. I love the Avengers, so I knew which part she was referring to, but she was adamant in showing me anyway.

"So, you know I'm always honest with you and you're always honest with me. Do you think it's a possibility that you might be pregnant?" The way her eyes popped open after I asked, showed me that she didn't even consider that. It would explain how emotional she has been lately.

"Me, pregnant? I highly doubt it," she said as she laughed at my question.

"It's not impossible though, Trice. Plus, it will help make sense understanding your newly emotional ass and all that nasty stuff you ate today."

"We had the same food!" she answered defensively.

"Yes, we did order the same thing, but all that extra stuff you added to your plate isn't you. You poured the leftover strawberry jelly on your eggs and dipped your sausages in the whipped cream. Now that is something, the normal Latrice would never do."

She sat quietly for a second, taking everything that I was saying in. After a few minutes in silence, she responded, "So what now?"

"Take a pregnancy test," I said.

"Ok. When I leave here I'll go get one."

"No need to. I have one already." Before she could even ask any questions or object, I was already running to my bedroom to grab the one I had stashed in my drawer. I honestly don't know why I even have it, but it was on sale and something told me it was going to come in handy one day. Today will be that day.

We followed the instructions and now were waiting for the results. I set the timer for five minutes as we sat around the table in silence. When the timer went off, she asked me to go and see what the test said. I walked nervously to the bathroom, read the results, and walked back into the living room.

"Bitch, you're pregnant!"

CHAPTER 23

STEPHAN
FAMILY REUNION

Kristen and I got to Virginia around ten last night. My mother waited up for us. My father apologized in advance that he would be calling it an early night. He was doing most of the heavy cooking and wanted to get as much rest as possible. We settled into the guest room and was asleep before eleven.

My father wasn't lying when he said he was doing most of the cooking. I woke up around six o'clock to use the bathroom and he was already in the kitchen cleaning and seasoning meat. Kristen was sound asleep and so was my mother. I ended up washing my hands and joining him.

"So Pops, what's on the menu this year? I'm happy to see that it's you in the kitchen."

"Well son, you know my specialties; fried chicken, baked chicken, whiting, catfish, shrimps, yellow rice, rice and peas, white rice, baked macaroni and cheese, potato salad, macaroni salad, ribs, honey glazed ham, vegetables, fruits, collard greens, beans, my famous biscuits, cornbread, candied yams, and this year, I'm making my rasta pasta. I think that's all."

"You think that's all? Pops, you're going to cook all of that?" I asked.

"Well, the beauty of owning your own restaurant is training

your cooks on how to make your signature dishes. I'll be making all the meats, but the rice's and other starches will be done by them," Dad said as he continued cleaning the chicken.

"That's smart. Sounds like we are going to have a feast today." I felt my stomach doing summersaults at the thought of it.

"Yes indeed. I love your momma and her sister's, but I can't go another family reunion having to sneak my own seasonings to pour on the food," he said as we both busted out laughing. We lowered our voices so we wouldn't wake the women. "I figured if I woke up earlier than everyone else that I could get all the cleaning and seasoning out the way, so even if they wanted to help, all they had to do was make sure the food didn't burn." We both tried not to laugh too loud.

The rest of the morning flew by so fast. We spent all morning cleaning and cooking. Thankfully, I took after my father, so he trusted me with seasoning and cooking. When my mom and Kristen finally woke up, he sent them to the backyard to get everything set up while we continued in the kitchen. My aunts, uncles, and cousins arrived shortly after and helped with setting up. By now, it was almost two in the afternoon. The rest of our families weren't due to arrive until three o'clock, but you know black people, they have to be fashionably late.

I left my father in the kitchen so I could shower and get ready. When I got dressed, I took over the cooking so he could do the same. My grandfather walked into the kitchen shortly after.

"Look at my favorite grandson." He patted me on the back as he went to take a seat at the table. It has been a while since I have seen my grandfather and I could see how age was getting the best of him. I was used to him walking and running after us, now he can barely walk and depending on a walker to get him from point A to point B. At eighty-seven, he was still the best dressed.

"Hey, Pop-Pop. How are you feeling today? You looking good!" I put the fork down and turned to face him.

"I'm hanging in there. Where's your father? He left you all alone in the kitchen?"

"He's in the shower. He's been in the kitchen before the sun came up."

"I'm not surprised. He is the hardest working man I know besides myself. Too bad that wife of his don't know nothing more than adding salt and pepper to her food," he said with pure disappointment in his voice.

"Pop-Pop, that's my mother you're referring to."

"Unfortunately. Now if your father would've married Tina, then he would've been outside enjoying a beer instead of slaving in this hot kitchen."

"Unfortunately? You do realize that if he did marry whoever Tina is, that I wouldn't be here?" I turned back around to flip over the chicken and to check on the ribs. It was the perfect opportunity to hide the feelings that I was sure was evident on my face.

"Stop being so sensitive boy. I was just joking. You know I love your mother. Neicy is good to your father and a good woman."

"Momma's name is Nancy, not Neicy." I couldn't help but shake my head.

Saved by the bell, my father was back. My grandfather wouldn't dare disrespect my mother in front of him.

♥♥♥

The family reunion was off to a great start. The food was a hit and my cousin Rashad was doing his thing as the DJ. We all had on our mustard-colored customized shirts that said *Moore Family, Moore Reunions*. My cousin Nicky designed the shirts. It was cute and corny at the same time. I paid thirty dollars for Kris' and mine so I was going to wear it regardless.

Everyone congratulated Kris and me on our engagement. My whole family loved her from the first time they met her. I was asked constantly when I was going to propose, so it felt good to not hear it this time. Just when I thought I was off the hook; the new question was when is the wedding? Feels like I can never win. I told them we were in no rush to get married and wanted to enjoy each stage of our relationship. I didn't want to wait more than two years for the wedding, but at least a year as her fiancé sounded fair enough. I'm sure planning weddings are no walk in the park. We were going to take our time and plan properly. Well, she would be doing most of the planning. I just want to be there to help pick out the place, the food, and the cake. She can do the rest that women love to do. Picking out flowers and all that other stuff was not for me.

Kristen pulled me out of my thoughts when the *Wobble* came on. Everyone got to their feet, fell in formation, and started dancing. From the young to the elderly, everyone was on the grass getting their wobble on. Rashad started playing old school dance songs and new school dance songs. Before I knew it, there was an old school versus new school singing/dance battle. He went real old school with songs like *Push-It, Let's Groove, Computer Love, It Takes Two, Can't Touch This, Back That Azz Up,* and *Before I Let Go.* Then he did dance throwbacks and played songs like *the Dougie, Walk It Out, Stanky Leg, Lean Back,* and *Swag Surfin'.* For the young ones and those who were still in tune with the new music, he played *Before I Let Go* (the Beyoncé version), *Savage Remix, Fall and If by Davido, the Shoot, Renegade* and *Big Drip.*

I couldn't stop laughing at all the old folks trying to keep up with the young ones. The goal was for everyone to have fun and that mission was accomplished. It was time to start playing traditional games. We played the Water Balloon Toss, the Egg Race, the Moore Family Scavenger Hunt, Kickball, and relay races.

Before we knew it, the streetlights were on. Little by little, people started exiting. You know it was time to go when everyone started crowding around the leftover food and making their to-go plates. I was the only smart one who made to-go plates for Kris and me while the food was being served. I was sitting down under the shaded area of the backyard when my grandfather made his way towards me.

"There goes my favorite grandson." I don't know why he always called me his favorite grandson, because I was his only grandson. One thing I know for sure though was that I am his favorite grandchild. Everyone knew it and no one bothered to fight me on it.

"Hey, Pop-Pop, you alright?" I asked as I got up to give him my seat.

"I'm as good as I'm going to be. No thanks, I don't want to sit out here. Do you mind walking me inside the house? I want to talk to you about something before I leave."

"I don't mind at all." I patted him on the shoulder as we headed inside.

Once we got inside the house, I followed him to the living room. He sat in the love seat and I sat across from him.

"What's going on, Pop-Pop?"

"I wish that you lived closer. This isn't a conversation that I wanted to have over the phone and I'm sorry that we are having this conversation after such a great day, but I don't know when the next time I'd see you. It was now or never. Please don't be mad at your father for not telling you, I told him that I needed to be the one to tell you."

"Pop-Pop, what's going on?" My grandfather never sits me down unless it was something serious he wanted to talk about. My chest began to tighten as I prepared for whatever was coming next.

"I just found out a few weeks ago that my prostate cancer has spread. Some days are good and some days are not so good. I'm grateful that today I was able to see my family enjoying themselves. I wish I was able to get up, dance, and play with you all, but these old bones don't work like they used to. After a long talk with my doctor and my children, I feel like the best decision is for me to be checked into a Nursing Home. They have a great one out here and one of the floors is strictly for elderly cancer patients, so I won't feel alone. Your father and your aunt Sharon were the hardest to convince that this was the best decision for me. Both of them wanted me to stay with either of them, but I didn't want to spend my last days being a burden to my children. Everyone has their own life to live and I refuse to have either one of them worrying and checking on me every second. I've visited the nursing home and it's just what I need. Now I called you in here not only to tell you that but to also ask you for a favor."

I sat beside him and placed his hand in mine. "Anything for you. Just tell me what it is," I said as I squeezed his hand.

"Your father and your aunt Sharon don't know this yet and the only reason why I'm telling you before him is because I know how he'll react. The chemo isn't helping to slow down the spread of cancer and I've decided to live out my final days while in the nursing home. I'm tired of fighting and I'm ready to be reunited with my wife. I know she misses me as much as I miss her. I have dreams of her waiting for me at Heaven's gates and it always ends with me telling her I will be with her soon. Please don't tell your father this. If he or Sharon knew, they would want me to live my final days with one of them. That is something I cannot do. They don't realize how traumatizing it is to watch someone die slowly each day. That's a memory I don't want them to have. So grandson, please don't tell either of them."

I tried to stop the tears from falling, but I couldn't. I love my father, but my grandfather is my true superhero. Losing my grandmother was hard and I can't even begin to think how much harder it'll be to lose him. I know he's telling me without directly telling me that he didn't have long to live. I didn't know what to say so I just hugged him and at that moment I knew this would be one of the last hugs I'd ever get from him.

He pulled back from me and said, "Now for the favor I need from you." He reached into his pocket and pulled something out of his wallet. "I know I am asking for a lot, but one thing I'd love to witness before I go is to see you marry that beautiful fiancé of yours. I know this is last minute and I can understand if it cannot be done." He opened my hand and placed the paper in it. "This is a check. It should be enough to take care of all the expenses and if you need more, just let me know. I just want to see my grandson carry on our legacy, so I can rest knowing I've done well by my family. I've also decided to transfer my share of the restaurant your dad owns into your name. What you decide to do with that is completely up to you. We can talk about that later this week. That I don't mind talking about over the phone, but this, I needed it to be face to face, man to man. You deserve that much."

I sat there quietly for a second. This was a lot to take in. I was losing my hero in a matter of months, I would have to speak to Kristen about having a wedding in the next three to four months and he wanted me to take over his part of the investment in the restaurant. Wow! Who would have thought that this night would end like this?

As if he was reading my mind, he said, "It's a lot to take in. I know. Speak with Kristen and let me know what she says. If it's a yes and everyone wants to know what the rush is on the wedding date, then you can tell them that once I'm in the nursing home, I won't be able to leave. Which isn't a full lie. You can make it sound good. As far as the restaurant, you can have your lawyer friend look over all the paperwork and make sure everything is ok. Come on and walk me out. They must be looking for us now."

The walk back to the backyard was quiet. I was grateful that he let me be alone in my thoughts. I needed to find a way to switch my mood so no one would come asking questions. Just as we reached the back door, I planted the fakest smile on my face as I said goodbye to the rest of my family members.

I started bringing dishes into the house to start washing. I was so deep into my thoughts that I didn't even know Kristen walked into the kitchen until she wrapped her arms around my waist.

"Hey, you," I said as I squeezed her arm with my elbow.

"You ok? Looks like something is troubling you," she said as she released me and stood on the side of me. She grabbed a towel and began drying the dishes that I had washed. My heart smiled for the first time in the last hour. Not only can she read past my fake smile, but she's also such a team player. She didn't have to jump in and dry the dishes, but she did. All the worry I had about having a wedding so soon quickly disappeared. I just hope she would agree.

I told her everything that Pop-Pop and I spoke about. I tried to whisper as best as I could so no one else would hear. Everyone was back and forth from outside to inside bringing in everything as they helped with the cleanup. We would switch the topic every time someone walked into the house. When I finally told her the full story, she had to go to the bathroom to wash her face. I knew she wasn't going to take the news well, but because of how time-sensitive it was, I had no choice but to tell her now.

When she came back into the kitchen, you could tell that she had been crying. She kept her back away from the door so no one would see her face.

"So a wedding before the year is over, wow!" she finally said.

"Babe, I know that's a lot to ask for, but please don't feel pressured or obligated. I know we just got engaged two months ago, but I still wanted to tell you his wish."

"You should know that I would get married to you right here and right now. I know I want to spend the rest of my life with you and a wedding tomorrow or the next three years is not the issue. The issue is that we are not financially ready to get married so soon. Unless we did a courthouse wedding. Which I don't mind, but I know how big your family is on tradition."

"I knew there was something I left out. Dig in my pants pocket," I said as I turned my body towards her for easy reach.

She pulled out the piece of paper and her eyes widen as she read what was written. "Pop-Pop is giving us fifty thousand dollars to have our wedding this year? Where the hell did he get this kind of money? Babe, that means he has given all of this thought and his mind is set."

I saw the tears forming in her eyes. I dried my hands and quickly wiped away her tears before they could fully fall. "Remember my grandfather is pretty wealthy. He's owned three restaurants even before I was born, not including the one my dad now owns. Plus, he sells his famous seasonings. His cookbook is still on the market. Aunt Sharon oversees all of that now, but he still makes a great profit off them and everything else he has invested in. I'm a little nervous to see how much money he'll leave over."

"Sounds like I have a lot of planning to do. If a wedding before he goes is what he wants, then let's give it to him." She leaned up to kiss me as she grabbed her phone. I had a feeling she was going to call Latrice.

"Girl, we'll be back in NY by tomorrow evening. I need you at my house as soon as I pull up. We have a wedding to plan, and it has to happen by November or December the absolute latest."

Yup, I was right. She was calling Latrice. I wiped down the counter, grabbed a beer, and joined my father and grandfather on the stoop. I needed to take advantage of this moment. Kris came out about a few minutes later and then ran back in to grab her phone. She played it cool and said she wanted to take a picture of the three most handsome men of the night. She winked at Pop-Pop as he gave her his million-dollar smile. My heart broke knowing that this will be one of the last times that we'd all be together like this, but I was grateful Kris was there to capture this moment.

Aunt Sharon was ready to go, so I helped walk Pop-Pop to her car. I hugged him before he got in and whispered in his ear that I will see him soon.

My father and I sat outside for a bit sipping on our beers while Kris and my mom went to go find my mom's wedding book. Kristen asked to see it so she can get ideas and my mom was more than happy to show off her wedding day. She even went into the attic and pulled out her wedding dress. My dad and I looked at each other and just shook our heads and said, "Women."

CHAPTER 24
KRISTEN
NOVEMBER

I don't know who told me that I could plan a wedding in four months and a gender reveal in three, but I did it! My wedding is next month, December 28, and Latrice's gender reveal is in a few hours. Stressed was beyond an understatement as to how I felt. Latrice has been at my house almost every day after work. We were calling different wedding venues until we found the perfect one. Thankfully looking for a place for her gender reveal wasn't a problem. Trent's law firm was more than happy to let him rent out one of their conference rooms. They gave him a very generous discount as well. I don't know how much because he took care of that expense, but he said it was an offer he couldn't refuse. The place was beautiful. I wish it was big enough for Stephan and my family because I would've had our reception there as well. The gender reveal was going to be very intimate. I think we had a guest list of a max of thirty people.

I'm the only one who knows the gender of her baby. She wanted it that way and that is how we kept it. It was so hard not even telling Stephan. I almost slipped up a few times, but always caught myself. To finally be able to reveal this secret today was going to be a relief!

I was beyond grateful that Trent's coworkers volunteered to help set up and decorate the room. I dropped off the decorations to them last night. All I had to worry about today was picking up the food, making sure the place was set to my liking and being there to help greet the guest. I got food catered from Fisherman Cove and Bedstuy Fish Fry. Stephan was going to pick up the food from Fisherman Cove and I was picking up the food from Bedstuy Fish Fry. I gave him the paper with the written order and told him to make sure they gave him extra jerk and sweet sauce. I ordered jerk chicken, oxtails, rice and peas, white rice, cabbage, and plantains. He also had to pick up the cake, which was next door. Lord's Bakery is one of the best bakery spots in Brooklyn. I checked my bag and made sure I had my order paper for Bedstuy Fish Fry. I ordered fried chicken, baked mac and cheese, collard greens, yellow rice, whiting, shrimps, and house salad. Laurence and his wife were bringing the party favors. I also went to BJ's last night to pick up drinks for the party and take-home plates. I know there's no way we were going to finish all the food I ordered. The take-home plates came with lids, which would make it so much easier to pack food securely instead of using a paper plate and buying a whole bunch of aluminum foil.

♥ ♥ ♥

The setup was better than I imagined. Seeing how beautiful everything turned out made me even more excited for my wedding day. Who would've known that the decorations I bought from Party City would make this place look like I spent thousands on it? The baby pink and baby blue decorations looked so beautiful together. I added a hint of silver to the decorations to help make the colors pop even more. I was so grateful that everyone was on time. I made it clear that I needed everyone there before the couple arrived. This was not an event to be fashionably late.

The DJ hopped on the mic and introduced Latrice and Trent as they walked into the room. Seeing her eyes light up the way that they did lets me know that all the hard work wasn't for nothing. They made their way around greeting and thanking everyone for coming. We ate, mingled, and danced a bit before the time came to reveal the gender.

I had the DJ get everyone's attention and brought Latrice and Trent to the front of the room. I pulled out the huge black balloon and put it against the wall. I told them where to stand, handed them a few darts, and had them aim it at the balloon. The balloon was filled with either pink or blue confetti. Everyone had their camera phones out recording. Latrice and Trent took turns trying to pop the balloon. Trent finally popped the balloon and pink confetti filled the room. Everyone started screaming and congratulating them.

When they turned around to see everyone, Laurence, her mom, Trent's dad, and I were all holding a briefcase. The look on their faces was full of confusion. I counted to three and everyone opened their briefcase and turned it upside down. Out came blue confetti.

"Surprise! You're actually having a boy!" I screamed. Everyone started jumping up and down, especially Trent. He looked happy to be having a girl, but when he found out that he was having a boy, that happiness increased by ten. My helpers didn't know what was in the briefcases. All I told them was that I had a second surprise and what they should do when I started the count down.

Everyone was mixing and mingling. The hardest part was done and I could now sit down and relax.

"You outdid yourself, sis," Monique said as she sat down next to me.

"Thank you, Mo. I'm just happy that it went better than I expected."

"It really did. How's everything coming along for the wedding? I know you're happy this is done so you can focus solely on that."

"Girl, yes! Planning the gender reveal was the easy part of the planning. All the invitations for the wedding went out about two weeks ago. I had to overnight all of them. Pretty much everyone has RSVP already. I think it worked out that I chose the week of the Christmas break because everyone is pretty much off and wouldn't have to use any of their days. I decided to go with the Platinum Package at the Princess Manor. It costs extra, but I wouldn't have to worry about hiring a wedding planner or finding a food catering service. That package takes care of it all. I also added the red carpet package to it. When the guest arrives, everyone will get his or her picture taken and greeted with champagne. Stephan and I are going next week to taste a few of the menu options and finalize the foods we want. I want to make sure we have enough options for the vegetarians in both our families. I don't need anyone saying that the place was beautiful but the food sucked. Not on my day. Thank you again for pulling strings in getting Carl's sister to make my dress. I can't wait for you to see it. Getting it made was my only option. Everywhere I went told me it would take too long to get my alterations done and sent back in time. But, I remembered how beautiful your wedding dress was and knew Stacy would bring my dream dress to life. Have you been back to her shop since she designed your dress? She has a beautiful picture of you in the dress she made hanging up on the wall."

"I've been meaning to check out her shop. She just opened this one last year. She's been doing well business-wise and needed a bigger space to expand her clientele."

"It's really beautiful and I was treated like royalty from the moment I walked in there. I love how comfortable she made me feel. We spoke about how I wanted the dress to be designed and the parts of my body I wanted to be covered. I told her I wanted to show skin but in the right places. She knew exactly what I meant too; hide the back fat and tummy as best you could. She told me how important material is. She said many times we don't realize that we can hide our flaws by the materials we wear. She took her time to make sure she got every detail. Her team is working on the bridesmaid's dresses. We all have to go next week for the final fittings. I gave Stephan a piece of the fabric from the dresses so he could make sure everything matched accordingly. I can't even begin to imagine the day of my wedding, seeing all of you ladies in beautiful wine-colored dresses and his men in bright red. Girl, I would faint!" We both busted out laughing.

"Stephan knows you too well. He wouldn't dare screw this up for you," Monique said still laughing.

"Sis, if he wants me to say *I do,* he better make sure he gets it right.

I went over the rest of the wedding plans with Monique as she wrote down a few things for me to remember to get or do before the wedding day. I'm glad I was finally able to pick her brain. She went all out for her wedding day and I wanted to make sure mine was up to her standards. Latrice was going to take care of hair and makeup. That was one less worry for me. We've always joked about her doing it since the day she graduated with her cosmetology license.

It was time to shut down the party, so I started helping

Latrice's mom, Diane, make to-go plates as everyone else helped cleaning. She kept thanking me for making this day special for her daughter and how she couldn't wait to see how the baby shower would turn out. More event planning was the last thing I wanted to think about.

Stephan and I were back home before nine. I went straight to the bathroom to take a shower. When I got out, Stephan was sitting on the couch watching the sports channel. I grabbed the bag of Doritos, poured me a glass of Barefoot Moscato, and sat on the other end of the couch. He placed my feet in his lap and gave me a much-needed foot massage. I was mentally and physically drained. I didn't want to do any wedding planning tonight. I didn't even want to see my phone or laptop. I ate a few chips, took a couple of sips, and rested my head on the couch. I felt my eyelids getting heavy and knew it was only a matter of time before it was lights out for me.

CHAPTER 25

KRISTEN

Time was flying! My wedding is less than two weeks away and I still have a few things on my to-do list that hasn't been completed yet.

Stephan is going to see our new apartment today and sign the lease. I have been to the apartment twice already and knew from the first time that it was the right one. Stephan brought Trent along with him to make sure the paperwork was legit and to read the fine print. Once everything was looked over and signed, all I had to do was sign my part via e-signature. Thank God for new technology.

I wish I could be there but I can't be two places at one time, and today is the only day that Stacy could fit all of us in for final fittings. I needed to be there to see how the dresses came out and how they fit the ladies.

I made Latrice my Maid of Honor. It worked out perfectly because Trent is Stephan's Best Man. Monique and Eva are two of my bridesmaids along with my two favorite twin cousins, Mia and Mya. Stephan had most of his college boys as his groomsmen; Will, Mathew, Nate, and Lucas.

I drove to pick up Latrice before heading to Stacy's shop. I texted her ten minutes ago saying that I was five minutes away knowing how bad she is with time. When I pulled up to her house, she still wasn't outside. I honked the horn and waited an extra five minutes. I should have called her twenty minutes ago and told her I was outside, maybe then she would have been ready by the time I pulled up. I'm glad she's having a boy. I could not imagine her and another girl in the house. They would never get anywhere on time.

She came out a few minutes later, threw her bag in the backseat, and sat in the passenger seat.

"Well about damn time," I said as I watched her put her seatbelt on.

"Girl, I'm so sorry. This baby is kicking my butt today," she said as she rubbed her belly.

I moved her hand and rubbed her belly. I can't wait to meet him. If being pregnant was going to be like this, I can wait for my turn.

Eva was the first to arrive and was already in the dressing room by the time we got there. My cousins got there a few minutes after Latrice and me. I waited in the sitting area while everyone went to try on their dresses. The only person who has seen my dress was my mother. I didn't want anyone else to see it until the day of the wedding. Once everyone did their final fitting and left, then I'll try on mine. The only person who hasn't shown yet was Monique. She already told me that she'd try her best to be here on time, but her being a detective now, I knew what came with the job. She had the day of my wedding off and that's all that mattered.

The tears in my eyes formed instantly when I saw how beautiful everyone looked in their dresses. The sketches and pictures of the dresses did no justice as to how beautiful everyone looked.

Monique walked in just as everyone was doing their last walk through with the dresses. She asked everyone to stay in their dresses until she got dressed. When she walked out of the dressing room, the tears came back. My sister looked absolutely beautiful. This wine color complemented each of their skin tones. I couldn't help but pat myself on the back for choosing such a beautiful color. I took pictures of how everyone looked before they took the dresses off. Thankfully, the only person's dress that needed a little alteration was Latrice. She just needed a little extra breathing room in the belly area. Stacy said making maternity dresses is easier than people think, and she would have it altered before the end of the week.

I sat back down in the sitting area and waited for everyone to come out. I couldn't stop staring at the pictures I took on my phone. All the stressing and planning was starting to pay off. Less than two weeks and I'll be Mrs. Stephan Moore. I can't wait!

Everyone was out of the dressing room except for Latrice.

"I don't know anyone that takes as long as Latrice. Thank God she's having a boy and not a girl," Eva said.

"Girl, I said the same thing earlier. I was waiting outside for over fifteen minutes. She did say that today was a rough day for her because of the baby though."

"Imagine having twins! Those girls made every day feel like a bad day. I tell Carl all the time that they get along so well now because they spent all their time fighting in the womb," Monique said.

All the pregnancy stories everyone was sharing had me

grateful for my birth control pills. I left the ladies to go check on Latrice. Mo had her partner waiting for her in the car and had to leave but wanted to say goodbye to Latrice before she left.

I called out to her a couple of times but got no answer. I knocked on the only dressing room door that was closed before opening it. She was sitting in her panties and bra crying. I wasn't sure if it was her hormones again or something else this time. It wasn't until I looked down that I saw why she was crying. Her hands and thighs were covered in blood. My heart dropped and I froze for a quick second. I screamed for Monique and everyone came running to the back. Monique moved me out of the way to check Latrice. She told Stacy to grab something to cover her up in as she called Mike to bring the car out front. We wrapped Latrice in the robe that Stacy handed to us and walked her out to the car. I can tell she was feeling weak because we were carrying most of her weight. We got her in the backseat, and I climbed in behind her. Mike called it in over the radio and turned on their sirens. Kings County is the closest hospital from where we were. Mike told the dispatcher that it was easier for us to take her there than to wait for an ambulance. They alerted the hospital that we were en route. I called Stephan and told him that they needed to meet us there ASAP. I heard the panic in Trent's voice when Stephan told him we were heading to the hospital.

We were at Kings County in less than ten minutes. The nurses put her on a gurney and took her to the back. One of the nurses stayed back to ask me personal questions about her health. I had Trent on the other line to help me fill in any missing blanks. This wasn't the hospital where she was going to give birth, so they didn't have any information on her and was relying on Trent and me to give them as much info as we could. Trent told me to tell them that she just found out at their last prenatal visit that she has preeclampsia and was only twenty-eight weeks. I don't know what that is but seeing the worried look on Monique's face was more than enough to let me know that preeclampsia wasn't a good thing. The nurse thanked us as she headed to where Latrice was taken. They wouldn't let me go back there so I had to stay in the waiting area. After waiting a few minutes and not hearing anything, Monique got up, flashed her badge, and demanded that someone told us something. One of the head nurses came out and told us that Latrice is in premature labor. She said at twenty-eight weeks and the amount of blood she has lost, this delivery is going to be a tricky one and the chances of the baby surviving are very slim. She told us that they will do the best that they can do and for us to remain hopeful.

I texted Stephan to see how far they were. I didn't want to keep calling and making Trent worry even more. Stephan texted me back and said that Trent was driving as fast as he could and that they should be there in less than ten minutes.

I was saying a silent prayer for Latrice and the baby when I heard her mother running through the maternity ward calling out for me. I leaped out of my seat and met her halfway. I told her what the head nurse told us, and she immediately started shaking. Monique came over and helped me walk her back to where we were sitting.

Minutes later, Mike and Monique got a call over the radio that there was a nearby collision. Since they were the closest to the scene, they had to be the first to respond. I told her it was ok and that I would keep her posted.

I walked to the vending machine to buy a bottle of water for Diane. I walked past all the happy family members waiting to meet their new family member. Seeing all their happy faces brought back hope that everything was going to be ok. I ended up buying two bottles of water. They were two dollars each and the smallest bill I had was a five-dollar bill. I was not about to be walking around with three dollars in change.

As soon as I bent down to pick up the second bottle from the vending machine, I heard someone scream out, "No!" I ran back to the waiting area where I saw the doctor holding up Diane. She looked at me as I approached them and flew into my arms screaming, "Not, my baby!"

At that moment, it all became clear to me. The baby didn't make it. All the hope I had just went out the window. I held onto Diane as best as I could as I consoled her.

"How's Latrice? Does she know her baby didn't make it? What happens now? Can I see her?" I had so many questions and felt myself talking faster than usual.

"Ma'am, the baby is in NICU, Latrice didn't make it. We tried everything we could do. She lost too much blood and her heart started failing on us in the process of delivering. We almost lost her and the baby. The baby is fighting as best as he could, but at twenty-eight weeks, he is going to have to fight hard."

My knees buckled on me as I felt myself going down. The nurse that was with the doctor caught me before I could hit the ground and placed me on the couch. They put Diane in the seat next to me as we both cried. They told us they would give us a few minutes alone and that they would be back to give us an update on the baby.

My best friend, my sister, my rock, my right hand; is gone. This couldn't be. God wouldn't do this to me. The tears wouldn't stop falling. The pain wouldn't stop increasing.

We sat in silence for a few minutes. Diane was still a mess, so I decided I would go to the reception desk and ask if I could speak to someone about the baby. She told me that she would page the nurse. I went back to my seat and impatiently waited. My hands and legs were shaking uncontrollably.

I looked up and Monique was approaching the waiting area. Her eyes were bloodshot red. They must have called and told her. After the show she put on earlier, I'm sure they didn't want to get on her bad side by not keeping her updated. I ran to her, buried my face into her shoulder, and cried.

She held me as I cried. She lifted my face and wiped my tears. "I'm so sorry, Kris. I don't know what to say to make things better, but I need you to come downstairs. It's Stephan."

As if my world wasn't already crumbling down, hearing that Trent and Stephan were in a car accident was too much for me to handle right now. I didn't want to leave Diane by herself, but I needed to see how Stephan and Trent were. Monique took me down to the floor where they were. I saw Trent first and ran to where he was. Mike was standing next to him taking the report. I kept asking where Stephan was and Trent just kept apologizing saying how it was his fault. If Stephan looked as bad as Trent did, I was going to lose it.

I ran to the reception and asked for Stephan Moore. I was told that he was just rushed to surgery. Monique was back at my side, flashing her badge again and asking for someone to come out and talk to us as soon as possible.

I went back to Trent and he finally stopped apologizing and told us what happened. "I was speeding, trying to get here as fast as I could. We were coming from the other side of Brooklyn. I promised Latrice that I would never let her go through any parts of her pregnancy alone. We were just a block and a half away. I went across the intersection and this truck came out of nowhere and hit us from the side. I swear I didn't see it. It pinned us up against a van and we were trapped. The fire department had to come to get us out. I tried to tell them to get Stephan first, but they said it was too risky to get him from his side and had to take him out from mine. Once they pulled me out, I tried to get up to see how Stephan was, but I couldn't move my legs or my neck. They wouldn't tell me how he was. Kris, I'm so sorry. I really am. This is all my fault. Can someone please tell Latrice that I will be there as soon as I can. Even if I have to wheel myself there, I'm coming. Is the baby ok? Were they able to tell you anything?"

The tears fell again. The way he cried after I told him what happened, was exactly why I wish it wasn't me to break the news. The tears and shock that flooded Monique's face told me that she didn't know either and that her tears from earlier were for Stephan. My heart broke in a thousand pieces. Trent tried to get out of the bed, but his body wouldn't let him. The doctor came just in time and said that he needed to take him to get a CT scan and run tests to make sure there was no internal bleeding. Trent put up a fight, screaming and hollering that he needed to go to the maternity ward. He was causing more harm to himself by resisting that they had to sedate him.

It felt like hours that I had to wait to hear something about Stephan. Mo's badge didn't hold that much weight on this floor as it did in the maternity ward. They made us wait for him to get out of surgery before we could talk to anyone.

The doctor finally came out and told me that they had to rush Stephan into surgery because of the head injury he got from the car accident. The truck hit his side of the car, pinning him in and causing him to lose consciousness. He told me that they are doing everything they can to keep the brain swelling down. I asked if I could see him and the doctor told me once they get him set up in a room that they will take me to him, but he won't be awake to talk to me because he slipped into a coma. He told me that Stephan is extremely lucky that this happened so close to the hospital. Another five minutes without performing surgery would've been too late for him. He told me it is still too early to tell if he would come out of the coma, but for me to remain hopeful. My world was crashing down on me. First my best friend and now my fiancé. This cannot be my life right now.

♥ ♥ ♥

I leaped up and scared Stephan. I looked around the room and seen that we were still on the couch and he was still massaging my feet.

"Babe, are you ok?" he asked as he reached for me.

I got up from my side of the couch and sat next to him. "You won't even begin to believe the dream that I just had. Latrice died and you...I don't even want to talk about it. I'm just so happy that you are ok. I wouldn't know what to do if something ever happened to you." I wrapped my arms around him and kissed him all over his head. "I promise you, I'm going to seek help tomorrow. This has to stop. I need to put a knot on my dreams!"

HAVE YOU READ...

♥ ♥ ♥

STAY CONNECTED...

Website
www.scriptedknots.com

Instagram
ScriptedKnots_Shyquana

Twitter
ScriptedKnots

Facebook
www.facebook.com/scriptedknots

ABOUT THE AUTHOR

Writing has always been her passion. As a child, it was her escape. When she couldn't express her feelings verbally, pen and paper came to her rescue. It started with poetry and that is how *A Knot On My Heart* was born.

She realized how therapeutic it was to sit with her laptop and just type chapter after chapter. She didn't have an outline, but a story that she wanted to share. With each word she typed, the more her creative juices started to flow and that is how *A Knot On My Dreams* came to life.

Journey along and let her imagination take you on a roller coaster ride...